T0279373

THE HYSTERICAL GIRLS OF ST. BERNA-DETTE'S

ALSO BY HANNA ALKAF

The Weight of Our Sky

The Girl and the Ghost

Queen of the Tiles

Hamra and the Jungle of Memories

THE HYSTERICAL GIRLS OF ST. BERNA-DETTE'S

HANNA ALKAF

SALAAM
READS

NEW YORK LONDON TORONTO SYDNEY NEW DELHI

An imprint of Simon & Schuster Children's Publishing Division
1230 Avenue of the Americas, New York, New York 10020

This book is a work of fiction. Any references to historical events, real people, or real places are used fictitiously. Other names, characters, places, and events are products of the author's imagination, and any resemblance to actual events or places or persons, living or dead, is entirely coincidental.

Text © 2024 by Hanna Alkaf
Jacket illustration © 2024 by Leo Nickolls
Jacket design by Sarah Creech
All rights reserved, including the right of reproduction in whole or in part in any form.
SALAAM READS and its logo are trademarks of Simon & Schuster, LLC.

Simon & Schuster: Celebrating 100 Years of Publishing in 2024
For information about special discounts for bulk purchases, please contact
Simon & Schuster Special Sales at 1-866-506-1949 or business@simonandschuster.com.
The Simon & Schuster Speakers Bureau can bring authors to your live event.
For more information or to book an event, contact the Simon & Schuster Speakers
Bureau at 1-866-248-3049 or visit our website at www.simonspeakers.com.
Interior design by Hilary Zarycky
The text for this book was set in Adobe Garamond Pro.
Manufactured in the United States of America
First Edition
2 4 6 8 10 9 7 5 3 1

Library of Congress Cataloging-in-Publication Data
Names: Hanna Alkaf, author.
Title: The hysterical girls of St. Bernadette's / Hanna Alkaf.
Description: New York : Salaam Reads, [2024] | Audience: Ages 14 up. | Audience: Grades 10-12. | Summary: "Two teenagers investigate the strange occurrences of mass hysteria plaguing their all-girls school"—Provided by publisher.
Identifiers: LCCN 2024009789 (print) | LCCN 2024009790 (ebook) |
ISBN 9781534494589 (hardcover) | ISBN 9781534494602 (ebook)
Subjects: LCSH: Teenage girls—Malaysia—Kuala Lumpur—Juvenile fiction.
| Interpersonal relations—Juvenile fiction. | Girls' schools—Malaysia—Kuala Lumpur—Juvenile fiction. | CYAC: Girls' schools—Fiction. | Schools—Fiction. | Interpersonal relations—Fiction. | Kuala Lumpur (Malaysia)—Fiction. | Malaysia—Fiction. | Mystery and detective stories. | LCGFT: Thrillers (Fiction) | Detective and mystery fiction. | Novels.
Classification: LCC PZ7.1.H36377 Hy 2024 (print) | LCC PZ7.1.H36377 (ebook) | DDC [Fic]—dc23
LC record available at https://lccn.loc.gov/2024009789
LC ebook record available at https://lccn.loc.gov/2024009790ISBN 97815344945890

For the ones who scream, and the ones who don't; for the ones who bare their teeth and the ones who grit them instead; for the ones who are scared and the ones who are angry and the ones who survive and especially, *especially* for the ones who don't.

For Malik and Maryam.

For you.

This is a story about ghosts and monsters, some of whom hide beneath human faces. It includes discussions and descriptions of sexual assault, trauma, and PTSD. If this is too much for you right now, please set this book down and come back to it when you can. There is no shame in protecting your scars.

And it'll be here waiting for you, when you're ready.

Love,
Hanna

The Beginning

It is 12:32 p.m., a little more than half an hour before the school day ends, and the classroom is swampier than a sinner's armpit in the depths of hell.

St. Bernadette's, with its grand arched doorways and windows, its gables, its ornate tiles and stone staircases, stands imposingly on a hilltop in the middle of Kuala Lumpur, as it has done for the past one hundred years—all the better to look down on everyone else, so the haters say, and St. Bernadette's has more than its fair share of those. That's just part of what it means to be the best. But even with the massive wooden double doors of each classroom flung wide open, there is simply no breeze to catch. Overhead, the ceiling fan spins in lazy circles, doing little to provide any kind of relief, and one by one, like the flowers for which each of the school's classes is named, the students of 3 Kenanga begin to wilt in the relentless heat. Heads droop closer and closer to desks, eyes glaze over, and though the teacher does her best, coordinate geometry simply has no power over a room full of post-recess fourteen- and fifteen-year-olds as torpid as cobras after a feeding, and who are unwilling—or unable—to pay attention.

It is 12:47 p.m., and Mrs. Lee is trying to explain something about "calculating the perpendicular" when the first scream makes the students all nearly jump out of their sweat-soaked skins.

The scream is not a pretty, perfectly pitched horror-movie scream. It is hoarse and low, and it shakes and skips, as if whatever is causing it is forcibly strangling it out of the screamer, shaking it out of them in fits and starts. And the source of it is a girl sitting in the third row, two desks from the left; a thin, pale girl with a mop of unruly hair that she wears hanging over her face as if she's trying to hide from the world; a girl so new and so quiet that the others sometimes have trouble remembering her name, or that she is there at all.

They will remember her now, though.

"Fatihah!" Mrs. Lee shakes off her surprise and strides over to the girl's desk. This is not a normal Thursday occurrence, but Mrs. Lee has been teaching for more than twelve years now, and the range of "normal" is so wide in a school full of teenage girls that little fazes her at this point. "Fatihah! What is happening? What's wrong? Aiyo, this girl!" She has to shout to make herself heard, because the girl known as Fatihah will not stop screaming. And the other girls, usually so eager for something, anything, to break up the monotony of the school day, begin to grow restless and fearful and uncertain. Because Fatihah's eyes are wide and staring, gazing up toward a specific spot in the corner of the ceiling as if fixed on something only she can see, something she desperately wishes she couldn't.

"Mrs. Lee, what do we do?"

"Should I call someone?"

"Teacher, maybe we can throw some water on her face."

"Teacher, please make her stop!"

The classroom erupts in confused commotion. Girls are covering their ears, girls are trying to offer solutions, girls are trying their best not to panic, girls are panicking without reservation.

Lily, who sits next to Fatihah, grabs Fatihah by the shoulders and shakes her hard so that her head bobs back and forth, back and forth. "Wake up, Fatihah!" she yells. "Stop it!"

"Don't do that!" Mrs. Lee snaps, frantic in her own helplessness, hands flapping uselessly in the air. "You might hurt her!"

Fatihah's eyes roll back so that only the whites show; her hands clench at the edge of her desk, so tight that the knuckles are white and it seems as if she may crush the wood into splinters; her body shudders, and blue-green veins bulge in her pale temples. And the girls of 3 Kenanga have no idea what to do. Some stare, transfixed, unable to tear their eyes away; some cannot bear to look at all, closing their eyes as if they can will the nightmare away; some cry, and some babble, and many just stand, silent and bewildered and helpless.

And then Lavanya, who sits by the wide open doors, pauses, frowns, and yells something over the chaos, something that silences all but Fatihah, who just keeps screaming.

"There's more."

And as 3 Kenanga listens, they begin to hear it: screams piercing the afternoon heat; screams of every pitch and timbre;

screams so raw and so terribly, profoundly afraid that they turn everyone's blood to ice.

It is now 1:05 p.m. The bell rings to signal the end of school, and nobody hears it.

They hear only the screams.

Khadijah

"This is not a good idea."

I pause, a spoonful of Koko Krunch halfway to my mouth. The problem with this as a statement is that my mother thinks many things are Not a Good Idea.

"Well?" she asks. She looks first at me, then at Aishah, then back at me. As if I'll be the one to say something. Mak is an optimist. She'll look at a weather forecast that says 80 percent chance of rain and say, "That means there's still 20 percent chance of sun!" And she'll look at me and believe, really believe, that I'll start talking now. On a random Monday. When I haven't said a word in three months. "What do you think, Khadijah?" she asks me.

Even if I wanted to talk—I don't—Mak has a way of asking me questions that makes me want to extremely not answer them. So I settle for another big bite of chocolate cereal and a shrug.

Mak frowns. She doesn't have her hijab on yet. The morning humidity makes stray strands of her hair zigzag out away from her head. Mad-scientist hair. "Don't you think it's just too soon? We don't even know yet what caused it. Those poor girls."

Ah. Now I get it. Mak is talking about the screamers.

Everyone is talking about the screamers.

Except me.

I don't want to talk about the screamers. I don't want to listen about the screamers. I don't want anything to do with the screamers. I want to be able to close my eyes and not remember what that day felt like. Not think about the way those screams echoed off the old stone walls of St. Bernadette's. The way it felt to see girls being carried out of their classrooms. Twenty-seven screamers, all crumpled and white like used tissues.

I just want everything to go back to normal. I think the universe owes me normal.

Mak is peering at me over the top of her steaming coffee mug. "Don't you have anything to say, Khadijah?" she asks. Her eyes are so hopeful. She still thinks she can reach through the layers of protection I have built around myself and yank me out.

For a moment I feel a twinge somewhere in my chest. *She's trying so hard, Khad. Maybe you should too. Maybe it's time.*

Then I remember the times I did try. When I did speak. And she didn't listen. And my heart hardens once more.

"So you'd rather we stay at home?" Aishah asks.

I shoot her a look. It's not like my little sister to jump in. That's my job.

Or at least it used to be.

Mak frowns. "To be safe."

"From what?" Aishah says it almost like it's a challenge.

Mak hesitates. "I don't know," she mutters finally, gathering up her things for work. "I don't know from what. That's the problem. How am I supposed to protect you from something I don't know enough ab—" She catches herself. Starts tying up her unruly hair and coughs. "Anyway. At least promise me you'll be vigilant. Watch out for each other. Read ayat Kursi if anything feels . . . off."

"Sure," Aishah mumbles.

I roll my eyes so hard, I think I see the back of my own skull. My mother works at a newspaper. Her job is literally dealing with facts, all day long. And she thinks we need to protect ourselves from what, exactly? Jinn? Ghosts?

"I saw that." Mak reaches out to whack me lightly on the arm. I shrug, because that was the point. I've never been good at hiding what I think. Even without using words. "I'm not saying that's what I believe," Mak continues. "I'm saying it's worth protecting yourself. Just because you don't believe in the unseen doesn't mean they don't believe in you."

"They already had people come in for that, anyway," Aishah says. "You know. To 'cleanse' the school. That's why it was closed on Friday. What?" she says in answer to my raised eyebrow. I have become an expert at saying a lot while saying nothing at all. "I heard about it from Wani. You know her mom's one of the teachers. Wani got all annoyed because she had to go to school over the weekend. This ustaz and, like, two or three assistants went around to every corner of the school and read doas or something everywhere." She pauses. "And a priest. And a monk, I think."

Oh good, I think. *Cover all the bases. Equal opportunity ghost-busting.*

"Hmm," Mak says. "They did mention something in the parents' WhatsApp group, but I was hazy on the details."

Aishah coughs. "My point is, whether you believe it or you don't believe it, it shouldn't be an issue anymore. Right?"

"Right," Mak says softly, patting Aishah's hand.

There is a rumble and splutter outside, the telltale signs of the ancient orange school bus making its way down the street. Aishah immediately gets up and heads to the sink with her dirty dishes. I follow right behind her.

"Wait." Mak frowns. "Are you su—"

"See you tonight, Mak," Aishah says. She bends low for salam, kissing our mother's hand.

I hoist my backpack on and head for the door. I don't kiss Mak's hands, and she doesn't expect me to. I don't like to touch, and I don't like to be touched, not anymore. I head out the door and don't look back.

I stopped looking back a long time ago.

We don't sit together on the bus. We never do. I hold my breath as I scurry past the driver. Make my way toward the very back left corner. I've been going to St. Bernadette's since I was seven. I know almost every kid on this bus at least by name. But not a single person looks up or says hi as I walk past. Not even Maria, who used to wipe her boogers on my skirt in standard one, on our very first day of school.

"Morning, stinkface!" Sumi yells, waving at me. She and Flo have used their backpacks to save a seat for me, as usual. Not that they need to. Everyone knows this spot belongs to the three of us.

Aishah sits down somewhere in the middle, with her own friends. She's in form three this year, and I'm in form four. At St. Bernadette's the younger kids—form one and form two, the thirteen- and fourteen-year-olds—go to afternoon session. The rest of us, from form three to form five, make up the morning session. Last year I'd be out the door by six forty-five a.m., and when I got home, Aishah would already be in class. We barely saw each other, and it made us sad. Back in the before times—as in Before the Incident—we used to get excited about the idea of being on the same schedule.

But that was back when we were still talking. When *I* was still talking.

"Yo," Sumi says as I approach, moving her backpack from the seat beside her and offering me a fist to bump.

"Morning, loser." Flo blinks at me sleepily, her head leaning against the window. She's never properly awake until at least the middle of second period.

I shrug off my backpack and settle into the spot between them. Immediately I feel myself relax. Sumi's bony butt is on my left, Flo's more padded one on my right. It used to be that whoever came last got the end seat. But ever since It happened,

Sumi and Flo make sure I am always in the middle. They take their bodies, their friendship, their love, and they use it to make me a cocoon. In here I am snug and protected and safe.

I frown as I glance around the bus. There are more empty seats than usual, I'm sure of it. Flo catches me.

"Yeah, I know," she says softly. "Some of them were screamers."

I feel my stomach clench at the mention of screamers.

Sumi yawns, mouth open so wide, I can see all three of her fillings. "And some of them are scared of becoming screamers, I guess," she adds.

"Close your mouth lah when you yawn," Flo says, wrinkling her nose. "You're so gross."

In answer, Sumi leans over me, gapes right in Flo's face, and breathes on her.

Flo gags theatrically. "I'm going to muntah all over this seat."

Sumi shrieks. "Don't you dare!"

I swat Flo away and grin at the sound of her laugh. The thing about being silent is that you hear a lot more than you used to. Some people have such scared, nervous little laughs. Flo's is deep and full. It wells up from somewhere inside her. It rips through the air as if it wants to touch everyone. Flo laughs like she means it.

"Anyway," Flo says, munching on half a karipap. "What do you mean, 'scared of becoming screamers'?"

"My ma said she heard of this happening somewhere else when she was younger," Sumi says. "She said she thinks sometimes it takes a few days for it to stop. So who knows? Maybe this isn't the end of it. Maybe there'll be more."

"This has happened before?" Flo's eyes are wide.

"Ya. She said this kind of thing is nothing new. She was so casual about it too." Sumi shakes her head. "She said she never went through the screaming exactly, but when she was in school, this girl started talking in this deep, hoarse voice. Like she was possessed."

Flo raises one eyebrow. "What does that have to do with the screaming?"

"I know, right?" Sumi shrugs. "I was like, 'Ma, why you so random?' But then she got all mysterious and was like, 'You know ah girl, sometimes old buildings have things living there you cannot see also.'" Sumi pauses to consider this. "Kesimpulannya, my ma is quite weird lah, sometimes."

"Actually, my mama was weird about it too." Flo shakes her head. "I tried talking to her about the screaming, right, and she shut me right down. Said what's done is done, and then took me to church to get a blessing." She makes a face. "I figured she'd be interested lah since she used to go to St. Bernadette's. But no. And since when does my mother not want to *talk*?"

I can feel my face getting warm, my palms getting clammy. I wipe them off on my baju kurung, then wipe them again. I don't know how to stop it.

"Khad?" It's Flo's hand that reaches out to tug my sleeve gently. They're careful, always so careful, not to touch me directly. They know I can't stand the feel of skin. That's when I realize I'm gripping the hem of my school top tight in both hands. When I let go, it's a labyrinth of wrinkles. "Are you okay?" I can feel the worried glances they're exchanging over my head.

I hate it.

"May I?" Sumi asks, her hand hovering uncertainly, and I nod. She rubs my back in slow, soothing circles. "There's no reason for the screaming to go on," she says quietly. "They said they've taken care of it. I'm sure it'll be fine, okay? Everything's going to be back to normal."

Normal, I think. Sure. Normal. Sumi and Flo keep talking, and I sit back and stare at the empty spaces. I can hear my mother's voice telling me this is not a good idea. And I feel a tightness in my chest, a weight I can't explain, gathering itself in the cavity behind my ribs so that it's hard to breathe.

Rachel

"This is not a good idea."

My mother shakes her head, then quickly pushes back a strand of hair that falls out of place. Mother does not like mess; not in her hair, which she is wearing in her usual bun; not in her home, where everything is spotless and has its place; and especially, especially not in me.

"But, Mother," I begin, then pause. *No, Rachel. Too needy, too much.* "Mother," I try again, ironing out all my emotions so my tone is calm and reasonable. *That's it, Rachel, that's the way.* "It is my last year in school. I think participating would really help with my extracurriculars, right, so that when it's time to apply to university—"

"Your extracurriculars don't need help, Rachel," Mother says, taking her time to sip hot tea from a fine china cup, which is milky white with gold around the rim. Her back is ramrod straight, her silk cheongsam is pristine, her pinky is held up delicately. Mother always says that appearances are everything, even when we're the only ones around to see them. "You play the violin and the piano. You are part of youth choir. You are a karate black belt. You tutor underprivileged children in your spare time. You are a prefect. You do not need some . . . play." She says it as if it tastes disgusting, as if she wants to spit it out. "Especially with SPM just around the corner."

"SPM is still a couple of months away," I mumble. My mother has been obsessed with making sure I get perfect results in the Sijil Pelajaran Malaysia since I first started secondary school. She used to cut out newspaper articles of high achievers and their results, and paste them on my wall, for "inspiration."

"You see this one?" she'd say, jabbing at the grainy photo of some kid grinning between his proud parents and teachers. "Thirteen A1s! This one got only eleven A1s, but has an inspirational sob story about their little sister. You have no sob story and no little sister, so you must work extra hard instead."

She stares at me now, her expression cold, stern. "This is the biggest exam of your life," she tells me, as she has done since I was thirteen. "This is the first step to determining your entire future. You cannot risk it all to dress up and play pretend on some stage."

There is a cold feeling in my chest. I do not say what I want to say, which is, *You chose all of those activities, not me.* I do not say, *My whole life has been yours to curate and calculate and cultivate. Just let me have this, just this one thing.* I do not say, *Surely nobody can determine their entire life based on questions you answer at age seventeen.* I have spent my entire life parsing my mother's words, her exact tone of voice, and none of this will sway her. I know this. But I try again anyway. "But, Mo—"

"No." My mother picks up her newspaper. Her expression is like a closed door. "The answer is no."

I know when a fight is lost. "Okay, Mother," I say quietly, standing up and smoothing the wrinkles from the skirt of my pinafore. "Okay. I'll go to school now."

"Pakcik Zakaria will pick you up after your prefect meeting and drop you off at orchestra rehearsal," she says from behind the paper. "Don't be late."

"Yes, Mother," I say.

"And, Rachel," she says as I'm about to walk out the door.

"Yes, Mother?"

"I want you to forget about the silly nonsense that happened last week."

"Last week?"

"You know." She puts the paper down long enough for me to see her lips all puckered up again, like she's tasting something sour. "Those girls. The . . . screaming. Don't let it distract you from your work. You understand?"

I blink. It didn't even occur to me that I should be thinking about it at all. "Yes, Mother."

We do not kiss each other goodbye. I don't remember the last time we did.

Pakcik Zakaria has just taken the car to be serviced, and the air conditioner is working like it's brand-new; it's freezing, even though he turns up the temperature when I ask him to. I wrap my legs in the baby-blue blanket I keep in here—I am always cold—and stare out the window as KL goes crawling by. When we get to the bottom of the hill, I lean forward and tap him on the shoulder. "Saya keluar sini sahaja, Pakcik." I do not like being dropped off at the gate; it makes me feel like everyone is looking at me, even though this is St. Bernadette's, and it's not like I'm the only student getting dropped off by a chauffeur. It's the premier all-girls school in Kuala Lumpur, after all. Everyone tries to get their child in here.

I grab my bag and join the crowd of girls walking slowly up to the school's heavy iron gates. There's a moment, as you're making your way up this hill, when you turn a corner and St. Bernadette's suddenly comes into view, in all its 112-year-old glory. It's not a tall building, but there is something about its arched stone windows and doorways and the massive double doors that open up on either side of each of the old classrooms. St. Bernadette's looms. Its center is its tallest point, a three-story building with a pointed gable topped with a cross. From here lower buildings sprawl left and right, as if St. Bernadette's is reaching out its arms to encompass as much as it can: land, trees, girls.

Sometimes it feels like my mother's grip on me is so tight, I cannot even breathe properly. But as soon as I'm back here within St. Bernadette's embrace, walking across the intricately embossed old red tiles, it gets easier to fill my lungs. I am here. I am in a safe space, a space where I belong. Everything will be fine.

I have been going to St. Bernadette's since primary school—a separate, newer building housing several hundred seven- to twelve-year-olds a little ways down the hill. There is a picture of me from the first day of standard one that sits on the piano at home in a golden frame, watching me every time I play. I'm not even seven years old yet in that photo, my hair in two long braids down my back, my face solemn, my bag almost as big as I am. Other children had parents waiting outside the hall or classroom, holding containers of food, ready to eat with them and ask them about their teachers and their friends; I had nobody. I remember Pakcik Zakaria driving us to school, Mother and me sitting in the back seat, me in my blue blanket. Pa was long gone by then, busy building his new family over in Canada. Sometimes I would creep out of bed in the middle of the night just to open my atlas and see where he was, trace an invisible line from Kuala Lumpur to some place called Vancouver. Vancouver had snow. I tried to picture my father in a big padded jacket, playing in the snow with some little girl who was not me.

Mother told me what was expected of me from the very beginning, that this is a good school, and that I was to study hard and listen to my teachers and not be an embarrassment to her and how she had raised me. Nobody explained what an assembly was; I walked along the corridors, admiring the patterns on the red tiles under my feet, ignoring the loud clanging of the bell, until a teacher came and yelled at me for not getting in line. When I asked my mother why she did not come the way the other mothers did, why she had not explained, why I was never told, she stared at me and just said, "Because you can handle all of this on your own, what. You are not a baby, Rachel."

I may only have been turning seven that year, but I was already learning to understand what my mother was really saying, the true meanings that lurked in the spaces between the words. It was not just about standard one. It was about everything. She wanted me to learn to handle everything on my own, just like she did.

And maybe it worked. Maybe she had a point. I don't know. I was sometimes jealous of the other children, whose parents always looked so happy and excited to see them.

But I was never afraid like they were, not of the teachers and not of St. Bernadette's itself, not even once I graduated from primary school and went on up the road to the secondary school with the rest of the thirteen- to seventeen-year-olds. Sekolah Menengah Kebangsaan St. Bernadette's is housed in the original Gothic building that a group of French nuns established as a mission school way back in the early 1900s, with more rooms added on over the years as the number of pupils swelled. I found no fear in its dark corners or its echoing stairwells, or in the bats that hung from the ceilings or in the piles of bat poop all of us had to step over in the corridors, or even in the monkeys that watched us from the trees beyond the fence.

Other kids whispered about the ghosts that roamed St. Bernadette's or waited in the shadows to scare us in the bathrooms, told stories about wailing nuns and headless Japanese soldiers that had died bloody deaths on school grounds during the occupation. Other kids went hunting for entrances to the maze of tunnels the soldiers had supposedly dug underneath the school to house ammunition and bodies. But I didn't bother listening. It changed nothing for me. I might not have fit in among the other girls. I might not have understood their jokes or their conversations or their ways. But it didn't matter. Within the walls of St. Bernadette's, I was happy, comforted, secure.

Now here I am, almost seventeen and in my last year of school. Everyone is busy making plans—college, university, matriculation, sixth form, public or private, overseas or local, self-funded or scholarships. This is what my mother also expects of me. Good grades, good job, good car, good house, good life. Then she can show her friends, the way she shows off her fancy branded handbags. *See what a good job I did, raising this perfect child? No husband also. See how I managed all on my own? See how she honors me and my sacrifices? See this life I have built, in which I want for nothing?* She doesn't mention the fact that she never needed to work at all, that my grandfather died when I was little and left her, his only daughter, with more money than she could spend in a lifetime.

Ahead of me three girls climb out of a school bus together. It's orange, the exact color of mandarins. They laugh and joke and take up much more of the sidewalk than they need to. "Come on!" they yell loudly at each other. "We have to go before it's too late!"

Before it's too late. I start walking faster, as if I'm the one they're talking to, as if they are waiting for me to catch up. For just one second I think about running up to them, putting an arm over one girl's shoulder, laughing and teasing like I'm one of them. Part of the group. What would they say? How would they react?

I check my watch. The first bell is about to ring. I walk faster, but not fast enough to keep pace with the girls ahead. My mind chants a mantra in time with my footsteps: *Before it's too late, before it's too late, before it's too late.*

Khadijah

"Earth to Khadijah," Sumi sing-songs right in my ear, making me jump. I look up to see the other girls filing slowly off the bus. "We're here. Save your daydreams for later, can?"

I stick out my tongue like I'm five, and grab my backpack. I pivot on my heel and walk straight into the soft bulk of Uncle Gan, the bus driver. He is standing and looking at us. Arms crossed, a sour expression on his face. I smell the fresh-laundry scent of his wrinkled striped shirt, and something else. Something that immediately makes my heart start leaping uncontrollably in my chest. Something that sets alarm bells clanging throughout my entire body.

Cigarettes.

He smoked cigarettes too. The smell filled my nostrils until it felt like it was part of my bloodstream. There was no way to avoid it, not with his weight pressed on top of me. Later I swore I could still smell it even when the sheets had been washed. Even after we'd thrown them away. Even after I'd burned the mattress.

Three months of therapy, and I still sleep on the sofa in

the living room. My nightmares are all damp, groping, reaching hands and the smell of cigarettes.

DANGER, the voice in my head screams. *DANGER, DANGER, DANGER.* And suddenly I'm back in the darkness, drowning in it, drowning beneath the heavy weight that pins me down and won't let go, drowning in my own silence, and I want to run and scream and cry and throw up all at once, and, and, and

And there is a gentle hand on my elbow. A reassuring presence at my back. Sumi, I think. Flo. And I take a deep breath and try to focus.

You are on the bus. You are here, at St. Bernadette's. You are safe.

"You're okay," Flo whispers. "We've got you."

"You girls can go faster or not?" Uncle Gan grumbles, as he does every morning.

"Relax, Uncle," Sumi says with a jaunty smile. She guides me gently past him—*Hold your breath, Khad; try not to smell him*—and toward the door. "We're going."

"Your friend okay, ah? She looks like she wants to vomit." He frowns. In his voice I hear the healthy fear of a man who doesn't want to spend the morning cleaning barf off peeling pleather seats.

"She's fine lah Uncle. Don't worry." Sumi turns to me. "You are, right?" she asks softly.

I nod, even though it feels like my legs are about to collapse under me. Aishah is gone; everyone is gone. We're the last ones to get off. Just ahead of us, farther up the hill, the wrought-iron gates of St. Bernadette's are flung open, like arms awaiting a hug. There is a tug, somewhere in my chest. *As usual,* I tell myself, clinging to it like a mantra. As usual.

The sharp *drrrrrrring* of the school bell sounds just as we step onto the pavement. Sumi swears under her breath.

"Come on," she says, already breaking into a run. "We're going to have to hurry so we can make it before the second bell. I can't afford another tardy slip. My mother already threatened to whack me with the feather duster last time."

"May I point out," Flo yells to her steadily advancing back as we struggle to keep up, "that not all of us are school runners like you, Miss Sumitra?"

But Sumi is too far ahead now, loping away from us on those long legs. Her cropped curls bounce in the wind. Flo might as well be talking to the shadows, or the monkeys chittering in the nearby trees.

"Typical," Flo mutters as she reaches up to retie her hair.

I grin a grin that's still a little wavy around the edges. I slip my arm through hers. *As usual,* I think. *All is as usual.*

"Come on," Flo tells me. "Let's go."

Assembly is uneventful, until the headmistress, Mrs. Beatrice, stands and walks to the podium. The tightness of her pencil skirt makes her steps small and forcefully dainty. The clack, clack, clack of her sensible black heels echoes through the silent hall. She clears her throat, and the mic whines in protest, making us all wince. "Good morning, young ladies."

"Good morning, Mrs. Beatrice," the hall murmurs back.

She clicks her tongue. "Are you still asleep? Again, with some energy, please."

"Good morning, Mrs. Beatrice," everyone around me says. It is marginally louder this time, and the headmistress smiles, thin-lipped and satisfied. "Very good," she says. "You will all, of course, recall the incident that happened in our school this past week."

An incident. Such an innocent word, as if someone lost their shoe or slipped in the corridor.

"I'm sure it was most distressing for many of you to see your friends afflicted in such a way." Mrs. Beatrice blinks as she scans the paper she's holding.

Someone has clearly laid out all the talking points she's sup-posed to hit. Afflicted. I close my eyes, just for a moment. I remember the sound of the screams. The way terror traced pat-terns on my skin. The trail of goose bumps it left in its wake.

"The teachers and staff of St. Bernadette's are, of course, always here for you. We have taken the appropriate steps to make sure all parts of the school have been, er, appropriately cleansed—"

Someone snorts, and soft laughter breaks through the hall.

Mrs. Beatrice raps the podium sternly. "Silence, please. Silence. As I said, the situation has been taken care of, and we are sure such occurrences will not happen again."

"I wonder what she thinks the actual cause was," Sumi whis-pers.

I manage a small shrug. I do not want to wonder.

"Shh." A prefect named Jane has somehow materialized at Sumi's elbow. Jane is the type of person who likes pointing out the teacher's mistakes. The type of person who takes particular pleasure in telling people what to do. "Stop talking. Pay attention." Bloody Jane.

Onstage, Mrs. Beatrice continues. "I understand it may be difficult, given what you have been through, so our school counselor, Mr. Bakri—" Mr. B half stands and gives an awkward wave. His grin is just a little too wide, a little too friendly. "Mr. Bakri will be on hand should you need someone to talk to, but of course you can also feel free to approach any teacher here. Otherwise, we trust in the resilience and strength of our girls and hope that you will go about your day as usual, always being sure to remember your role as representatives and ambassadors of our prestigious St. Bernadette's School."

Flo leans in. "In case you were wondering, she means, 'Don't embarrass us or make us look bad, because the whole world thinks we're cursed.'"

"Quiet!" Jane hisses.

"All right. Chill lah."

Once the speech is done, the teachers get the rest of assembly over with and send us off to our classes. 4 Cempaka is one floor up, sandwiched between 4 Anggerik and 4 Melati. The newer blocks, like the library and the form-five block, have slatted windows that open up to let the air in. But like in all the older classrooms at St. Bernadette's, there are no windows here.

Instead each of the rooms in the form-four block boasts two sets of massive wooden double doors opening up to narrow corridors. If you look to the right, you'll see the green hills; to the left, you'll see the canteen and tennis courts.

The three of us separate to settle into our seats. Teachers learned a long time ago to keep us apart. I'm surprised they allow us to be in the same class at all, to be honest.

I slide into place between Ranjeetha and Balqis. Ranjeetha is bland and inoffensive, like plain rice porridge your mom makes you when you're sick. Balqis breathes loudly through her mouth and is prone to telling stories that are entirely too personal.

"Morning, Khad," Ranjeetha says with a sunny smile.

I smile half-heartedly back. I know Ranjeetha doesn't expect a response. I like her a little more for it. Most of my classmates are used to this now, the whole me-not-talking thing. It's just that some are nicer about it than others.

"I am so tired," Balqis moans. "I don't know what I ate yesterday, but I cirit birit all night. Bathroom every hour. And the smell . . ."

I nod politely and keep my mouth even more firmly shut than before. This will not help me. Balqis doesn't need encouragement to overshare. She just needs an audience. The audience doesn't even really need to pay attention. They just have to be in her vicinity.

Thankfully, Puan Ramlah strides into the room right then. Puan Ramlah is both our class teacher and our English teacher. She can always be relied on for three things: motivational clichés, smelling overwhelmingly of rose perfume, and an increasingly creative string of Malay curses when riled. It is therefore 4 Cempaka's solemn duty to rile her up as often as we can.

Today, however, Puan Ramlah doesn't seem to need riling. Her large chest heaves beneath the shiny satin of her baju kurung. She waves away the singsong of "Good mor-ning, Puan Ram-lah" as if it doesn't matter.

"Good morning, class," she says, sitting heavily in her chair at the front of the room. "How are you? How is everyone?"

"Good," the class choruses back.

"No, no, don't give me that." Puan Ramlah sits back and fans herself. I can see beads of sweat forming on her forehead. "I know some of you must still be dwelling on what happened last week. I thought we could take some time to talk about it. You know. Clear the air."

I feel my blood freeze in my veins. *I don't want to talk about it,* I think, clenching my teeth hard. My jaw begins to throb. I don't. I don't. I don't.

Balqis takes the bait. Of course it would be Balqis. "I feel pretty sad about it," she volunteers. "For all those girls, you know? One of them was this girl I know in 5 Anggerik. She used to live near my house in Ampang. Her brother played badminton with my brother in the evening. It was weird seeing her being carried out of her class like that, all sweaty and all. She looked like she didn't even know what happened to her. Kind of dazed macam tu . . ."

I squeeze my eyes shut. For just a moment I remember what

it was like. How I was in the bathroom washing my hands when the screams began. The way the sounds bounced off the tiles. The way I ran out, looking about wildly for the source of the noise, only to realize it was coming from everywhere, everywhere, all around.

"Khadijah?" Puan Ramlah is talking to me now.

She's talking to you, Khad. Pull yourself together. I look up at her questioningly.

"You look like you might have something to share." Puan Ramlah leans forward. She steeples her fingers together like some kind of movie villain. "Something you might want to talk about."

Oh no, not you too. Let's just say that some teachers haven't been willing to accommodate this new Khadijah.

Two rows ahead I see Flo turn back to look at me. Concern is written all over her face. I can tell she wants to step in. To save me. I hate how much I want her to. I look at Puan Ramlah and shake my head quickly. *Please leave me alone.*

Balqis leans over to stare at my face. She is so close that I can smell the Milo she had this morning. "You sure?" she says. "Your face looks kind of funny."

I jerk back quickly, and my chair makes a harsh scraping sound against the concrete floor. I'm starting to break into a cold sweat.

"Khadijah—" Puan Ramlah begins.

"Cikgu, I'm sure she's fine," I hear someone say. Sumi, I think. But it's hard to be sure over the roaring in my ears. Why are they pressuring me like this? It's there again, that free-falling feeling. That sense of losing control.

And I hate losing control.

Puan Ramlah bristles as if we've hurt her feelings. "I was only going to say to you, and to everyone else here, that if you ever want to reach out for a private conversation . . ."

From my left I suddenly hear a soft gurgling. And when I look over, Ranjeetha is swaying back and forth, back and forth. She's pale, staring at a corner of the ceiling as if nothing can make her turn away. She gurgles again. It's a small, strange sound that comes from deep in her throat. As if there's something lodged there that she's trying to shake free.

And I feel a cold, cold fear stealing its way all over my body.

Oh no. Oh no. Oh no. *Say something, Khad. She's in trouble, and you need to say something.*

The words catch in my throat, almost choking me.

In the background Puan Ramlah is still going on in aggrieved tones. "And furthermore, there is really no need to interrupt, Sumitra. Was my question directed at you? No, it was not. You girls, really, ah, sometimes tak fikir, this Khadijah for example . . ."

But I'm not listening. I'm not even looking at her. I can only stare at Ranjeetha's face. And for a second—for just one brief second—Ranjeetha looks back at me. And the expression in her eyes is one that I recognize. A look of pure terror, a look that begs, *Save me. Please save me. Please. It's going to happen and I can't stop it. Please, Khad. Please—*

And then her eyes glaze over and become wide and staring. And there's absolutely nothing I can do but watch as Ranjeetha opens her mouth and begins to scream.

"It wasn't your fault," Sumi and Flo take turns saying to me. "You couldn't have done anything to help her. Nobody could have."

I want to tell them I know, and I was right there, and stop fussing. But I don't. Or maybe I can't. Is there a difference? I'm not sure anymore, really.

All I can think about is Ranjeetha's face as she screamed. The desperation in her eyes. Her mouth, open so wide, I swear I could see the back of her throat.

I don't remember if I screamed when It happened. I remember screams, the way they echoed in my ears, the way they tore through the silence until my mother flung open my bedroom door and saw the monster in my bed. I just don't remember if they were his or mine. Maybe both.

But the desperation. That, I recognized.

There is a long line of girls outside the office. Everyone is waiting to use the phone to call home. *I'm scared. Please come pick me up. I don't want to be here anymore.* Twelve more screamers today to add to the twenty-seven from last week. Thirty-nine in all, and nobody wants to be lucky number forty.

I feel Flo's hand on my hand, and I wince. I can't help it. She immediately withdraws, her expression apologetic. "Sorry," she whispers. "You want us to call your mom for you? We can. If that's what you want."

I think about this for a bit. I imagine my mother rushing to school to pick me and Aishah up. The overbearing concern, the pride at being needed again, at being asked for help. I shake my head. Absolutely not.

"Suit yourself," Sumi says. "We'll stay all day, just like always." That will have sounded convincing to everyone but us. Unfortunately, I've known Sumi since the time when she still watched *Didi & Friends*. I know all her tells. She keeps looking back at the line and clenching and unclenching her fists. Never mind the words she's saying; even the unflappable Sumitra wants out of here. But Sumi has spent a lot of the past three months following my lead. Watching my back. She will not leave me now.

"That's right," Flo says, linking her arms through ours. "Just like always. Like it's just another day. Forget it ever happened."

And so we go about our business and pretend everything is fine.

Which is a thing I'm really good at doing.

Rachel

The thing is, if someone came to me and asked me straight out, *Why? Why do you want to be in this play? Why do you want to act so much?* I'm not even sure I would have an answer. I don't know if acting is something I'll be good at. And usually I don't even try when I'm not sure I'll be good at something, because when you're used to being the best at things, being just okay feels a lot like failure.

But this. This is different. I saw the poster at the theater where we were rehearsing for choir, and I could not look away. RODGERS AND HAMMERSTEIN'S THE SOUND OF MUSIC, it said in big blue letters against a backdrop of green hills and clear skies. AUDITIONS NOW OPEN FOR THE VON TRAPP CHILDREN. I have watched *The Sound of Music*—it was on Mother's list of approved movies—and I know the story. I imagined myself as Liesl in a filmy white dress, floating prettily across the stage. Never mind that I have never danced in my life. *I am sixteen going on seventeen. I know that I'm naïve. . . .*

My choir mates walked past me then, bringing me back to reality.

"See you next week, Rachel," one girl said politely.

"Have a good weekend."

"Good work today."

I nodded and smiled but didn't reply. For the first time I was thinking, *What if I do something just for me? Just because I want to?*

Anyway, then Pakcik Zakaria sounded the horn and I woke up. Because in what universe would Mother let me do something so useless as be in some play? Every step I've ever taken has been toward a goal she has set for me.

That's why it was silly of me to even try. She was never going to say yes.

There is no teacher when I get back to class after my prefect duties, even though Puan Latifah is supposed to be there, explaining to us the history of the Malaysian constitution. And Puan Latifah is never late.

Everybody is busy talking and laughing, and nobody looks at me as I slip into my seat. I tap the shoulder of the girl in front of me, a girl named Dahlia, whose shoulder-length hair whips into my face as she turns around.

"What?" she says.

Rude, the Mother in my head sniffs. "Where's the teacher?" I ask her.

Dahlia stares at me. "You serious?"

"What do you mean?"

"Don't you know?"

I try not to click my tongue the way Mother does when she's irritated at something. "No. Otherwise I wouldn't be asking, what."

Dahlia sighs as if she's doing me a big favor. "There were more screamers just now," she says. "Not sure how many. But mostly over in the form-four block, I think."

"Oh." Come to think of it, I was wondering why everyone seemed a little more frantic than usual this morning. "I guess I wasn't paying attention."

"Figures." Dahlia snorts and turns back like she's trying to tell me the conversation is over. I tap her shoulder again.

"But where is everybody?"

She frowns at me. "What do you mean?"

I gesture to the empty seats all around us. "There are a lot of people absent today, aren't there? I mean, like, more than usual?"

"Well. Yeah." She looks at me like I have heads growing out of my armpits. "It's because of the screaming."

"But our class doesn't have any screamers."

"Yet." Dahlia examines her nails, which are shiny and perfectly rounded at the tips. "I guess people just didn't want to take any chances. So they stayed home. Lucky! I wish my mom would've let me ponteng also." She peers at me. "Aren't you even a little bit scared?"

I blink at her. "Of what?"

"I mean!" She leans in close. "Isn't it a liiiiittle terrifying, all this screaming, not knowing what's causing it, not knowing who will be next?" She grins. She does not look very scared to me.

"It's like something out of *Goosebumps* or, like, True Singapore Ghost Stories or something."

"It's just a case of mass hysteria," I tell her. "This is nothing new. There have been cases like this going back to the 1500s. In 1962, schools got closed down somewhere in Tanganyika because there was a laughing epidemic that affected almost a thousand children, with symptoms that lasted anywhere from two hours to sixteen days." I shrug.

Dahlia stares at me. "No shit, Little Miss Wikipedia."

I shift uncomfortably in my seat. I don't know why people look at me like this when I provide information they've been looking for. Like I'm weird or wrong for doing my research and knowing things. "What? I looked it up on the internet. You know. When it first started. Anyway, the point is, it's never gone longer than sixteen days. If it isn't over by today, it will be in, like, two weeks."

"I guess." She nibbles on one of her perfect nails. "So, what causes mass hysteria, then?"

"Nobody really knows." The Mother in my head sneers, *They just want attention. What else?*

Dahlia grins. "Then it could still be ghosts, couldn't it?"

I'm about to reply when Puan Latifah comes in, all breathless like she was running up the stairs. "Sorry, girls," she says, setting her things down on the table at the front of the class. "Please open up your books and copy these notes down. We will discuss after." She begins writing on the board, and I take out my notebook and dutifully begin writing everything down.

But even while my hands are busy, my head is full of all these empty seats around me. Are people really this afraid? Are we really this superstitious, these brilliant minds of St. Bernadette's, one of the best schools in Kuala Lumpur? I wonder what Mother would say if I told her, if I wanted to be one of those girls who stayed home because they didn't want to be next. Stay home? What for? You are scared of what, actually?

I wonder what those girls are scared of.

"Rachel."

I jump. Just a little. "Yes, Puan Latifah?"

"Are you still with us, or have you left this plane of existence for a more exciting one?" This is how Puan Latifah is, sarcastic and snide and supremely irritating. Everyone is looking at me, and I can feel my ears getting hot. The Mother in my head says, *You see? You see what happens when you sibuk thinking about other people's problems? Focus, Rachel.*

"I'm here, Cikgu." My tone is perfectly polite, but irritation bubbles just below the surface of my skin. Why is she picking on me? No teacher has ever had to worry about me and my string of straight As. I've never failed a thing in my life, except maybe making friends. And standing up to my mother.

The bell rings. The next period is about to begin, and our math teacher taps her foot impatiently outside, waiting to start. Puan Latifah gets her things and exits without another word, and I am saved.

But it is hard for me to glance up at the seats where my classmates should be and not wonder every time what it is that scared them away.

Khadijah

"Did your mom complain when you said you wanted to go to school today?" Sumi asks on Tuesday morning. "Because I had a hell of a time convincing my mother, let me tell you. Thought she was going to tie me up just to keep me from leaving."

I snort. Mak had a lot to say this morning about the school and all the things happening within its walls. "Why would you walk into a place that isn't safe?" she yelled. "Why would you walk straight into a situation where you might place yourself in danger, again? Why, Khadijah?"

Not that I answered her. But if I had, if I'd felt inclined to open my mouth, I might have told her that St. Bernadette's is the only place where I do feel safe, despite everything. I might have told her that it feels like the only place I really need to be. But I didn't say anything, which only made her madder.

She shook her head, hair flying all over the place. "I don't understand," I heard her mutter. "I don't understand this at all."

I assumed Aishah wouldn't come. Aishah obeys, that's her whole thing. But she just slung her backpack on and followed me out of the house without a word. And there she is, just ahead of us, arm in arm with her best friend, Sarah.

Sometimes my sister surprises me.

Flo laughs. "Really, ah? Because my mama was like, 'Please lah don't let some hysterical girls get in the way of you learning. You need it.'" She sniffs. "She could have said it without the insult. But you know Mama."

Sumi snorts. "Lucky. My mother kept going on and on about this so-called hold St. Bernie's has on us. 'You girls possessed aa? Why must go even with all these so scary, scary things happening? Why cannot just stay home nicely? You see this girl, Appa? So stubborn!' She wants to take me to the temple to pray later." Sumi's Aunty Nirmala impersonation has improved tremendously. I'm impressed.

I pat the pocket of my baju kurung. My mother made me stash a list of surahs and doas there this morning. Like a life vest or a fire extinguisher. In case of haunting, break glass.

"Did you see?" Flo asks. "There's a hashtag now. #StBerniesScreamers. We were trending the whole night. Higher than the latest episode of *Gegar Vaganza*. Higher than Jimin."

"You shouldn't pay any attention to that stuff," Sumi says, wrinkling her nose.

"How can you not?" Flo says, shrugging. "We're everywhere. Everyone's talking about us. You know it's viral when every influencer has an opinion. Even the food reviewers. Even the mommy bloggers."

Out of the corner of my eye, I see Sumi shoot Flo a glance

and shake her head slightly. "All the more reason for us to talk about something else, then," Sumi says. I don't know whether to be grateful or annoyed. I love them for protecting me, and I resent needing to be protected at all. "Get back to normal."

"Okay, okay," Flo says. "You know what else was trending?"

But I never find out. The road loops left and St. Bernadette's is right there, and for some reason I stop in my tracks.

Today the school doesn't look like the safe, welcoming place it's always been. Not even with all the lights on to ward off the gloom of impending rain.

Today, with any trace of sunlight smothered by the dark clouds gathering overhead, it looks foreboding.

Angry.

As I watch, just for a moment all the lights flicker off, then on again. Like a wink. Or a warning.

I blink.

In the distance the second bell rings, and Flo groans. "Not again. Come on, time to run for it."

It takes a few steps for them to realize that I'm not with them, and Sumi turns back with a confused look on her face. "Khad? Hurry up!"

But my feet feel like they're trying to walk through jelly. I feel brittle, as if with the slightest touch I might crumble into dust and be borne away on the breeze.

I shake my head and gesture at them to go ahead.

I should have known better, honestly. They never listen to me, after all. They march right back and link arms with me on either side. As if they're shoring me up. As if their energy is transferable. "Nonsense," Flo says, tossing her head so her bangs fly left and right. "You get into trouble, we all get into trouble. Together."

That's not what I'm afraid of. At least I don't think so. I'm not really sure why I'm afraid. I just feel like we are teetering on the precipice of something. But what that something is, I can't be sure.

"Agreed," Sumi says as she shortens her strides to match ours, falling into step, left, right, left, right. "And all it'll cost you is buying us ayam goreng from the canteen every recess for the rest of the week. Kan, Flo?"

"Right."

I manage to strangle out a laugh. Even to my own ears, it sounds pathetic.

"Sure." Flo nods. "It'll clog our arteries in, like, two days. But we'll die with grease on our fingers and a smile on our faces."

By the time I will myself to walk through the gates, we're hopelessly late, which means being forced to spend our time after assembly sweeping the hall and picking up stray rubbish on school grounds. The worst part of this is putting up with Jane's gleeful smirk.

"Next time maybe try to show up on time, ladies," she says snidely as she bosses us around.

Flo and Sumi pull faces behind her back. The lights stay firmly on.

As usual, I try to tell myself. All is as usual.

But it doesn't work.

Rachel

During Bahasa Melayu, our teacher has a meeting and tells us to go to the library and keep ourselves busy. I wonder if this is about the screamers again and feel a wave of irritation wash over me. I know it's not their fault or whatever, but do those girls have to take over everything?

I set my things down on a large table by the window, right in the corner, out of the path of the ancient air conditioner belching out gasps of cold air. (Mother would say, *Who knows when is the last time they cleaned that thing? So much dust. So much germs.*) The other girls are in little groups, chatting and gossiping and taking advantage of this unexpected freedom. But I figure it is as good a time as any to finish up my physics homework.

Clare the librarian passes by and smiles. "You are always working so hard!" she says, and I smile politely back, even though what I really want to say is, *Please stop. Please don't tell people how much time I spend in here doing homework by myself.* "It's okay to spend some time with your friends once in a while, you know!" she continues. She does not seem to realize the suffering she's causing me. "They tell you girls that failing these exams is like the end of the world, but it's really not lah! There is plenty more to life than doing well on some tests, okay? You're more than your achievements!"

The Mother in my head laughs a humorless laugh and whispers, *And what does she know about achievement?*

I swallow hard. I know Clare means well. But she has no idea. None.

"It's okay," I mumble. "I just have a little more to get done."

"But why don't you at least study with your friends?" she asks.

"Because I don't have any," I say. I don't mean to make her feel bad for me. I'm just telling her the truth. But I can tell she feels bad anyway. "It's not a big deal," I say quickly. "I'm used to doing stuff by myself. I don't mind. I can manage just fine."

There is a pause. "I know you can, Rachel," Clare says finally. "I know you can. But you're only this age once, and school ends for you soon enough. Don't you want to make some memories here? For yourself? Before it's too late?" She doesn't wait for an answer, just pats me on the head before walking away.

For a while all I can do is stare at her retreating back.

Before it's too late.

But what if it already is?

The handwriting in my notebook blurs for a second, and my heart starts hammering in my chest like a lion dance. Is this all there is? Just a constant need to fulfill Mother's expectations for me for my whole life? The right SPM results, the right university, the right degree, the right job, the right partner, the right life? It's suddenly hard to breathe. I snatch up a pen and push back my chair with a loud scrape that, just for a moment, makes the room go quiet. Then I march up to the bulletin board by the door. I saw it earlier when we came in, tried not to think about how it made me feel, how much I wanted to do it. SIGN UP SHEET, the paper reads in fat black letters. FORENSICS TOURNAMENT. I know all about this competition; the school enters a bunch of girls in it every year. It takes place at a fancy international school in KL, half an hour away. I've never taken part, never even let myself dream of signing up.

Until now.

I run my finger down the list of categories: ORIGINAL ORATORY, EXTEMPORANEOUS SPEAKING, DUET ACTING . . . My finger stops.

SOLO ACTING.

The Mother in my head is yelling now, her voice ringing in my ears. *Don't be stupid, Rachel,* she says. *This is a waste of your time,* she says. *Will you really disobey your mother this way?* she says. *Will you really disappoint me?*

I ask myself, *But what would you say, Rachel? What do you want to say?*

Before it's too late.

Quickly, before I can change my mind, I uncap my pen and carefully write my name, big and bold, on the line below SOLO ACTING. Rachel Lian.

Then I walk back to my seat. It's just two words, just one step. A small one. But already I'm finding it easier to breathe.

Khadijah

For a while the school day proceeds as normal. In 4 Cempaka we work away at math, and art, and biology. There are no screams. Well, except for one girl. She bought a packet of sugar doughnuts to eat before afternoon session began. A monkey snuck in and jumped down from the roof of the canteen to snatch the packet right off the table. That kind of scream happens often enough. Another note in the school's everyday symphony.

But this time all of St. Bernadette's goes silent.

You can see the exact moment when we go tense. The way we all hold our breaths, grip our tables a little harder. Straining as we wait for the next one. When it never comes, we allow ourselves to breathe. But anticipation ripples through every nerve, and any loud sound still makes us jump.

In the middle of English class I am called to the headmistress's office. Nobody tells me why. My footsteps echo oddly in my ears as I walk down the school's long corridors. I give every shadow a wide berth and try to pretend it's not because I'm scared.

Mrs. Beatrice awaits me with Puan Ani, the head of the English department. The school counselor, Mr. Bakri, hovers awkwardly in one corner. ("Call me Mr. B!" he always says, grinning like a talk show host. He is all white teeth and fake niceness. I have never been less inclined to call anyone anything in my life.)

"Sit," Mrs. Beatrice says.

I perch as little of my butt as possible on the chair across from her desk. I am ready for a quick getaway. All three of them look at me and smile as if I'm a contestant on some kind of nightmare version of *American Idol*.

"Khadijah," Mrs. Beatrice begins, and then stops. She taps loudly on the table with her pen when I fail to meet her eye. "Look at me, please. Thank you. Khadijah, we wanted to speak with you about the big debate that is coming up. As you know, St. Bernadette's has been at the forefront of competitive debate for many years, and it is our wish that in the national finals we are able to field our very best team."

Somewhere in the school someone shrieks loudly. My heart leaps into my throat as I count down the seconds, waiting for another scream. *Why are we talking about this right now?* I think. *Don't we have bigger things to worry about? Screaming girls, for example?*

No second scream comes, and I allow myself to slowly unclench, and attempt to listen to what Mrs. Beatrice is saying.

"You should know, Khadijah, that the reputation of St. Bernadette's is one we would like to maintain, particularly at this . . . trying time." She glances over at Puan Ani, who clears her throat.

I shift uneasily in my seat. They're acting like it isn't over. Like they're expecting more screams.

"Yes, Khadijah," Puan Ani says, "we've missed your presence very much in the regionals, and though we've pulled through, we really don't want to take any chances at the national level." She smiles at me. I think I smile back. I'm not sure. Puan Ani has always been nice to me. But I have a feeling I know what they're about to ask, and it's making me want to throw up.

"Do you think you'd be able to do that?" Puan Ani's smile wavers a little at the edges. "Khadijah? We've still been listing you as reserve, as you know, so technically you're still part of the team."

I look down. There's a hole forming in the canvas of my left shoe. Right there, right over the little toe. If I focus on that, maybe they'll stop expecting me to answer.

I see a pair of shoes shuffle over next to mine. Glossy brown leather with a perforated pattern on the toes. Mr. B. "Look, Khad—can I call you that? I've heard your friends call you 'Khad' instead of 'Khadijah.'"

No.

"I know about your . . . incident . . . a couple of months ago."

My pulse quickens. I try not to let it show. *Shut up. Shut up, shut up, shut up.*

"And I know how hard it must have been for you ever since.

But we—all the teachers and I—we're very worried about how you've been acting since then."

He smells of cheap cologne and cigarettes. He is too close. Too close. I grip the arms of the chair hard and focus on the glossy brown leather. *I am going to throw up all over your shoes.*

"I told you this before, but my door is always open if you want to talk about . . . everything."

I would rather eat rotten eggs. *Focus on the shoes, Khad. Focus on the hole in the canvas. Hold your breath and don't think about the smell of cigarettes and the weight on your chest and the sweat on your skin that isn't yours.*

"Don't you think it's been long enough now? Don't you think it's time to get back to your life?" he asks quietly. "Don't you miss the person you used to be?"

I push my chair back so fast, it almost topples over. And I push past Mr. B. And I run all the way to the bathroom, where I promptly heave up chunks of the cereal I ate for breakfast.

Debate, my mother always said, was the perfect activity for me. "You came out of me arguing with the doctor and all the nurses," she'd say. She delights in describing my red, puckered face. The way I howled like I was mad at the world for forcing me out of my safe refuge. And it's true. I didn't debate because I loved to talk. I debated because I loved to fight.

Maybe the teachers knew this too. I'd been earmarked for the team even before I got to form three. The youngest kid not only on the St. Bernadette's team but on any team. Most debaters were fourth and fifth formers. Pretentious, lofty sixteen- and seventeen-year-olds. And I loved beating them back down to the ground. I loved strategizing. I loved trying to figure out what they'd say, how we could poke holes in their argument, how they might counter us, how we would fight back. I made my words into fists, and in my eight minutes of talk time I punched like Tyson. I could tear apart their points in one or two well-timed sentences. Government or opposition—this was British parliamentary style, after all—I was Best Speaker more often than I wasn't.

I wasn't popular the way Flo was, but everyone, everyone at St. Bernadette's knew me as "the debater."

Until I became something else. Someone else. The girl who stopped talking. Which was slightly better than my other options: The girl whose stepfather did *that* to her. The girl who was abused. The girl *that* happened to.

At least "the girl who stopped talking" is an active thing. The result of something I did, not something that was done to me.

I can still taste bile on my tongue. I splash cool water onto my face. Mr. B's voice echoes in my head. *Don't you miss the person you used to be?*

I stare at the contours of my face in the chipped mirror above the sink. *He does not know,* I tell myself. He does not know that this is the one question I have avoided asking myself.

There is a flash of lightning outside. Seconds later, an answering crack of thunder.

In the bathroom the lights flicker off, one by one.

I am suddenly cold.

My skin is a map of goose bumps. My breathing is loud and ragged, my pulse deafening in my ears. I squeeze my eyes shut and try to get my body back under control. *Don't you miss the person you used to be?* I did not used to be the person who was afraid of the dark. I did not used to be like this.

A sudden gust of wind blows through. Each stall door slams shut, one by one by one.

Something lands on my face, sharp edges biting into my skin. I reach up with trembling fingers to remove it.

It is a leaf, nestled in the palm of my hand, brown and dry and curling into itself.

Outside, the rain keeps falling.

That night, after a silent family dinner and Isyak prayers, I lie on the couch, turning the leaf over and over in my hands. Waiting for sleep that will not come.

I do not sleep in my bedroom anymore. A few days after it happened, Mak came home and found me trying to burn my mattress in the backyard. I'd already stabbed it a few times. Ripped at its skin and exposed its insides. It wasn't destroyed enough for me. The next day she came home with lighter fluid and a brand-new blowtorch. She figured out how to use both, drove us somewhere safe and secluded in a borrowed pickup, and said not one word about the black smoke and ashes that we left behind. We never bought a new mattress.

Something about the leaf, about the feel of it on my skin,

makes me anxious. And the worst of it is, I cannot explain why.

I check my phone. The glow of the screen almost blinds me. 2:57 a.m. I give up on sleep, the way it has given up on me, and sit up.

Don't you miss the person you used to be?

Who was that person? I try to remember her, and get fleeting glimpses. Cobwebs of memories. Running through the corridors of St. Bernadette's with Sumi and Flo, laughing so hard, my stomach hurt. Making cookies with my mother. Asking for her advice. Eager to laugh with her, to tell her my stories. Helping Aishah—first with her shoelaces, then with her math homework, then with girls who were mean to her and with teachers who were unfair, then with our stepfather and his steady, disconcerting gaze. Raising my hand during a debate, stretching it up high so I would be noticed, desperate to make my point. Desperate to fight back. To be heard.

Now it is three forty-five a.m. I crumple the leaf up in my hand until it is nothing but dust. Then I tuck my phone under my pillow and go to sleep.

I dream of dark shadows and the rustle of dry, dry leaves.

Rachel

SOLO ACTING

Rachel Lian

I am practically vibrating as I wait in the hall for our briefing to begin. They made the announcement at the end of assembly. "All students who have signed up to participate in the forensics tournament this year, please stay back in the hall." *Me,* I think. *I'm one of those people, that's me, it's me.* For once the Mother in my head is silent. Or perhaps my euphoria is enough to drown out her admonishments. I keep remembering the way it felt to write down my name, to see it right there, in bold black ink you cannot erase. Of course I couldn't be in *The Sound of Music.* That was a big production, with tons of people involved and permissions needed to do all kinds of things. But this? Solo? Alone? That's nobody else that I have to work with. That, I can do. And that, I can hide from my mother.

There are a few of us waiting here for the teacher to appear. Everyone else is in pairs, or little groups, settling into an easy familiarity that tells me they know each other, they've done this before. I hover awkwardly beside the piano, half hiding behind its bulk, trying my best to appear nonchalant, like I belong here.

A teacher bustles up to us, and I recognize her as Puan Ani, who taught me English in form three. "Good morning, girls," she booms, and immediately everyone sing-songs their good mornings back. "One, two, three . . ." She counts us off under her breath, then jots it down in her notebook. "Right. You are all here because you signed up for this year's forensics competition. Now, some of you have participated in this before and will know the rules and the process, etcetera, etcetera." She waves a hand vaguely in the air. "But there are some of you who have never done this, and anyway, it's good for everyone to get a refresher." She clears her throat.

"Every year we are one of the few government schools invited to participate in what is considered quite an elite competition, with the bulk of competitors coming from international schools not just in Malaysia but all over South- east Asia." She looks around at all of us, making sure to peer directly into our eyes. "This is an honor, and we must not let the name of St. Bernadette's down. Especially now, when . . . so much has been happening." She coughs delicately. "I'm sure I don't need to tell you just how much it would mean for us to go to this tournament and do really, really well. Perhaps even win. Yes?"

Everyone mumbles an answering yes, and she nods in approval.

"Very well. Next steps. You are to select the pieces you wish to perform, or to write them if the category requires it, such as for original oratory. If at any point you find that you need some help, I and any of the other English teachers would be happy to . . ."

A piece, I think. *I need a piece to perform.* My mind is buzzing happily, and I feel almost giddy, like a little girl opening presents on her birthday. Or like some little girls, I suppose, the kinds that get Barbie dream houses and McDonald's birthday parties. My birthdays were just for the two of us. There was nobody else to invite. And Mother always gave practical gifts—books on great inventions, or biographies of world leaders, tickets to symphonies and recitals where I knew I was expected to study the movements of the lead violinist or pianist.

For a moment the Mother in my head moves restlessly. *Bad daughter,* she hisses. *Bad, bad daughter.* But even she isn't enough to quell my excitement.

"We will let you know once we finalize a rehearsal date," Puan Ani finishes with a flourish. "Any questions?"

One girl raises her hand. "How come there's a rehearsal this year?" she asks. "We didn't have one last year."

Puan Ani nods. "Yes, but this year we thought it would be helpful for us to see your pieces before competition so that we may give you any pointers for improvement as necessary."

"Oh." The girl shrugs. "Okay."

"Any other questions?"

Everyone stays silent, and Puan Ani beams at us.

"All right, then! I look forward to seeing you all up on that stage!"

Me too, I think. *Me too.*

The euphoria sends me wafting down the school corridors, propelling me gently through my duties in a pleasant pink haze. I sink into daydreams of hot stage lights and full theaters. Who do I want to be? What do I want the audience to feel? Am I going to be flashy and hilarious, dramatic and glamorous, restrained and emotional? Do I want to move them to tears, or have them laughing in the aisles? There are so many possibilities, so many new identities to explore, so many ways to shed this old cocoon that imprisons me, and emerge with new wings, a Rachel Lian reborn.

I let myself drift through class, through recess, through school, the thoughts of my budding stage career embracing me like a hug. I think of snatches of dialogue as I go to the bathroom, imagine myself drenched in the bright glow of a spotlight as I wash my hands. In the empty seats of the classroom where my classmates have headed to biology lab without me, I see rows of spectators watching me in awe, and I imagine their rapturous applause as I gather my books. I think about the new Rachel Lian as I walk past other classrooms full of bent heads and the soft scratches of pen against paper, and as I turn the corner to go up the stairs, and as I see the girl.

She is standing at the bottom of the staircase, right foot placed almost perfectly in the center of the first step, hands clenched by her sides, head bowed. And she sways, rocking softly back and forth, so that her straight hair, which hangs to just above her shoulders, sways too. It's as if she's gearing herself up to move, to take that first step.

The haze around me shimmers slightly, and I frown at this disruption to my plans and daydreams. "Hey," I say. "Are you all right?"

The girl doesn't respond. She just keeps swaying.

I try to ignore the tendril of resentment that wiggles its way through the crack in my daydreams, the little hint of frustration that blossoms in my stomach. She might be hurt, I tell myself, or sick, or having a mental health moment, and you know, who am I to judge her for that? "Hey," I say again. "Do you need help? Do you want me to call a teacher, or take you to the sick-room or something?"

Still she doesn't answer, but in the silence that stretches on after my words, I can hear her ragged breathing. She's panting as if she just ran a marathon.

Not your business, the Mother in my head sniffs. *Get past her and go to your class. Is one act of irresponsibility not enough for you today?*

I do my best to ignore Mother's words. I reach out a hand tentatively—I know some people don't like being touched, after all—and grab the girl's shoulder. "I'm sorry, but are you—"

In one swift, sudden move, the girl snaps her head around to look at me. Suddenly there is a roaring in my ears, and I can feel my heart begin to pound like a drum.

Because the girl's eyes are wide and staring; blue-green veins are bulging in her pale, sweaty temples; and her lips are curled in a snarl. She throws her head back and turns her glassy eyes to the ceiling just above me.

And then she begins to scream, and scream, and scream, as if she will never stop.

Khadijah

It's Wednesday. I keep forgetting. I glance over at Balqis's exercise book to make sure over and over again, searching for the rounded ballpoint letters that spell it out neatly in the top left corner. Eventually even Balqis gets impatient. She writes it for me in big black felt tip letters on a pale pink sticky note. Then she smacks it onto the corner of my desk. *WEDNESDAY.* The paper smells like strawberries.

The gaps in the classroom feel like black holes. The teachers try to hide the spaces where girls are missing by getting us to switch seats so we're all clumped together. They act like it's an idea that just dawned on them. "Isn't that better?" they say. "You're all so much closer now!"

They teach and call on students and berate us for work undone, and my classmates talk and laugh. Everything seems so normal. Everyone seems so normal. At one point someone raises her hand to ask about a screaming girl, and the teacher shushes her. "Let's not talk about them anymore," she says brightly. "I think it's time we all move on, don't you?"

I just stare at her. I don't know how to move on, how nobody else seems afraid, how they don't feel the very air within St. Bernadette's pressing down on their skin like it wants to keep us still, quiet.

Mr. B pokes his head in at some point during the day and clears his throat. "I'm always here if anyone wants to talk." I try very hard not to meet his eye. To appear invisible. Nobody replies. My fingers are still trembling. I sit on them to make them stop. Sumi and Flo shoot worried looks in my direction that I pretend not to see. Even if they asked, which they don't, I cannot explain what is making me so anxious.

Maybe it's that I know what it's like to sit in the shadow of a monster and hope it doesn't appear. Hope it doesn't notice you. Hope it isn't hungry.

It has stopped raining, but the clouds linger, painting everything in shades of gray. The girls chat about silly, inconsequential things between classes. The latest IVE video, a pair of shoes Flo is begging her mother to let her buy, Asha from 5 Orked's new girlfriend. I don't know if I'm the only one to glance outside and notice it. But the monkeys in the trees make no sound. They sit on the branches and stare at us from a distance. As though they know something we don't. As though they are waiting.

I wait too, my body tense and as tightly coiled as a spring.

But when it happens, it's still a shock.

It's like that scream wakes everyone up. From daydreams straight into this shared nightmare. Backs straight, heads snapping to attention, alert and afraid. The scream is long, low, the kind that's so hoarse, it feels like it's ripping the screamer's throat into shreds.

"How many do you think today?" whispers May Ling.

"Don't know," Jacintha says quietly. "Could be five. Could be fifty. No way to tell."

Puan Aminah, who has still been valiantly trying to teach us Malaysian history, clicks her tongue. "Let's just stay together here and hope for the best," she says gently. "And perhaps . . . perhaps we ought to close the doors." She pauses. "And lock them."

What are we trying to keep out? I wonder. And then, fleetingly, *Or what are we trapping in?* I remember what locked doors mean; they mean hidden things, for better or worse.

No matter. Everyone is desperate for something to do. Something other than waiting for the screams to end. So we close the doors and slide the deadbolts into place and huddle together, trying to find some kind of comfort in each other's familiar presence. In one corner Zulaikha begins to recite Ayat Kursi under her breath. Protection. I find myself following along, though my lips are chapped and dry. Mak would be proud, I think wildly. She'd be proud that I'm finally doing what she told me to do.

"There's another one," Flo says. This one is high-pitched and stuttering. As if the screamer needs time to take a breath, to gear up before each section.

"I wonder who it is," Jacintha says. Nobody answers. I can feel my heartbeat in my entire body. In my temples. In the tips of my fingers. In the soles of my feet. I'm sweating. It's hot. It's so hot.

Another one. This one is less scream, more sob. The kind that racks the entire body, makes your chest ache. The screams are starting to layer now, crisscrossing, twisting, weaving into each other. I wonder how long we'll all sit here. Counting off each one like in some kind of twisted *Sesame Street* episode. One scream! Two screams! Ha-ha-ha! I wonder if one of us will be next. I wonder if it will be me. I wonder what it feels like. I wonder if I would feel terrified, or free. I had screamed, before. When It happened. The scream stuck in my throat at first, choked me as much as his hands around my neck. It had been hard, so hard, to push it out. To make myself heard. There is a sudden ache in my right forearm. I look down and realize I've dug my nails into the flesh so hard that I've drawn blood. Red spots bloom on the white fabric of my sleeve. *Mak is going to kill me,* I think.

We are at scream number six—piercing, shrill—when there's a clattering in the corridor outside. And then a pounding on the door that makes us all jump and forces a tiny shriek out of Zulaikha.

"Open up!" a voice yells, tear-soaked and frantic. "Please, please open up!"

Puan Aminah wrenches the door open. We blink as sunlight streams into the classroom. It takes a minute to make out the figure standing silhouetted in the doorway. Her chest is heaving, and tears are streaming down her cheeks.

I know this girl. This is Sarah. I've seen her around school, arm linked through my sister's. I've seen her with her hijab off and laughing with Aishah over random TikToks on our couch after school. She has eaten off our plates, slept over at our house, sat through our annual Lord of the Rings marathon.

Why is she here?

I feel my heart leap into my throat. I rise to my feet.

Sarah's face crumples as soon as she sees me. "Kak Khad," she sobs. "Kak Khad. I was there, I was right next to her, I saw her scream. I couldn't stop her. I . . . I . . ."

I am trembling all over now. Who? I will her silently to tell me. Who?

And even though I know in my heart and in my bones who she's talking about, that there could be only one person she could be talking about, it still feels like a knife twisting in my gut when she says it.

"Aishah."

Rachel

I don't believe in the supernatural. I don't. I refuse to fall victim to the same madness that plagues so many of my schoolmates.

But there is something about the memory of that screaming face, the way the girl's spittle misted against my skin, that unsettles me.

The screams brought a teacher running, and I watched silently as the teacher tried her hardest to bring the girl to her senses, to talk to her, to make her stop. More than anything else, that was what I wanted, for it all to end. But it seemed to take hours—*That doesn't make sense. It was probably just a few minutes, Rachel. Don't be silly,* the Mother in my head says—before the girl finally shut her mouth and crumpled into a heap on the floor, like she'd finally run out of batteries.

"Rachel." The teacher looked at me as if she'd just realized I was there. It was Cik Diana, and she was youngish and new and pretty, and very popular among the student body because of all these things. She also looked vaguely sick and as though she were feeling utterly out of her depth. "Help me get her to the sickroom."

And we walked together, shouldering this limp body between us, as more screams echoed through the rafters of St. Bernadette's. We weren't even able to get her into the sickroom, a musty little room with two hard plastic chairs and a single bed covered in sheets of dubious cleanliness, all of which were already occupied. The teachers were lining more chairs up outside, and we placed her carefully on one of them. There were eleven new screamers today.

I was still trembling when I came home. I'm still trembling now, and the ladle clinks loudly against the side of the bowl over and over again as I try to put beef and broccoli onto my plate.

Mother raises an eyebrow after yet another loud clink.

"Sorry," I mumble. Then "Sorry" again, but clearer this time. Mother hates when people mumble. *Ridiculous, Rachel. So utterly ridiculous to let some silly overly emotional girl throw you off this badly.*

I spend the rest of the meal being as silent as I can, which really isn't as difficult as it sounds. I'm used to keeping quiet around Mother, after all, used to nodding and making sounds of polite agreement and saying nothing at all that is real or true, over a meal that I barely eat.

"What is the matter with you?" she suddenly asks, and I look up, surprised.

"Hmm?" My mind was far, far away from the broccoli in oyster sauce that I am pushing around on my plate. I was thinking about the girl's face, the way her mouth opened so big that I could see all the way to the back of her throat. I was thinking about the way her screams ripped through my eardrums, deafening me for a moment. I didn't think Mother would notice.

But of course Mother noticed. Mother notices everything.

Some actress you are, Rachel Lian.

"You are acting strange tonight," Mother says, frowning at me. "What's wrong?"

"Nothing," I say automatically. I am conditioned to tell my mother nothing.

She peers at me closely, and I have the distinct feeling she's seeing everything, from the dirt in my pores to my innermost emotions. "This is not true," she pronounces after she's done scanning me. "You are not telling me something. What is it you are thinking about so much?"

"I'm not thinking about anything, Mother," I say, trying my best to maintain eye contact, keep my expression open and honest. *Think of it as practice, Rachel. Think of it as playing a part.*

"Really?" She raises one eyebrow at me, a trademark Mother move. "Hmm. You sure these . . . these screaming girls are not distracting you?"

I try to shake off the memory of the look in the girl's eyes, the way her baby hairs rose in crazy zigzags from her sweaty face. "I'm not distracted," I lie. I haven't figured out the girl's name, and for some reason this is bothering me, that we shared such an intimate moment and I don't even know who she is.

"Then what is wrong with you?" Mother leans forward and presses a cold hand to my forehead. This is a rare moment;

Mother is not a person who touches. "Are you sick? Do we need to pay a visit to Dr. Priya?"

"Everything's okay, Mother," I say. "Really. I'm absolutely fine." I spear the broccoli with my fork, take a bite, and set the fork down, just to prove how fine I really am.

Mother puts down her own fork and spoon and sighs. "Rachel," she says. "You have just put a piece of broccoli into your water."

"What?" I look down, and there it is, a lump of green sitting at the bottom of my glass. "Oh," I say.

"So I will ask you again." Mother picks up a piece of beef with her fork and lays it gently on the bed of rice in her spoon. "Got anything you want to tell me, or not?"

I grit my teeth. *Get a grip, Rachel. This is your last chance, your last opportunity to do something, and be something besides Mother's perfect daughter. You can't let some hysterical girls stop you.*

Lights. Camera. Action.

"Actually, yes." I set my own utensils down. *Okay, Rachel. You can do this. You're not lying to Mother. You're acting.* "There are going to be a lot of extra classes in the next few weeks," I say carefully. "You know. Since SPM trials are coming up. The classes are optional, but I thought it would be good for me to go. They're free anyway. And the teachers always discuss questions from past papers. And I thought it might be good to get more one-on-one time with my teachers. Especially if I'll need reference letters for university." *Babbling, Rachel. You're babbling.* I steal a glance at Mother's face, but as usual I can't tell what she is thinking. "Is that okay?" I ask, and then kick myself mentally for it. People like Jane probably don't ask. They just tell people what they want to do and expect everyone to go along with it.

"Hmm," Mother says. It is not an answer. I'm not sure what it is or what it means, and it feels like years before she asks her next question. "Will it affect your activities?" she asks.

I almost want to hold my breath. That she is even asking means there's a chance. That she's considering it. "It will not affect violin lessons," I tell her carefully. "Or piano. My karate coach is going back home to Taiwan for a bit. There's the choir Christmas performance—"

Mother waves this away like a mosquito. "Christmas is not as important as university," she says.

"There's the volunteering."

"I can talk to them," she says. "Those poor children need help, I know, but you're the one with a chance at Harvard or Cambridge. You've got your own needs to think about."

I bite my lip. I hate every time Mother talks like other people just don't matter.

"What? Don't make that face at me. It's true." She dabs at her mouth with one of the cloth napkins that are laid out for us at every meal, the ones she makes Kak Tini wash and iron before every use. "Anyway, keep me and Pakcik Zakaria informed of your schedule at all times. And study hard. SPM is only the first step; you know this. There are many, many steps to go. And it is very important to build these good study habits now. University will be easier to manage later on if you can do that."

"Yes, Mother." I'm not really listening. All my anxieties, all the memories of screaming girls have faded away. In their place are amazement, wonder, joy. I cannot believe I pulled this off. I am not used to this feeling, this world where I know something my mother does not, where I have something she cannot take away from me. It feels a lot like victory.

Khadijah

They call Mak.

I hear her before I see her. I am sitting cross-legged on the cold floor, and Aishah is leaning against me in the sickroom. This is all the space there is. Three girls are already sitting side by side on the bed. Two more sit on scratched-up plastic chairs. The rest are outside. Aishah's sweat soaks into my shoulder. I don't move her. This seems like the least I can do. And I have done so little, so little to protect her. The screams have wrung her out like a wet rag. She doesn't speak. I wonder if she'll be like me and decide that silence is better than the alternative.

Outside the door, my mother is not silent. "Where is my daughter?" I hear her say. She is high-pitched, frantic. "Where is she? What happened to her?"

"We don't know," the kind-faced ladies at the office say, stricken. "We're so sorry, Puan. We just don't know."

The ride home is strange and silent. It reminds me in painful ways of the time after It happened. Aishah is playing the role formerly played by yours truly. She is the victim, stretched across the back seat of our car, pale and wan. Eyes closed like Sleeping Beauty waiting for someone to wake her up from the nightmare.

I kept mine closed too.

My guilt is a stone in the pit of my stomach. It is a vise around my neck that chokes me. It is iron bands around my chest, tightening with every minute. You protect your little sister. That's what you do. Beside me my mother drives her car as if she's possessed. Her eyes are laser focused on the road ahead. The rage that comes from her is so palpable, it's like gasoline shimmering in the air all around her. "I knew it," she mutters. "I should have made you both stay home. I should have made you listen to me."

I understand this too, the search for control in a world that continues to fall apart around you. I could tell her this does not work. That the world will keep breaking regardless.

But I don't speak. I never speak. It begins to rain, and my mother turns on the windshield wipers. In my head I chant along to their rhythm: *I have failed. I have failed. I have failed.*

My mother tries and fails to get either of us to eat some lunch. Her anxiety, her constant fluttering—all of it clogs up the air and makes it even harder to breathe. When she finally sends Aishah to bed and announces she is going back to the office, it is a relief. "Look after your sister," she tells me as she heads out the door. As if I need to be told. As if I haven't been doing exactly that my whole life. As if it isn't another reminder of how I have let my sister down.

In Mak's wake, she leaves quiet, but no peace.

My guilt makes me restless. It is no longer a stone, or a vise, or iron bands. It is ants in my veins. It forces me up, sends me pacing in circles around the room. Even prayer doesn't calm me down.

Why is this happening? Why would it happen to Aishah?

Aishah and I have phones—beat-up old models Mak bought secondhand off Carousell. As long as homework is done, we're allowed to use them after school. My homework isn't exactly done. But Mak isn't here, so how would she know?

I take my phone and open up the browser. Type "screaming schoolgirls" into the search bar. The top news results are all about St. Bernadette's. They're all the same: Careful reports from people who observe us from a distance. Like zoo animals.

As I scroll farther down, I realize that the articles are no longer about us. They date back years and years. I click on one. THE MYSTERY OF SCREAMING SCHOOLGIRLS IN MALAYSIA, the headline reads. A British expert calls Malaysia "the mass hysteria capital of the world." I wonder what makes him an expert. I learn about April 2016, when the screams spread from school to school, seemingly without reason. I learn about 2019, when hysteria broke out among girls at a school in Kelantan. And I read this, an account from one of those 2019 screamers:

> I was at my desk feeling sleepy when I felt a hard, sharp tap on my shoulder.
>
> I turned round to see who it was and the room went dark.

Before I knew it, I was looking into the "other-world." Scenes of blood, gore and violence.

The scariest thing I saw was a face of pure evil.

It was haunting me, I couldn't escape.

The only thing I don't learn is why—what is causing these episodes of collective hysteria in places with no obvious connection to one another.

And I need to know the why. I need to know what I can do to stop it from happening again. So I can keep Aishah safe.

I click and scroll and click and scroll, and somehow I find myself on a Facebook page. St. Bernie's Old Girls, the banner across the top reads. The text is splayed in bold across a grainy picture of the school. It's very Graphic Design Is My Passion. As with most Facebook groups, it seems to have started out promisingly. But now it's the same handful of people commenting on everything. There's the one who posts relentlessly optimistic daily good mornings. There's the one shilling MLMs.

And there's one more.

Someone has posted a link to an article about the screamers of St. Bernadette's. I find her in the comments section. Under rows of OMGs and all the usual thoughts and prayers, her reply is short and to the point.

So St. Bernadette's is screaming again.

Again?

My guilt is still there, but it is overshadowed by something else. A new feeling. It's the way I feel when I'm worrying away at an argument. When I'm systematically unpicking an opponent's carefully woven statements. Here is the start of the thread, and if I pull at it enough, I will unravel it all. Adrenaline is coursing through my veins. I click on her username, which is "Sasha A." The display picture is nondescript; a woman in a hijab, back turned to the camera, facing the setting sun. There are no details of her life on display. No full name, no age, no city. No cherubic, beaming children, no adored pets. No pictures with friends or family. No unnecessary comments on the hot-button topic of the day. No breadcrumbs to follow.

I bring up the messenger box. My thumbs hover over the keypad. I'm hesitant, anxious. But only for a second.

What happened at St. Bernadette's when you were there?

I hit send. And then I wait. And wait. And wait. I fall asleep waiting.

When I wake up, there is still no reply.

Rachel

Later that night Mother sits, her back perfectly straight, and switches on the news, as is her custom. I excuse myself to go to my room and study. I'm not, of course, actually going to study. I'm looking for that piece, that magical piece that will allow me to unleash everything inside me, truly show myself on the stage for everyone to see for the first time in my life. My unease from the screams has been forgotten; my brain is too busy turning cartwheels.

I still can't believe it worked. My little trick worked. I scroll through pages and pages of monologues, mouthing the words, picturing myself onstage, a spotlight shining right on me. Solo acting, Rachel Lian.

And then I find it. The perfect one, the one I feel in my bones was meant for me. Made for me.

I skim the words, my excitement, delight, adrenaline growing with every second. This is the one. This is the one. I know this girl, recognize her voice and all the layers and nuances of her emotions, feel her heart beat. I can act her.

I can become her.

With trembling hands I grab some loose sheets of writing paper and a pen. I cannot use the printer for this. Mother will hear it and glide into the room and start asking questions, things like, *What are you doing using the printer late at night?* And, *What for?* And, *Show me.* It's not a risk I'm willing to take.

And so I begin to write, carefully copying the whole thing out by hand, in my neatest handwriting, double- and triple-checking every word to make sure I get each one right.

And then I hear it.

"This is the mass hysteria capital of the world."

"St. Bernadette's in the heart of Kuala Lumpur . . ."

St. Bernadette's?

I set down my pen and walk out of my room. "What are you watching?"

"Oh." Mother shrugs. "Some talk show. They're talking about the thing that keeps happening at your school." Her upper lip curls in an expression of utter contempt. "As if this is important. As if this is news."

I sit on the edge of the couch. The bland TV host has hair so sprayed down that it doesn't move at all, and perfect red lipstick. She gestures enthusiastically as she talks to a panel consisting of a man with the most luxuriant mustache I've ever seen, a lady in a lavender hijab, and an overly loud American sweating slightly in a checkered suit jacket.

"I don't know how I feel about that," the lady in the hijab is saying, and the American shakes his head. The patterned jacket was a mistake; it makes him look like he's glitching every time he moves.

"You simply cannot deny it," he says. I think I see the other two panelists wince at the sound of his voice. "Say what you like, but you simply cannot deny that this is an overwhelmingly female phenomenon. Most cases of mass hysteria in modern times happen among women and girls."

"Now, now," Mustache says jokingly. "You're going to get us into trouble with our viewers, you know. All the feminists will be after our heads. Better be careful."

"They're welcome to review the literature themselves," the American says stiffly. "I'm merely telling you what the data shows us."

"Indeed." Mustache nods, stroking his upper lip. "Well. Women are the weaker sex, after all, ha-ha, and perhaps more prone to spiritual affliction—"

The American's eyes look like they might bulge out of his head. "Spiritual affliction?" he repeats.

At the exact same time, the hijabi bristles as she says, "Weaker sex?"

"But what do you think is causing all of this?" the host asks, interrupting smoothly. "St. Bernadette's is hardly the first." My stomach contracts at the mention of the school, of us. "We've all heard of this phenomenon, particularly in schools, for years and years now. Kelantan in 2019 was of course the last major case that sparked international attention, but there have been reports of smaller incidents since. What do we think is causing these waves of hysteria?"

"A bunch of hysterical girls looking for attention," Mother scoffs as she sips on her tea, served as always in a fine china cup hand-painted with delicate flowers.

I think back to the girl's wide-open mouth, the strange blank look in her eyes that gave way to terror once she was herself again. *You would not say that if you saw what I saw,* I think. But I don't say it aloud. Mother doesn't like when you talk back.

"Well, the science—" the American begins, before he is interrupted by the hijabi.

"It's stress," she says, nodding firmly. "Plain and simple. We put far too much stress on children these days to do well, to excel in their exams. We tell them SPM means everything. And the effects of that—"

The TV blips off, and I blink. I didn't realize I'd been clenching my fists the whole time. *What gives them the right?* I wonder. What gives them the confidence, this panel of "experts," to speak about us and our experiences, without so much as asking us what we think or feel?

"Nonsense," Mother pronounces, picking up her book of sudoku puzzles and a pen. "All nonsense. Waste of time, discussing all this. Just ignore and move on." She looks at me, her eyes all narrow, and wags a finger in my direction. "I know you found yourself unfortunately mixed up in all this." She waves one hand vaguely in the air. "And I know you helped that girl out of the goodness of your heart. But you do not need to get involved. Stay away from those troublesome girls."

Troublesome is one of Mother's least-favorite attributes.

It is how she describes children who do not behave in restaurants, people on motorcycles, and a large swath of politicians. It is how she probably thought of me when I called her from school. Cik Diana told me to call my mother. "She might want to take you home," the teacher said to me, all warm sympathy. I already knew how Mother would respond, but I called because the teacher was there with me, "for moral support." And it felt like not calling Mother would be letting the teacher down somehow. Cik Diana listened, nodding encouragingly, while I told my mother what had happened. I was glad she couldn't hear Mother's response: "So?"

So I stayed until the school day was over and Pakcik Zakaria came to take me home.

Troublesome. There is no redeeming the screamers in her eyes. There is something about the way she says it, the discontented twist of her mouth, the quick expelling of breath through her nose.

"I don't think that's fair," I say.

Mother stares at me, eyebrows raised. "Oh?" she says.

I wipe my clammy palms surreptitiously on my napkin. My mouth is suddenly dry. "I don't think those girls chose to be screamers," I say. It's hard to look directly at Mother, so I focus on bits and pieces of her, anything so I don't have to meet her gaze. "I don't think it's fair to blame them for something they couldn't control," I say to her chin.

"Really." Why won't she stop staring at me? I can feel my face growing hot. "And what makes you say that, Rachel? What about these girls has you suddenly rushing to defend them, hmm?"

"Um." I focus on the pearl earring on my mother's right lobe. "I . . . I guess . . . I mean, I think . . ." I am trying to stand up to her, trying to tell her what I think, and it's all unraveling so fast, and I don't know why my heart is pounding, but suddenly I'm not sure what to do.

"You think?" She sniffs. "Because it seems to me like you haven't been thinking very much at all. Don't you agree?"

When I finally look up to meet Mother's eyes, there is a steely glint in them I recognize. My heart sinks. *Now you've done it, Rachel.* But I don't say anything. I just nod.

"Good." She turns her attention back to her book. "That man said girls are weak. But you know better. You are strong. And you don't let any of these silly things distract you. All right?"

I get to my feet. "All right, Mother."

"Go to your room."

I head back to my room and close the door. The euphoric rush I felt when I found my acting piece is gone; even the sight of the papers tucked into my textbook and covered in rows and rows of neatly handwritten lines brings no joy. Instead I wrestle with so many thoughts that I'm not even sure how to feel: thoughts of screaming and hysteria and an overwhelmingly female phenomenon; thoughts of stress and exams and expectations; thoughts of the stage and thoughts of Mother and thoughts of St. Bernadette's itself, standing tall on the hill in the middle of the city. A place where I've always been safe. Where I will always be safe.

Right?

My head is starting to hurt; there's no way I'm getting any work done tonight. I slip out of my room to head to the bathroom and brush my teeth.

From the couch my mother looks at me and raises a single perfectly shaped eyebrow. "And just what do you think you're doing?" she asks.

"I'm getting ready for bed," I say, but already that itchy, unsure feeling is coming back.

"Hmm." She taps her pen against her book. "Are you sure that's a good idea?"

I hesitate. I know what she wants, what's expected of me. "Maybe . . . um. Maybe I can study for another fifteen minutes first?"

She nods approvingly. "This sounds good," she says, and I hate the way this makes me feel like I've won some kind of prize. "Another fifteen minutes of revision, and then you can sleep."

"Okay," I say, nodding. "Okay. I'll go do that now."

"And, Rachel . . ."

I turn to face her. "Yes, Mother?"

"Do not ever talk to me like that again."

I sit at my desk and take my physics book back off the shelf. The Mother in my head hums approvingly as I get to work.

THURSDAY
7 DAYS AFTER

Khadijah

I spend the next day at home with Aishah.

It isn't really something we planned. She just doesn't get out of bed. Not when the alarms go off, first Mak's, then mine, then her own. Not when our mother goes in there to wake her up for Subuh prayers. Mak has a big meeting she can't skip. And there is no way in hell she's letting Aishah stay home alone. That leaves me, world's most mediocre caretaker, to be with her. But since taking care of Aishah just means poking my head in every once in a while to make sure she's still breathing, and making a bowl of instant noodles for lunch that she won't touch, it works out.

And it allows me time to figure out how to assuage my guilt.

I did not sleep last night. I stared at the ceiling and thought in circles instead. About how it was always the two of us. How Mak was always busy working, ever since Baba died when we were little. How I used to tie Aishah's shoelaces. Learned how to braid her hair from watching YouTube videos. Made sandwiches when she was hungry. Made the monsters go away, real and imaginary. "You take care of your sister, okay?" Mak would say before she left for work. And I always did. Until now.

I need to find out what is going on. I need to know. I need to know that I can stop it from happening again.

Sasha A's lack of response makes me itch. The thread she left sits there, mocking me with its possibilities.

So St. Bernadette's is screaming again.

When did it happen before? Why is it happening now?

I open up my laptop. I search every possible combination of "St. Bernadette's" and "screaming" and "mass hysteria." I plug the words into an online thesaurus and search all their synonyms. I scroll through pages of trash. I'm pretty sure I almost give the laptop a virus a couple of times.

But I find nothing that will help me unravel the thread.

I slip into Aishah's room. The curtains are drawn tight. The only light is from the sleepy cat lamp on her nightstand. It glows in the darkness, fat and content. Aishah lies on her back, eyes wide open. I sit on the edge of her bed and take her hand in mine. I want to lean in and whisper into her ear, *What happened? What was it like?* I want to tell her that everything will be okay. That I'll take care of everything. I want to be able to do this for her.

But I can't. And all she does is pull her hand away.

I get up and walk to the door. Before I leave, I pause. Try to find the words. Try to make myself say them.

In the end, I just close the door.

I flop onto the couch and shut my eyes. I am tired, so tired. My sister lies in her bed, silent and still. I do not know what shadows she sees when she closes her eyes. I do not know how to help her.

My phone vibrates noisily on the coffee table. A new message. Mak, probably. Asking how we are. Asking what Aishah is doing, for the twentieth time today. Asking if we have eaten.

But it is not Mak. Not this time.

> **Khadijah Rahmat**
> What happened at St. Bernadette's
> when you were there?

Sasha A
The girls screamed. Just like they're screaming now.

Instantly I feel my whole body start to tremble. I try to type, but my fingers are clumsy. Every word comes out wrong. I force myself to take a deep breath. *Calm down, Khad. Calm down.*

> **Khadijah Rahmat**
> Why can't I find anything about it any-
> where?

Sasha A
I guess the school made sure it was all hush-
hush. They were worried about their rep
The glorious name of St. Bernadette's
Can't start having us be known as the school
for freaks

I think of Mrs. Beatrice and "maintaining the stellar reputation of St. Bernadette's."

> ### Khadijah Rahmat
> They still worry about that now

Sasha A

Nothing changes as much as you think it
does

> ### Khadijah Rahmat
> Can you tell me what happened?

Sasha A

Exactly what you think. Girls started screaming bloody murder one day, one after another.
Not as many as you guys though, probably
lik . . . 20, 30 total? Lasted three days. Then it
just stopped. They figured the bomoh they
called to bless the school must have worked.

> ### Khadijah Rahmat
> When was this?

Sasha A

I was in form 4. So like . . . 9 years ago? God
I'm old.

> ### Khadijah Rahmat
> Did they ever figure out why they
> screamed?

Sasha A

The girls didn't remember a thing. The adults

told us it was either a jinn or a disease. I remember thinking how weird it was that you
could catch a scream like you catch a cold

>**Khadijah Rahmat**
>What were the girls like, when they
>came back? The ones who screamed?
>Did they remember anything?

Sasha A
Are you a reporter or something
?
You ask a looooot of questions
There were some reporters back then and
they were just like this
Like you

I pause. I wonder how much I should tell her.

>**Khadijah Rahmat**
>I'm just looking for answers. My sister
>was one of the screamers.

There's a long pause.

Sasha A
I'm really sorry to hear that
But you should really be careful
Stop poking around

And watch out for your sister
Don't let her go anywhere by herself
It's important, just trust me

I'm shaking again now. I'm not sure why.

Khadijah Rahmat
Why?

Now there's an even longer pause.

Sasha A
They never said it was connected
But the timing
It was too much of a coincidence
        Khadijah Rahmat
        What are you talking about?

Three dots appear, then disappear. Appear, then disappear. Whatever it is she's trying to say, Sasha A is taking her time saying it.

Another ping. Message received.

Sasha A
The girl who disappeared.

Rachel

I don't study for just fifteen minutes. I study for hours, late into the night. Every time I try to stop, every time I even think about acting, or about screamers, the Mother in my head chants, *Bad daughter, bad daughter, bad daughter* until I turn back to the pages before me and all the other thoughts disappear. In the morning I wake up and get ready as usual, and Mother sits at the breakfast table and nods approvingly when I tell her what time I finally went to bed.

"Good," she pronounces. "Achievement is built on the altar of sacrifice."

I nod and smile and pretend that I'm not about to fall asleep in my eggs.

Sacrifice, Rachel, I tell myself. *That's what it takes. Forget the screamers. This is your chance, remember? Rachel reborn. And the only way to do this, the only way not to get caught, is to make sure nothing slips. Not your grades, not whatever activities you still have. Nothing. You'll just have to push yourself that much harder.*

So I grit my teeth and go through the school day, concentrating so fiercely in every class that my head hurts. I answer questions and turn in perfectly done homework and ignore Dahlia's snide asides. *Sacrifice,* I think. *This is sacrifice.*

And when the last bell rings, and I realize it's time to do it, to actually do it, to begin acting, it feels like I've earned it.

I wait in the canteen, sitting at a back table, sipping from my water and pretending to read my history textbook while everyone else slowly streams out of school. It's not an after-school cocurriculars day; most kids from the morning session will be heading home, or wherever it is everyone goes when classes are done for the day. And the afternoon-session kids are already milling into class. There is less noise than usual—the screamers have dampened everyone's spirits, and everyone seems more muted, more controlled. But the girls cannot be completely contained, and there is still laughing and teasing and talking. Sometimes I look at them and wonder what it is they have to say to each other, what it means to speak so freely with other people.

Finally the canteen empties out, except for a few students working on their homework, or sitting around tables talking to each other. In the hall a group of girls practice some kind of traditional Malay dance onstage. ("Five, six, seven, eight, and tuuuuuurn," a voice yells.) On the field another group is working on their cheerleading moves ("You CANNOT be so sloppy, or we will LOSE," a voice calls firmly). Even in the in-between moments, even after everything, St. Bernadette's pulses with warmth and life.

I make my way up the stairs to the third floor of the form-five block and peek into empty classrooms until I finally pick one right at the end of the block, near a teacher's bathroom we aren't allowed to enter, and a smaller side staircase. It's a science lab, with rows and rows of beakers, scratched-up surfaces, and wobbly wooden stools. I sit on one and wait for a little while, but not a single person wanders past, not one teacher or student. And why should they? The form ones and form twos occupy the form-three and -four blocks in the afternoons. I can hear laughing and talking, but it's coming from far away. Like another world.

I smile. Perfect.

From my bag I pull out the folder that contains the pages of my monologue. I put the papers on the table, flattening out any wrinkles with my palm. I must have skimmed a hundred different pieces before I found it, trying them on and tossing them aside like T-shirts that don't fit right. Seeing every word, every line, makes me remember anew what it felt like to find this one, the sensation of slipping on a costume that fits perfectly and becoming the person I want to be. Bruce Wayne to Batman. Rachel Lian to . . . to . . . I don't know. Someone better.

I read it again, and again, and then again. It's the same thing I do with history notes or math formulas. Over and over and over, until the words are burned into my memory. It's one scene, a girl emceeing her big sister's wedding. At first it's just a regular emceeing gig—she's a little awkward, she makes some lame jokes, shouts out to some of the people who are there. But as time goes on, she gradually reveals more and more of the family dynamics at play, the ones the audience cannot see. The uncle who appears only to borrow money. The rigid, overbearing mother using her tears to manipulate everyone around her. The absentee father trying to make amends. And through it all, there's a bond between sisters. You laugh at first, but suddenly you're crying because it feels too real, all these feelings. Too real and too much. At least it will feel that way if I do it right.

"So, ladies and gentlemen, I invite you to raise your glasses," I say aloud, raising my own, picturing it in my hand. It's so real, I can see the light glint off the rim, feel the cold smoothness of it, hear the slosh of the drink inside—Coke only, of course. I must be responsible. It is my sister's big day, after all. "And give your blessings to my new brother-in-law, and to my sister. And to me. Because we made it. All the way here, to fucking happily ever after." I bring my imaginary glass to my lips and swallow the liquid all in a single gulp. Then I run the back of my hand across my mouth. I imagine smeared lipstick on my hand, a streak of bright pink scraped from lips to cheek. *I should buy pink lipstick,* I think. That's what she's wearing. Pink lipstick.

The Mother in my head is saying something, but I don't hear her. Outside, life goes on as it normally does. But here, in this safe little cocoon in the middle of the school, I am in control. I get to decide who I want to be.

And I will make my audience love me. Just watch.

Later that evening, when I'm finally back home, Mother pushes open the door of my bedroom, and I quickly shove the pages of my script beneath an English essay I can't seem to get done.

"How was it?" she asks, and I almost choke. Her top lip curls up just a little while she watches me cough spittle all over my books. "Are you all right?"

I take a sip of water from my bottle. "I'm fine," I say. My voice is a squeak. "Sorry."

She nods. "How was the extra class?" she asks.

That's what she's asking you about, Rachel. Relief floods through my whole body. "It was good, actually," I say.

"And you found it helpful?"

I think of hot-pink lipstick smeared against pale skin. *It's acting,* I tell myself. Just acting. "Yes," I say. "Yes, I thought it was very helpful."

That night I sleep with the pages of dialogue under my pillow and dream of stage lights and endless applause.

Khadijah

Julianna Chin.

Her name was Julianna Chin. And when she disappeared, she was sixteen. The same age I am now.

Sasha A sends me a picture she snaps of a newspaper article. **I saved it,** she says. **Don't know why, but here you go.** It takes a couple of tries because her hand shakes. When I get a decent enough copy, I pore over it like it's a treasure map. The picture is grainy. It's hard to make out details. Julianna has long, dark hair and wears a pale T-shirt. A little heart—gold or silver, you can't tell in black-and-white—hangs from a chain around her neck.

Julianna Chin went to school as she always did, and had to stay afterward to practice for a show she was taking part in later that month. Her mother drove to school to pick her up at four p.m., as she usually did when Julianna had extracurricular activities. But this time, even though the mother waited and waited for over half an hour, Julianna never appeared.

Never appeared. She'd gone into St. Bernadette's that morning. And then she simply never came out again. As if she had vanished. As if she had been swallowed whole.

> **Khadijah Rahmat**
> What happened to her?

Sasha A
Nobody really knows
Her parents went all in trying to find her
Posters, media appearances. Promised a
reward and everything
Some say some rando came into the school
and took her
Some say she ran away
Me, I feel like she just got sucked into the
walls

> **Khadijah Rahmat**
> Into the walls???

Sasha A
Don't you feel it?
That school gives off VIBES
I only had a year left after it happened, other-
wise I would have made my dad transfer me

I pause, my thumbs hovering over the phone keypad. *Are you really getting information from someone who believes St. Bernadette's ate one of its students, Khadijah? Seriously?*

Khadijah Rahmat

This is really, um, sad, and also kind of strange

But what does it have to do with the screamers?

Sasha A

Didn't u read the article?

Keep scrolling

I frown as I scroll, squinting at the screen. Reading bits of phrases aloud. "A form-four student at the prestigious St. Bernadette's school . . . reignited the debate on Kuala Lumpur's vagrant problem . . . the school is cooperating with investigations . . ."

And then I pause.

Mrs. Chin confirmed that though Julianna was still recovering from feeling unwell a week or two prior, she seemed in high spirits when she went to school that morning.

Sasha A

See it now?

You know what "feeling unwell" is code for right?

First Julianna was a screamer

And then she was gone

Julianna Chin may be long gone, but she is all I can think about. My brain itches for answers.

Where did you go, Julianna?

Why did you scream?

My sister screamed. Is she going to disappear too?

The questions swirl in my head, round and round. I'm still thinking about them at dinner. Until a gasp from my mother derails my train of thought. I look up. Aishah is standing in the doorway of her bedroom. Just staring at us.

"Sayang!" Mak stands, hands clasped together. She looks hopeful. Delighted. "Are you feeling any better? Do you want something to eat? I can—"

"No." Aishah cuts her off. My little sister always did know how to get to the point. "I'm just telling you. I'm going back to school tomorrow."

Mak frowns. "But, Aishah, sayang, don't you want to rest a couple more days? The doctor said—"

"I'm fine," Aishah says. "I just want to go to school. Go to band practice. Get back to normal."

Under the table I grip my knees so tight, I think I may break a kneecap. What if Aishah disappears? How am I supposed to protect her? How can I accept that I might fail, when failure might mean never seeing my sister again? And then, another, smaller voice: *How come she can get back to normal when you can't?*

My mother sighs. "Fine. But it's Friday tomorrow. Can you at least give it the weekend? Really rest up properly before going back?"

Aishah shrugs. "I guess."

"And I'm dropping you off and picking you up." Mak glares at me. "Both of you."

"You're working."

"I'll talk to my boss." Mak takes her plate of unfinished food over to the counter. Starts rummaging around in the cupboard for containers. She swears softly every time she can't find a matching lid. Aishah turns and goes back into her room. The door closes firmly behind her.

And I sit at the table and wonder, *What the hell do I do now?*

Rachel

Everything will go the way I want, the way I intend, the way I dream. I will make it through the day, completing my prefect duties, taking notes in class, raising my hand to answer questions just as the teachers expect of me. After school St. Bernadette's will show me its hidden enclaves, and I will become her, bold and beautiful and incandescent with emotion. And at night I will be my mother's perfect daughter, engaging in polite conversation at the dinner table, completing my homework and studying long into the night without being told. I will. I will make this happen. *Athletes do this,* I tell myself. K-pop idols, Hollywood superstars, astronauts about to be launched into space, scientists on the brink of a brand-new discovery. Achievement is built on the altar of sacrifice. *This is what it takes, and you'll do anything it takes, Rachel. Anything.*

And it is true. I am flying, I am focused, I am untouchable. I buy a tube of lipstick from the Watson's down the street, in a bold, brilliant pink. Her pink. I keep it in my pocket, feeling the reassuring weight of it, the glossy smoothness of its plastic exterior against my fingertips. I have never owned my own lipstick before, not like this—it's nothing like the tinted balms or glosses Mother lets me wear on special occasions. *Trashy,* the Mother in my head hisses. *Trashy and inappropriate and bad, bad, bad girl.*

I run a finger along the lipstick's gold rim and ignore her. *Now you can be her anytime you want,* I think. *Now you can transform whenever you like.* And I laugh aloud at the sheer delight of it.

"What?" Dahlia says, raising one eyebrow at me.

"Nothing," I say back. "Nothing," but I am intoxicated by all the possibilities laid out before me. The girl in the pink lipstick would stand up for what she wanted. The girl in the pink lipstick would know how to make Mother understand. All around me, girls bend over their work, concentrating on the values of a and b, x and y. The tube is smooth and warm in my hand. *I could be her,* I think. *I could be her.*

After school St. Bernadette's presents me with a new rehearsal spot, a gap between the library building and the edge of the grounds, where the concrete floor ends in a storm drain, and a narrow strip of grass gradually slopes upward toward the fence that surrounds the school. I almost miss it; I am wandering around the school checking out various nooks and crannies when something draws me through the narrow passageway that opens up into the gap. Like invisible hands, gently guiding me toward my destiny. The drain itself is littered with cigarette butts; clearly this is a place the school's adults visit regularly.

It's quiet, and nobody can see me unless they actually turn the corner, or somehow make out who I am through the library's heavily frosted glass windows. And anyway, the windows are dark; Clare must have turned off the lights in the very back, in the section of the library with the ancient reference computers that nobody really uses.

There is nobody around. I take the tube of lipstick from where it lies nestled in the depths of my pocket. I swipe it across my lips, just like I practiced. It feels like wax and smells like strawberries. I shake my hair loose from its ponytail. And then I take a deep breath and try to relax, feel myself slipping into her skin. When I open my eyes, they're steely, cold. I am about to confront my mother, about to tear into her for the way she treats us all, the way my sisters and I have never found a shred of comfort in her embrace, the way she's killing us with her expectations of a life we have no desire to live. My hand clenches tight around the stem of an imaginary wineglass. "A wedding is meant to be a happy occasion, Mommy," I say, ice dripping from each word. "So set aside your desire for the last word and paste a smile onto that face. Eat, drink, and be f-fucking merry, for once in your life."

I stop and bite my lip, still clutching a glass that isn't there. The Mother in my head stirs restlessly. *Language,* she tuts. *Is this the way you were raised?* But the funny thing is, the more I ignore her the softer she seems to get.

It's not about the morality, but I wonder if the judges will take off points for bad language since the competition is being held at a school. Sure, it's an international school, and those are probably less conservative than a place like St. Bernadette's. But still.

I am leaning against the library wall, lost in thought, when there is a loud thump against the window next to me, as if something has slammed against it from the inside. Something big.

My heart is suddenly racing. A squirrel, maybe, a squirrel that got trapped inside, I tell myself. Or a large rat, or a cat. A snake, or a civet.

I'm not sure what it is that makes me hesitate. But it takes me a long time to work up the courage to peer through the panes and confirm my suspicions. So many possibilities, I remind myself. So many possible reasons. *There's nothing to be afraid of, nothing to worry about, Rachel. You're being silly.*

I lift my eyes to the glass. A stranger stares back at me from the window.

The pages of my script slip from my hands, and I reel backward, almost tripping over my own feet.

And then I laugh, breathless and relieved. *Rachel, you are truly losing it if even your own reflection gives you a heart attack.*

I take another look at the girl in the glass, her pink lipstick, the way her hair hangs on either side of her face. Traces of my fear linger in the contours of her face. I raise one hand and wave, then pull it back, embarrassed by my own shenanigans. *Complain when people treat you like a child, then act like a child,* the Mother in my head says.

I bend down to pick up the scattered pages of my script. Then I pause.

The pages aren't scattered at all. They lie on the ground, neatly stacked, surrounded by a perfect circle of dried leaves, for all the world as if I put them there.

I look around, frowning, as if someone is here, as if someone has done this and is hiding, waiting to laugh at my bewilderment. But all around there is nobody, and I hear nothing but the sound of sweeping in the distance.

Khadijah

I wake up on Friday and immediately begin searching for her name on the internet. As if I can find her. As if the next time I hit that button something will miraculously appear. Something I missed.

She had no social media. No clumsy posts, no ill-constructed GIF-laden websites. Her disappearance doesn't turn up in any digital archives. It's not discussed in online forums. Nobody ever seems to have talked about the old screamers of St Bernadette's.

In a world where everyone has an internet footprint, Julianna Chin doesn't exist.

I toss my phone onto the sofa. Bury my head in my hands. If I am going to do this, if I am going to find out what's happening and protect my sister, I am going to have to do what I least want to do.

I am going to have to ask for help.

Sumi and Flo are staring at me like I have lost my mind.

This is not anything new. But the reason this time is a little different than usual.

"A girl disappeared?" Sumi says. She's trying to keep her voice low so Aishah doesn't hear us. They are each draped over an end of the sofa, Sumi and Flo. I asked them to come by after school. They told me they'd bring homework over. I spent hours pacing the floor, anxious to see them. To present them with what I know, carefully written on a piece of paper.

I nod.

"And only nine years ago?" Flo shakes her head, bewildered. "How have we never heard anything about this? Or about a whole other screaming incident? Like, you'd think someone would tell us if it happened before."

I shrug.

"And she was a screamer?" Flo asks.

I nod again. *They'll see the connection immediately,* I tell myself. They'll understand. They always do.

Sumi and Flo exchange glances, and my certainty suddenly wavers. They get it, don't they? Don't they?

"But there's no real proof that the screaming had anything to do with why she disappeared, right?" Sumi asks. "None of the other screamers disappeared?"

I bite my lip.

"Because otherwise . . . ," Sumi continues. "Well, otherwise you're just kind of going off something some random person on the internet said happened. Just seems kind of cra—"

"What Sumi means . . . ," Flo says, cutting in smoothly. I pretend not to notice the way she reaches over to jab Sumi hard in the arm. Pretend that my hands didn't convulse automatically into hard fists when Sumi bit back that word. *Crazy.* "What Sumi means is that this isn't a lot to go on. And I mean, it's been a couple of days since we've had any screaming. Maybe it's over. Are you sure about this?"

I don't look at either of them. I stare down at my fingers. At the dry skin around my cuticles, at the hangnails. I've picked at one so much that it's bleeding, a thin red line in a sea of pale. I don't know how to explain that I can feel the wrongness in my gut. That I know something will happen to Aishah. Again. Unless I stop it.

Sumi lays a hand on my shoulder. "Look, we're here for you. We always are. If you want us to help with this, well . . ." The pause lingers in the air for just a little too long. "That's what we'll do," she finishes.

"Right." Flo slides down to kneel on the floor beside me. "So what's the plan?"

Relief floods through my whole body. They may be reluctant, they may think I've lost my mind, but they're here. They're here, the way they always have been. And part of love is showing up. I pick up my pen and begin writing.

Sumi joins us on the floor and frowns. "Okay. So we'll put together a complete list of screamers. And you'll try to find out as much as you can about this Julianna person."

"Which you'll pull off by telling your mom you're back on the debate team," Flo finishes. "A genius touch, I might add. She has been not-so-subtly nudging you to get back to your old activities. And this way she'll actually let you go."

"She'll never say no," Sumi agrees. "It's the perfect plan."

"It is." Flo slips her arm through mine. "And if there is a connection between being a screamer and Julianna disappearing, we'll find it. And if we find it, we'll stop it. As simple as that."

As simple as that, I think. As simple as that.

The note says, *I am rejoining the debate team.*

My mother reads it with her jaw hanging slightly open. She looks up at me. Then at the note. Then at me. Even her blinks are confused.

"What?" she begins. Then, "How . . . ?"

I reach over to flip the paper. There is more text for her to see. Mak frowns. I track the movement of her eyes. The note is not long; I know each word by heart. I should. I spent hours choosing each one. I strategized their placements like they were chess pieces on a board. *I would like to help the team with research and speech preparation. I am not ready to speak yet, but I think I am ready to try to get back to my old life.* It's carefully constructed to echo my mother's own wishes for me. She will not say no.

And she doesn't. Instead she springs up from her chair and clasps me close. I try to stop myself from stiffening at her touch. At the feeling of skin on skin. I don't think she notices. "Oh, sayang," she says. Over and over, her voice muffled against the top of my head. I can hear the tears in every quiver. "Oh, sayang. I'm so proud of you."

I try to smother my guilt. *It's for Aishah,* I tell myself. It's to keep her safe.

My mother doesn't need to know I'm lying.

Rachel

I brushed off the strangeness of Friday—*Just your imagination working overtime, Rachel. It's nothing*—and spent the weekend alternating between memorizing my script and making plans. I need plans, schedules, lists, strategies. The only way this will work is if my mother doesn't see my studies suffer, doesn't see me get distracted. The moment I lose my focus, the moment I let my concentration slip, everything fails, and the new Rachel will be nothing but a dream I had once upon a time.

So I am dismayed today when Cik Diana pulls me out of class for a "quick chat" in the corridor. I can feel all the eyes of my classmates burning into my back. I try very hard to ignore them.

"I'm sorry to interrupt you in the middle of your lesson," Cik Diana begins, and you can tell just how new she is, how fresh, because she apologizes. No teacher has ever apologized for wanting me to do something. "I just finished a meeting with the headmistress, and I really wanted to make sure I spoke to you as soon as possible."

"Okay," I say slowly. "About what?"

She smiles, and dimples appear in the creamy smoothness of her cheeks. "Well! After everything the students have been through in the past few days, I was talking to Mrs. Beatrice about how it would be nice to do a kind of Community Day, where we invite parents to the school and let the girls really feel how much they are loved and supported and held up by everyone around them. 'Stronger Together,' that kind of thing. Do you see?" Her eyes actually sparkle. I thought that was a thing that only happened in stories.

"Sure," I say, because I don't quite understand what I'm supposed to do with this information.

"Now, how you come into it is that I know you play the piano, Mrs. Beatrice tells me quite beautifully."

"Uh-huh," I say, and I blush like some kind of idiot because I'm not used to compliments.

"So I was wondering if you'd like to be part of a special musical performance for the event!" Cik Diana looks at me expectantly, as if I'm supposed to react with enthusiasm to this idea. She has the grace to not show her disappointment at my lack of enthusiasm. "Don't you think it's a great idea? We'll put together something really lovely and tasteful, something that combines students and teachers and parents all working together to make beautiful music. The symbolism in that can be so powerful." She smiles at me. "I know how kind you are, Rachel. I saw it the day we helped that girl. Do you remember?"

"I remember," I say quickly. I try not to shudder.

"I could tell that day just how much empathy you have, and I think that will translate into a truly memorable performance." She pats me on the shoulder. "I won't keep you for much longer. Get back to class, and I'll let you know the details later, all right? I'm so excited to be working with you on this!" And she zooms off, curly ponytail bobbing behind her.

For a while I just stand there, trying to take deep breaths, trying to fill my lungs as much as possible. She didn't even wait for me to say yes. The Mother in my head hisses, *She didn't need to, silly girl. This is a good opportunity for you. Your teachers trust you to do this. You cannot say no.*

I can't?

You can't.

I can't, so I'm just going to have to manage, aren't I? *It'll be worth it in the end,* I tell myself. It will. It will be worth it.

Khadijah

It's like the ideal group project. The perfect splitting of tasks. Sumi and Flo get to work on putting together a complete list of screamers. "They must have something in common," Flo muses. "Something that ties them together, and to Julianna and the others before. Maybe we can try to figure out what that is."

I nod. I have my own mission.

I am hunting for Julianna Chin. And I know exactly where to head first.

I find her in the library. On a shelf of yearbooks, in a room in the very back. The books are spine out. Each one stamped with *The Beacon* and its year of publication. I count backward. Last year's, 2023. Then 2022, 2021, 2020. . . . I keep going until my eye hits 2015.

The yearbooks are wedged in together tight to save space. The tops are covered in dust. Above me the air conditioner hums. The shelf vibrates slightly. I wonder if the humming and vibrating are the school reacting, St. Bernadette's anticipating what I'll find. I work the 2015 book out slowly, until it lands in my hands.

The cover is a watercolor illustration of marguerite daisies. The little white flowers that adorn our school badge.

I take a deep breath, and sneeze. It smells like dust and stale air.

I take the book to a quiet corner and crack it open. Skim through introductory text from the usual suspects: headmistress, head of the parent-teacher association, head prefect. I see a younger incarnation of Mrs. Beatrice. Hair more severe, clothes less stylish. She was an assistant headmistress back then.

I keep flipping until I reach the form-four class pictures. Then I run my finger under every name until I find her. She's so normal. Just another teenage girl in a row of teenage girls. Julianna, with white ribbons in her pigtails and a wide smile.

You were my age, I think. My age, and then gone forever. I think of the same thing happening to Aishah, and my heart constricts.

I look for her everywhere then. In every picture of every club and every activity. It's as if I'm trying to reach out across the years between us, score her image into my memories. She was in 4 Melati. She was a runner, poised at the starting line, serious face on. She was an actress. Mouth slick with pink lipstick, dressed up as Dorothy in *The Wizard of Oz.* Blue gingham and white ribbons twirling across the stage. She was . . . She was . . . I squint at the page.

She was a student counselor. The ones you're supposed to go to if you just need someone to talk to. There she is, front row, right next to the teacher. Hands on her knees, beaming smile pasted onto her face. I read the name, even though I know every curve of it, every line. Julianna Chin.

And then I pause at the name beside it.

Teacher Adviser: Encik Bakri.

Encik Bakri.

Mr. B?

I peer closely at the page. Trying to see the Mr. B I know in the contours of this face. It's a grainy black-and-white smudge in a sea of faces. It's hard to tell.

Is that really Mr. B? Our Mr. B?

I wonder just how old he is. How long he's been around. How many of the girls of St. Bernadette's have passed through his classrooms. His counseling room.

And then I wonder, if that's him, what he can tell me about the screamers. And about Julianna.

Rachel

"Hello, Rachel," the man says, offering me a hand to shake. Cik Diana mentioned his name, but I've already forgotten it, mostly because I wasn't paying attention. Instead I am thinking about how long this will take, wondering when I can get back to my precious monologue.

Pay attention, the Mother in my head hisses. *Be polite.*

"It's nice to meet you, sir," I say automatically.

"Call me 'Uncle' lah," he says, a genial twinkle in his eye. He wears a shirt and tie, dark slacks, leather shoes. Clearly he's taken time out of a busy schedule to be here, to do this with us. A part of me feels a small twang of guilt. *The least you can do is focus, Rachel.*

"Okay, Uncle," I say.

"I see you're all getting acquainted," Cik Diana says, bustling up to where we're all gathered in the hall, by the piano in front of the stage. "But I'll do a round of introductions to be sure we're all on the same page."

We go around the circle, saying our names. I recognize a nervous-looking form-three girl who is always getting into trouble for long nails; apparently she plays the violin. The man who told me to call him Uncle plays the guitar; together we make up the musical trio. A small group of fourth formers will perform a dance to our music, to be choreographed by someone's mother. And Mr. B, who isn't here right now but who is apparently handy with a computer and Canva, will create visuals to be projected onto the large screen behind them. "And I will oversee the whole thing," Cik Diana finishes. "Any questions?"

"What did I get myself into?" Uncle says with a quirk of his mouth, and then everyone laughs. I try to smile too, but I can't help the sour feeling growing in the pit of my stomach. This doesn't sound like some little project; this sounds like weeks of extra work, work that cuts into my precious rehearsal time. *What do I do?* I think desperately. *What do I do?*

"Now, now, sir," says Cik Diana with a smile. "You should be used to all this."

"I don't know," he says, shaking his head, although he's smiling in the way adults do when they know they're being funny. "It's been a lot of years since my daughter studied here, you know. I thought I was done with the whole taking-part-in-things thing. But now my niece goes here too, and well . . ." He spreads his arms out helplessly.

The girl in the pink lipstick curves my mouth into a smile, and before I know it, I say, "Once a sucker, always a sucker."

Silence falls over the room, and I can feel myself turning hot. *Why, Rachel? Why?* That isn't something I'd ever do, something I'd ever allow myself to say aloud.

Then Uncle starts to laugh, and after a beat the others join him. "I guess I deserve that one," he chuckles. "I look forward to us working together, Rachel."

I try to laugh too, but it comes out strange and strangled. "Me too," I say. "Me too."

It's a short meeting, so I'm relieved when we are dismissed and I can finally, finally practice. I walk briskly away from the hall, trying to shake off that unsettling moment from earlier. *It's a good sign, Rachel,* I tell myself. *You're starting to really understand this character, to feel her, to be her. That's what a good actor does.*

I need a place to practice—though, if I'm being honest, I've already been practicing in my head all day, reciting the words to myself on prefect duties or on my way to the bathroom or in the library or between classes.

Or even during classes.

The Mother in my head clicks her tongue, but I'm getting very used to ignoring her.

But today I'm late, and though St. Bernadette's has been kind to me before this, there don't seem to be any empty spots to be found. For a second I think about going to the library and actually studying. Like I told Mother I was doing.

Mother.

There it is, that familiar feeling of guilt.

But no. I have to practice. It's my last shot, my only chance to do something different, something that's just for me. That's what I tell myself every time she brings me hot tea, or carefully cut fruits as a study snack—when I quickly put my script away and pretend I was working on Malay literature essays all along. *After this I will be her perfect girl again,* I tell myself as she rubs the ache out of my hunched shoulders. After this. I promise. Just this one time, before it's too late.

So where can I go?

Then I know.

Brede's House.

Brede's House is the oldest building at St. Bernadette's, built as a residence for the nuns who founded this place over a hundred years ago, and named after the school's first headmistress. There have been rumors for years that the Japanese soldiers dug their tunnels here, that Brede's House guards the entrance to an entire world below ground. It stands in the very back corner of the school, a little ways up from the field and closer to the sloping hillside, a nondescript building with peeling paint slightly obscured behind some towering frangipani trees. Because it is so old and the school can't really afford to repair it, it's not used for much. Girls would dare each other to go inside and stay there, alone, front door closed, for five minutes—especially in the evenings, after practices or extra classes, when the shadows were starting to grow deeper and longer. "You'll never survive Brede's House," they would say to each other.

I always thought it was silly. But one year some girl twisted her ankle trying to run from the imaginary ghosts in Brede's House, and another girl fractured her elbow trying to find the fabled tunnel entrance, and the teachers told us that if anyone did this again, they'd be in massive amounts of trouble. So there were no more silly dares and screeching girls and heart-pounding quests, and Brede's House stands alone, and empty, and almost forgotten.

Until today, anyway.

I walk slowly past classrooms, past the tennis/volleyball/badminton/whatever sport we need it for court, past the counseling room, where Mr. B looks up hopefully, like he's just waiting for someone to come inside and tell him all their problems. I walk past the library and the two blooming frangipani trees dropping their leaves and flowers to the ground, and all the way across the field where the netball team is practicing, and up the shallow stairs set into the slope, and there it is.

From the outside Brede's House doesn't look like much. It's a narrow two-story building that stretches out long in the back, with wide wooden double doors, and walls that used to be white once upon a time. It's gone through a few renovations, so the windows are now the regular slatted glass windows you see in most of the school's newer blocks. But the one thing they kept was the large round stained-glass window on the second floor, right over the front doors. You can't quite tell what the colors of the glass are anymore because of all the dirt and dust on it. But you can tell it used to be beautiful. The school's motto arches over the window: SIMPLE IN VIRTUE, STEADFAST IN DUTY. I've never figured out what it means, and when I once googled it to try to find out, I realized that almost every other convent school in Malaysia has the exact same motto. It made me feel cheated, like we try to sell how special we are, when really we're just the same as anyone else.

I make sure nobody's watching me, then push open the double doors, step inside, and close them carefully behind me. They're not locked; there's nothing here but rooms full of cobwebs and spiders and broken furniture. Inside, the narrow passageway leads to a set of stairs, with doors to my left and right, three per side. I think about going upstairs—I'd probably be even less likely to be found there—but decide against it just in case any of these floorboards have gone rotten. The Mother in my head says through gritted teeth, *Asking for trouble, isn't it? You fall down and break your neck, and then what?* In this stillness, here in Brede's House, it's somehow harder to ignore her.

As I step carefully through the building, the floor creaks under my weight, and I hear something scurry away. It's quiet, and there's nobody here, I tell myself, trying to pretend I didn't hear a thing. That's what matters.

Eventually I pick the third door on the left and open it to reveal a little room with a large dust-covered teacher's desk in the corner, a blackboard on the front wall, and a massive pile of broken chairs and desks right in the center. Sunlight struggles to get through the grimy windows. I set my things on the desk, kicking up a cloud of dust, and flick the switches by the door until the ancient ceiling fan begins to move slowly, wheezing as it goes. "Perfect," I say out loud. "It's perfect."

Now time to get to work.

I close my eyes, ready to become her again, ready to lay my emotions bare.

And then I open them. And frown.

It's right there, right on the edge of my hearing—faint, but persistent. Once I notice it, I can't not hear it.

The sound of sweeping.

I shake my head, as if that will help me get rid of the noise. *Focus, Rachel. Try to bring yourself back to her.* When I look up again, there's a wide, toothy smile on my face, one that I know doesn't quite reach my eyes. A pageant-queen smile. "Our uncle Alfred is here today," I say, scanning the room. So many faces, and I only really like about five of them. Wait. Pause. I don't like how I sound there. I clear my throat and try again. "Our uncle Alfred is here today," I say, this time gesturing to Uncle Al, who waves to the crowd, changing my intonation just a little. "Not that I'm one to care about looks, but Uncle Al's looking great! He's lost a ton of weight—about sixty-five kilograms of ex-wife." I imagine a smattering of limp ha-has, and shuffle my cue cards frantically, desperate not to lose this crowd, not to ruin it for my big sister. My smile goes all wobbly at the edges. I glance down at my notes and take a deep breath.

Sweep, sweep, sweep.

I grit my teeth. I know the frangipani trees tend to make a mess, but maybe if I ask politely, the aunty can . . . go and sweep somewhere else for a while? It's worth a try, right?

I head toward the main doors. Outside the room, the air is still; every step I take, the sweeping gets louder and louder. *She must be right outside the door,* I think. The cleaner aunty. She must be right there.

I grab the door handle and pull it open.

There is nobody there.

I take a step outside and look left and right. A carpet of dry leaves and dead blossoms crunches beneath my feet.

I am suddenly very cold.

Quickly I turn and walk back to the room where my things still lie on the desk. One by one—*Come on, Rachel. Don't be silly. There's no need to rush*—I place everything back into my bag, as neatly as I can. Everything in its place. I try to ignore my trembling fingers, and the fact that I can hear the sweeping again now, louder than ever. Only, it's not outside anymore.

It's coming from upstairs. Right above my head.

I think about taking a look. I think about what I might find, what I might see. I think about Mother and what she would say: *You don't itchy backside go looking for trouble.*

I sling my bag over my shoulder, then walk out of Brede's House, shutting the door firmly behind me. Then I keep walking. *That's right, Rachel, that's right, even though your legs feel like they're going to give out any minute now.*

It's only when I'm far enough away, when the sunshine has chased away my goose bumps and when my teeth have stopped chattering, that I turn to look.

And maybe it's the late afternoon sun in my eyes—maybe it's a trick of the light—but I could almost swear I see a shadow move behind the dusty panes of the stained-glass window on the second floor.

Khadijah

I've been at St. Bernadette's secondary school since I was thirteen. This is the first time I've ever set foot in Mr. B's office. I headed here as soon as I made the connection. No time like the present.

I'm not actually sure how many kids have been in here at all. Voluntarily, anyway. I feel like someone on National Geographic. Trying to observe a creature in its natural habitat.

Mr. B, on the other hand, is all fidgety. This is a big deal for him. I can tell by the way his eyes widened when he looked up and saw me standing in the doorway. He's been wanting me to come see him, hasn't he? And here I am. Just not quite for what he wanted, or expected. But he doesn't need to know that.

Yet.

"I'm so glad you came to see me, Khadijah," he says earnestly, straightening his tie. "You know my door has been open for you—well, for any student, of course, but especially for you, given the . . . well . . . ever since . . ."

I nod quickly.

And then we both sit in silence.

Mr. B coughs. "I have to admit, when I imagined these visits, I assumed you would be . . . ready to talk."

I shrug.

"Yes, yes, I suppose that's my own fault. You know what they say. When you assume, you make an ass out of *U* and 'me'!" He chuckles, then stops abruptly. "Maybe I shouldn't have . . . Pretend you didn't hear me say that word."

I nod again, and he sighs.

"I have to tell you, Khadijah, I'm not sure how I can help you if you won't speak." He runs a hand through his hair. It's much messier than usual. He's been doing this a lot, I think.

"Though, to be honest with you, I'm not sure I can help even when kids do talk to me. Odd things happening in this school lately, you know?"

My heart leaps. Yes, yes, get him talking about the screamers. My nods are so vigorous, it feels like my head might snap off my neck. Thankfully, he notices.

"So that's what's bothering you? All this screaming?" He nods sagely, an *Ah, that's what I thought* kind of nod. "I don't blame you. It's unnerving, especially when we have no idea what's causing it. You can often feel helpless from not being able to help your friends, or perhaps scared that it may happen to you." He leans forward to look me straight in the eye. He is equal parts sincerity and cheap cologne. Both make me feel like I cannot breathe. "But, Khadijah, you must understand that you are not alone. These feelings are valid, and normal, and allowing yourself to feel them and breathe through them is an important part of processing these events."

Mr. B talks like my therapist. At least I know he's gotten some training.

I reach into my pocket for the note I prepared. I silently hand it to him across the table.

Has this happened before?

Something flickers in those eyes when he reads it. I don't know if I imagine it, but when he looks back up at me, he seems more controlled. More wary. "What makes you ask that?" His tone is light. Pleasant, even.

From my backpack I pull out the yearbook. *The Beacon* 2015. I open it up to Julianna's class picture. Lay it gently on his desk. Take a pen from his cup, circle her face.

Then I wait.

Mr. B looks at it for a long time. In the distance I hear the sound of sweeping. Stiff bristles on hard concrete. He doesn't say a word. But that's okay. I'm used to silence.

When he does talk again, he doesn't look at me. "Ah yes, Julianna Chin," he says. His tone is still so perfectly bland. So airy. "A fine student. One of my counselors, and an actress as well. Did you know her?"

I shake my head. *But you did,* I want to say.

"A lovely girl. It's truly a tragedy that they never figured out what happened to her." He shuts the yearbook with a firm snap.

"I'm not quite sure what it has to do with anything, though, or why you would want to hear about such an unfortunate incident."

I feel a sudden fiery flame of angry kinship with Julianna, this poor missing girl. They called my trauma an "incident" too, after all. I take the same pen and scribble quickly on my note from before.

Was she a screamer too?

I push the note back across the desk toward him. I see his eyes flick toward the paper. But he makes a big show of pulling a stack of exercise books closer. "This has been a very pleasant conversation, Khadijah, but I'm sure you need to get back home. And I myself have a whole lot of marking to do."

I grit my teeth. Snatch the paper and scribble one last note. This time in all caps. The scratch of pen on paper matches the rhythm of the sweeping outside.

HOW MANY WERE THERE? WHY DIDN'T THE SCHOOL TELL US THIS HAPPENED BEFORE?

"Have a great day, Khadijah," Mr. B tells me. "Feel free to stop by again anytime. When you're ready to . . . talk."

I shoulder my backpack and walk away, the paper crumpled in my hand. I am so angry, I think my heart may burst from my chest. Why won't he talk about it? About her? Why has nobody ever mentioned the old screamers to us? What are the teachers hiding?

It takes a while for me to calm down. Longer still for me to realize my hand is still clenched into a tight fist.

Except, when I open it, there is no paper. Only one brown leaf, so dry that it feels like it may crumble to dust.

TUESDAY
12 DAYS AFTER

Rachel

I wake from a restless night of tossing and turning, my mind still lingering in the shadows of Brede's House.

You see? Going mental already, the Mother in my head says viciously. *Never do what I tell you. Never listen to me. You add more and more things, and you break. That's what happens.*

I shake my head, almost angrily. I do not break. I cannot break. This is just me being overtired and anxious about things I can't control. But you know what I can control? I can control myself. I can control how hard I work, how much effort I put into things, how I organize, how I schedule. I can make all this work, I know I can. I'm Rachel Lian, aren't I? Perfect student, every teacher's dream, the vessel for all my mother's aspirations. I can do it all.

So I say, *Fine, fine, it's all fine.* I just keep lying. Once you start, it's actually really easy to keep going. Or maybe that's her talking. Not me.

It's not fine, I think, staring at the paper Mrs. Dev has just placed on my desk. It's the quiz she surprised us with in her last class, a quiz going over all the biology concepts we've been learning in the past three months.

A quiz on which I have somehow gotten a C.

I blink, in case I'm seeing it wrong. But it's still there in the top right corner, a bright red C in a circle. I get a cold feeling somewhere deep in my stomach. I'm Rachel Lian. I don't get Cs. I just don't. I wait to hear what the Mother in my head will say to this, but she's silent and cold.

At the desk beside me Melissa leans over, trying to eye my paper. "What did you get, ah?" she says with great interest. "Can I copy your answers? I got a B. I just want to make sure I know what I did wrong, and since your papers are always so perfect wan—"

"Sorry," I mutter. "She said we'll discuss the answers later anyway."

Melissa sniffs. "Oh. Okay. Sure." I can tell she's not impressed.

"Typical," I hear Dahlia whisper.

Something inside me stirs.

No, not something. Someone.

The girl in the pink lipstick floats to the surface, takes over, makes my skin prickle with irritation, makes my mouth open and say, "And exactly what do you mean by that?"

Dahlia blinks at me. "Excuse me?"

"You heard me." The girl crosses my arms—I cross my arms. My arms are crossed, whoever is doing it. I am appalled and embarrassed and somehow also thrilled to be hearing these words come out of my mouth, these words I would never say otherwise. "What is your problem?"

Unfortunately, I fail to realize that crossing my arms means uncovering my test, and that damning, eye-wateringly bright C.

Dahlia's eyes flicker to it, then to me, and she snickers. "I've got no problem right now. In fact, it's nice to see Little Miss Perfect finally fail at something."

"A C is hardly failure," I hear myself say, and I imagine the words coming from lips painted a brilliant pink. "And one C won't make a dent in my perfect record. But, hey, maybe I should listen to you. You are, after all, the expert on failure." I gesture at her own paper, where she hasn't bothered to cover the F in the corner. "Unless you're going to try to convince me that F stands for 'Fabulous.' In fact, I'm surprised you still answer to 'Dahlia' at all."

Dahlia's face creases slightly in confusion, and the girl with the pink lipstick curves my mouth into a perfect, demure smile.

"Isn't that what your mother calls you at home? 'Failure'?"

Dahlia looks like she's about to launch herself at my throat when Mrs. Dev coughs delicately behind me. The girl subsides; I am me again, wholly, fully me, trembling slightly from the adrenaline.

"Is there a problem here, ladies?" Mrs. Dev asks.

"No problem, Mrs. Dev," I mutter, and Dahlia scowls but says nothing.

"Very good." Mrs. Dev pats me on the shoulder. "See me after school, please."

Every last bit of the pink-lipstick-girl's boldness disappears. I want to crawl into a hole and never come out.

I fold the quiz paper in half, then in half again, then again, until it's as small as I can possibly make it. Then I stuff it right to the bottom of my backpack, hidden under textbooks and gum wrappers and old pencil shavings. *Who are you?* the Mother in my head asks, her tone bewildered. *What was that?* But I ignore her, because I have no real answers myself.

After the last bell rings, I walk to the teacher's room to find Mrs. Dev. I shuffle slowly between the rows of desks piled high with books and papers, as if I'm making my way to my own execution. *A C, Rachel. You got a C. And the way you just talked to Dahlia! Who are you right now?*

I find Mrs. Dev sitting at a table carefully covered in a plastic topper decorated with technicolor ocean scenes. She's grabbing workbooks from a stack and marking with a bright red pen. *The same red pen that wrote that C,* I think, the C that is burned into my brain like a tattoo.

"Selamat sejahtera, Cikgu," I say.

"Mm? Ah, Rachel." Mrs. Dev sets down her red pen and stares at me over the top of her rimless glasses, which somehow always seem to slide about halfway down her nose. "Mind telling me what is happening with you? Mm?"

"What do you mean, Mrs. Dev?"

She pushes her glasses to the top of her head, where they get tangled in her thinning burgundy-dyed hair. "My dear girl," she says, "surely you don't take me for a fool. If one of the school's top students suddenly starts getting Cs, surely there must be something wrong lah right? Mm?" She leans forward, concern written all over her face. "So tell me. What is it? Got friend problem? Boy problem—or girl problem?" she amends quickly. "We live in a modern world, I know, I know."

I shake my head.

"Then? Home problems? Mm?"

I really don't need this right now. "No, Cikgu, no problem," I say. "Just . . . just had an off day, I guess."

"Off day, eh?" Mrs. Dev leans back, and her chair creaks like it's complaining about it. "Your other classes, how? All okay?"

"Fine," I say. "All fine."

Mrs. Dev snorts. "You don't bullshit me, please, girl. You think teachers don't talk to each other? No space in here, all the desks so close together. You think we don't hear things? Something is affecting your studies, and we just want to know how we can help you." She glares at me. "You think SPM cares about your off days, ah?"

"No, Cikgu." I don't say anything more, just look down and shift my weight from one foot to the other until she sighs.

"Look, girl, if you want me to help you, you know you can just ask, right?"

I can feel the girl in the pink lipstick moving restlessly just below my skin, waiting to say something back, waiting to pounce. I bite back her comments, swallow her sarcasm. "I know, Mrs. Dev."

"You are big already, after all. Besar panjang, almost leaving school already, mm? I cannot force you to tell me also if you don't want to. But if this keeps happening, I might have to call your mother—"

"It won't," I say quickly. "It won't happen again. I swear."

"Mm." Mrs. Dev shoves her glasses back onto her nose and picks up that damn red pen. "All right, then. Give you one more chance, ya. The next quiz, I expect better. Now go. I got a lot of work to do."

I murmur my thanks and walk quickly back outside. I'm sweating. *If you keep this up, Rachel, Mother is going to find out everything—EVERYTHING—and all the practicing and planning will be for nothing.* I think about not being able to get onstage, not being able to be the pink-lipstick-girl again, and shiver. I can't let that happen.

I'm just going to have to do better.

Khadijah

"We are going to get caught," Flo hisses.

"We are not," Sumi hisses back. The three of us are hanging out in the main stairwell of the admin building. The broad stone steps are cold and hard against our butts. It isn't comfortable, but it does offer a perfect line of sight to our target, Mrs. Beatrice's office.

"This does not feel like a good idea." Flo fiddles with the handle of the paper bag at her feet. She's always been the most risk averse of us. "Is this even worth it? There haven't been any screams in the past few days. Like, maybe it's over. We can just forget it and move on."

"It's fine. I told you." Sumi's eyes gleam in the dim light of the stairwell. This is her moment. Nobody loves a good scheme more than Sumi. For a second I wonder if she's this excited because she wants to help me or because she craves the adrenaline of chasing the forbidden. "Mrs. Beatrice is going to the forensics thing in the assembly hall. Her office will be empty. As long as we follow the plan, it'll all work out. And then we'll know for sure. Just like Khad wants."

Flo sighs. "Remind me again what the plan is."

Sumi pulls a crumpled piece of paper out of her pocket with a flourish. "With pleasure." She smooths out the creases of the hand-drawn floor plan as best she can. She ripped the paper out of her accounts notebook. "Here." She jabs at the right spot. "Here's Mrs. Beatrice's office. Right next door—they share a room—are the two assistant headmistresses. Puan Zaini is away this week, so there's only Mrs. Siva. I'll go in there and talk to her about, like, sports scholarships or something. She's been on my case about those, and planning my future or whatever." Sumi rolls her eyes.

I reach over and tap the rectangle she's drawn across from Mrs. Beatrice's office.

She nods. "Right, so that's where all the administrative staff sit. There's, like, three of them. Flo's in charge of that room."

Flo peeks into her paper bag. "I've got, like, a whole bag of cupcakes and kuih and stuff, and I'm supposed to tell them that I brought a ton because it's my birthday, and I wanted to share the leftovers with them since they work so hard and deserve a little treat." She wrinkles her nose. "And then I'll, like, chitchat with them, I guess?"

"Exactly what you're so good at, my love," Sumi says. And it's true. Flo oozes so much charm, she could get a brick wall to tell her its life story.

"And while we do all this, Khad . . ." Flo glances at me.

Sumi replies, "Khad will make her way into Mrs. Beatrice's room, quickly and quietly, and see what she can find. About

Julianna. Or about any of the screamers." Sumi looks like she's absolutely gleeful at the idea of pulling off this heist. Searching Mrs. Beatrice's office was her idea. She read my messages about Mr. B, about Julianna. Understood my need to know more. And decided to take action. It's a typical Sumi move, and I love her for it.

She nods to where we can see Mrs. Beatrice mulling over some documents, pen in hand. The headmistress isn't particularly tech savvy. She still insists on keeping hard copies of student files in an old file cabinet behind her desk.

"I know this," Sumi told us with a smirk, "because she pulled mine out that time I poured ink down Puteri's baju kurung because she was bullying that form-two girl, remember? She waved that file around the whole time she was scolding me about wasting my 'potential.' Kept talking about my 'permanent record.'" Sumi rolled her eyes and said, "Like I give a shit."

Now she reaches over, pats me on the arm. "If there's any info on Julianna, it's going to be in those files."

I must look as anxious as I feel. Flo leans against me, all warmth and comfort. "You can do it, Khad," she whispers.

"Just be quick," Sumi says. "We don't know how long we can keep them busy. Or when Mrs. Beatrice will come back."

I nod.

As soon as Mrs. Beatrice leaves, tap-tap-tapping past us down the stairwell without even a glance in our direction, we make our move.

I wait for Sumi and Flo to work their magic. It's not until I can hear the sounds of low, earnest conversation from one room and the squeals of delight from the other that I slip into Mrs. Beatrice's office.

It is not locked—it never is, unless the headmistress has left for the day. The room itself isn't particularly large. This is a public school, after all. Her desk is by the window, and there are two hard-backed chairs for people who come to see her. But there is also a low coffee table and a small sofa. And in the corner, the infamous file cabinet.

I don't realize until then that I am trembling.

I walk over to it with quick steps. My knees feel like they may give way. *Hurry, Khad. Hurry up. Stop wasting time.* I tug at each drawer, but the cool metal will not give under my fingers. Locked. As expected.

I scan the room, looking for the key. "It has to be in there somewhere," Sumi insisted. But where? Where? My anxiety makes me feel like I'm moving in slow motion, like I'm wading through jelly. *The desk, Khad. Check the desk.*

Mrs. Beatrice's desk is a study in angles and lines. Everything is in its place. A small pile of books is lined up at the exact center, stacked from largest to smallest, on top of a closed laptop. A cup of pens and pencils sits in the top right corner. In the top left, two trays, labeled IN and OUT. The IN tray has a sheaf of documents requiring her attention. The OUT tray is empty. I give the whole thing a good once-over, but it's easy to see that there are no keys here.

The drawers, then. I open them one by one, being careful

to move them slowly, softly. I am wary of a too-loud thud that may call attention to my presence. The bottom drawer is a surprisingly relatable mess. The kind I wouldn't expect from Mrs. Beatrice. It's a deep well of randomness—scrap paper, rubber bands, a ladle, two plastic food containers, a deflated rubber ball. But no key.

The second drawer houses nothing but program booklets. I sift through them and find booklets for St. Bernadette's events and concerts dating back at least eleven years. I pull out one from ten years ago. *St. Bernadette's End-of-Year Concert Extravaganza!* Someone designed the type in big bold letters, all cartoony like all they had was a vision and Microsoft Paint. I flip the pages until I find her name. I know where she will be, and there she is. Part of the ensemble cast for the school's production of *Bawang Putih, Bawang Merah.* Julianna Chin.

Focus, Khad. Focusing will get you close to her more than anything else will.

I shove the program into my backpack and carefully slide the drawer shut. Then I open the top drawer.

Here there's a tray, each of its compartments filled with office supplies. This compartment for paper clips. This one for staples and a small stapler, bright yellow. This one for highlighters. This one for a two-hole punch. And this one, in the very back, for . . . for . . .

For a key.

"What are you doing here?"

I whirl around, slamming the drawer shut at the same time,

bumping hard into the desk to hide the noise. Pain blooms across my right hip. My gasp sounds so loud in the silence.

Mrs. Beatrice stands in the doorway. Her forehead is creased; her pale green suit is not. "Khadijah?" she says. "Why are you here?"

My heart is beating wildly in my chest. This is not something we planned for. *Think, Khad, think.* I put out a hand to say, *Wait,* then bend over to rifle through my backpack. As if I'm looking for something. As if the answer is in here somewhere.

My hands close over a piece of paper. And I realize what it is. And I don't know if this is a good idea, but right now it's the only way I can see out of this.

So I straighten up. And I hand it to Mrs. Beatrice. And I close my eyes briefly as I hear her read it aloud, "I am rejoining the debate team."

Rachel

All through my ride home, through a silent lunch where I barely eat and Kak Tini clucks worriedly around me like an anxious mother hen, I cannot stop thinking about her. About how easily she slipped into my skin and took over. About how it felt to have her float to the surface, how naturally her words came from my lips. How it felt to be her, bold and outspoken, taking no shit. Saying the things I have always wanted to say. Being the girl I have always wanted to be. I keep stealing one hand into my pocket, feeling for the reassuring weight of the pink lipstick. Telling myself that I still have everything under control.

After dinner I am wrestling with my homework when Mother comes into my room and places something on my desk. I pick it up and read the label, frowning. "Facial masks?"

"Korean," she says. "Very good brand."

"Um. Okay." I set the packet down. I'm not really sure what to make of this. But then again, I've spent most of the night feeling unsure. The harder I try to concentrate on my assignments, the less able I am to do them. It's like I'm trying to catch fish with my bare hands, and they just keep wriggling and slipping out of my grasp. And I don't want to catch fish. I want to slip into the pink-lipstick-girl's world, into her head, into her skin. I don't want to be me anymore, sitting here staring at biology notes and a facial mask and wondering how I have disappointed my mother this time.

"I see you, you know," Mother says. "Staying up so late, working so hard."

I hold my breath. I wonder if she'll tell me to stop. I wonder if she'll say, *Take a break, Rachel. I can tell this is taking a toll on you.* Pat me consolingly on the shoulder, let me know she loves me no matter what. Say grades are not everything, after all.

But no.

"I think it's good," she says firmly. "It shows me that you are finally having the hunger you need to succeed." She stops when she sees the look on my face. "What?"

"I thought . . ." I pause. The girl with the pink lipstick fights for control of my tongue, wants so badly to say something I know I will regret, even if she won't. "I thought you were going to tell me to rest more."

Mother waves this away, scoffing a little as if it's the most ridiculous idea. "There will be time to rest later. When SPM is done."

I look at the packet on the table. *Soothing and Moisture Replenishing*, it says. "What is this for?"

Mother sniffs. "Really, Rachel, is this how you act when someone gets you a gift? I've taught you better than that, no?"

There it is, her magical ability to take an almost fully grown teenage girl and shrink her down to size. "Sorry, Mother."

"That's all right," she says, all martyred and long-suffering. "Just remember, Rachel, gratitude and politeness will always win the day." She bends down slightly to look at herself in the mirror that hangs above my vanity. "The facial masks are for your skin, of course. All this lack of sleep is wreaking havoc on your face, you know. All rough and dull. And got pimple here and here, and one here." She points out the exact location of every blemish, and I want to scream, and I want to snap, and I hold my tongue until the girl with the pink lipstick loosens it for me.

"Stop that," I say.

The look on Mother's face is as if I've hit her. "What did you say?" she asks.

"Stop. That." The girl enunciates each word carefully. She isn't rude or snarky about it, but her voice is firm and clear, and does not tremble the way my fingers do.

Mother just stares at me for a moment before seeming to come to a decision. "You are overtired," she tells me. "You must take better care. Appearances are everything. You know that." She straightens up again. "I am going to bed now," she says abruptly. "Study hard." And then she's gone.

I get up and walk over to the mirror. My face looks pale and tired; dark shadows are smudged under my eyes like I've been punched. There is no pink lipstick on me. But somewhere beneath my skin I feel her watching me out of my own eyes.

"It's all going to be worth it," I whisper to the girl in the mirror. "You'll see." I don't know if she believes me.

Khadijah

I am waiting for my mother to arrive, keeping an eye on Aishah, who stands a ways apart from me, alone and silent.

"I can't believe that you actually have to rejoin the debate team now," Sumi says breathlessly. "Like, damn, bro. Are they really going to let you get away with not talking?"

I bite my lip. Nod tentatively. Mrs. Beatrice beamed when she read that note. Patted me heartily on the shoulder. "What a tremendous decision you've made, Khadijah," she said. "I will be sure to let Puan Ani know right away." I felt sick to my stomach, and tried my best not to show it. Who has ever heard of a silent debater?

"It's just so weird. You lie about being on the debate team, and then the universe somehow rearranges itself to make it so you're actually telling the truth." Sumi shakes her head. "Wild."

I feel a twinge of annoyance. What's wild is that I allowed her to talk me into a heist that would never have worked anyway.

Flo passes me a slip of paper. "Before we head to the bus,"

she says. It's a list of names. Around us the stone walls of St. Bernadette's seem to lean closer. Like it's trying to take a peek. Like it's trying to catch every word. I hunch over the paper protectively, trace each name with my finger, count them off. I pause next to Aishah's name. Twenty-seven in all.

I look up at them, my face a question in itself.

"We couldn't find them all just yet," Flo says. There is something comforting in how she immediately understands. "We're still working on it."

"But not bad lah, right?" Sumi says, nudging me with her elbow. "I think we did a pretty good job so far lah. All things considered."

There is just the tiniest of pauses before I nod. Just the smallest little thought of, *Are you sure you did?* And I banish it immediately. Of course they did.

"Now we just have to look through them all and dig a little deeper into how they're connected," Sumi continues. "What they were doing when they were screaming, who they met, what they saw, what the experience was like. Anything they might have in common. And more to the point, anything they might have in common with Julianna."

I sigh. I can't even think her name without feeling a pang of frustration. I know that I need to unlock the mystery of Julianna Chin, and I'm not even sure where to start looking for the key.

"That's fine," Flo says. "Even if they're still not back at school, we can ask around, start talking to people, get a better idea of what it was like before they started screaming." Flo licks her dry lips. "You know, when it comes to figuring all this out, you have a primary source right there at home. Your very own screamer."

I look over to where Aishah stands. She fidgets with the key chain on her backpack, keeps her eyes on the horizon for Mak's car. Alone and silent, just like me.

"You should talk to her," Sumi says very definitely. "You should ask what happened. How she felt. What she was doing when it happened."

I think Flo clocks the expression on my face. She slips a hand into mine. I know she wants to comfort me. But somehow I do not feel comforted. I do not want the feel of her skin, her closeness. I leave my hand limp and unwelcoming in her grasp. "You don't have to talk," she tells me. "There are other ways to ask. You know?"

I nod again. I know. Of course I know. I'm just not sure Aishah will respond to them.

Ask her. I have to ask her. It's all I think about after we get home. It's playing in my head like a mantra, *Ask her, ask her, ask her, ask her.* Aishah does not talk to me, barely acknowledges I'm there. She moves around me as though I am a piece of furniture. An awkwardly placed chair or side table. She grabs the food Mak has left for us in the fridge—homemade pizza—and takes it to her room. I guess she doesn't mind it cold. Or maybe she minds cold pizza less than she minds being around me. My brain tells me it's because I failed to protect her. Failed to stop the screaming from getting her. Failed at being her big sister. I torture myself with this idea for hours.

Eventually she emerges from her bedroom. She walks to the sliding glass doors that lead from our living room to the back garden. Without even a glance in my direction, she slips outside.

Just ask her.

I walk over to the open doors. She's sitting right there on the grass. Almost perfectly in the center of the garden. She's wearing stripy green pajama pants and an oversized Totoro T-shirt. Her hair is disheveled; her eyes are closed. She must have taken a nap. Laid herself down, shut her eyes, tried to forget the world.

I step outside. Then I shuffle over to her in my bare feet and sit down beside her. She does not acknowledge my presence.

Our mother is not a gardener. The grass out here is more brown than green. And no plants survive. She tried to grow pandan and lemongrass and chilis once. The sad row of empty pots serves as a monument to her failures. The one frangipani tree that blooms red in the corner was there when we moved in, too grown to kill.

Aishah and I just sit there together for a while. With every breath I take, I try to summon more courage. Try to bring myself to open my mouth. To speak. I'm not sure when it got so hard, when talking started to scare me. I never thought I'd stop forever. But I never planned when it would end. So few people really understand why. The quiet is nice, and safe. Nobody twists your words when there are none to twist. Nobody reacts. Nobody gets too close.

But quiet cannot save her. Not now, not back then. I faced the danger, screamed our fear, and then embraced the silence. And now I must break my silence, my fear of my own voice. Or Aishah's screams may put her in danger.

Sweat leaves trails on Aishah's face as it drips down her forehead and cheeks. She peels one eye open and looks at me. "What do you want?" she says.

I pause. I pause for so long, she looks away, as though she's given up. As though she knew I wouldn't answer.

Come on, Khad.

I force the words past my lips. "What was it like?" I ask her. I haven't heard my own voice in so long. What a strange sound. What a strange feeling.

There is no trace of surprise on Aishah's face. "What was what like?" she asks.

"The screaming," I say.

She opens both eyes to study the sky. If this were a movie, it would be a brilliant blue. There'd be fluffy white Ghibli clouds. It would be the perfect backdrop for two sisters to open their hearts up to each other. They'd heal their relationship, end with a tight hug. The music would swell, the signal for the audience to weep, reach for their phones, and text their own sisters.

But this is not a movie. So the sky is a dirty gray and smells like smoke. And I don't reach out for Aishah. And she doesn't reach out for me. And I cannot stop myself from thinking: *This was not a good idea.* I cannot stop myself from thinking: *I should have stayed quiet.*

"I don't remember," she says.

"You must remember something."

"Not much." She tears at blades of grass, shredding them into teeny, tiny pieces. Mak would kill her if she knew. Mak is always talking about how frustrating it is that she can't make anything grow right. That all you can see when you look back here is brown.

I want to get up and walk away. I know what Aishah is like when she doesn't want to talk. But I promised Sumi and Flo I'd try, right? So I try. "What was happening before you screamed?"

Aishah snorts. "Look at you, Nancy Drew. Why does it matter, anyway?"

I wonder when she got so hard. So cold. "I just want to know."

She sighs and rakes a hand through her messy hair. "Fine. I was on my way back to class. I remember feeling a little weird, kind of lightheaded. My legs got a little wobbly, and I tripped near the frangipani trees." She rolls her left pant leg up to reveal a scrape, skin blooming purple around angry red lines like claw marks. "There, see? And then—nothing."

I blink. "Nothing?"

"Nope." Aishah stretches her long legs out and leans back on her elbows. "Nothing. From that point on, my mind's a blank until the moment when I was in the sickroom and you were next to me."

Sweat pools underneath my hijab. I reach up to scratch my head irritably.

"Just take it off," Aishah says.

"We're outside."

"Nobody can see you."

I leave it on. Something's bothering me more than the itch. "I'm sorry," I say finally.

She glances at me. "For what?"

I search for the right words. "That it happened. That I wasn't there. That I couldn't protect you. But I'm going to protect you from now on. I'm going to fix everything."

It takes her a long time to answer. When she does, it's so soft, I barely hear it. "It's not your job to protect me," she says. "It never was."

I curl my toes into the dirt. "It's what big sisters are supposed to do."

"I never asked you to do it." Her face is blank. But there is the slightest hint of a telltale tremor in her voice, just below the surface. The first sign that the ice she's covered herself with like armor has cracks. You'd have to know Aishah really well to hear it. You'd have to have known her all her life. And I think, *All this time I have protected myself with silence. But I am not the only one the incident had an effect on.* I was not the only recipient of our stepfather's hungry gaze, his wandering hands. It was me he acted upon, in the end. But only because of my own scheming.

The incident happened to Aishah, too. She had to watch it unfold. Watch what happened to me. Realize what could have happened to her. How close the danger was.

That must change a person too.

"It's not a thing you have to ask for. It's just how things

work." I pause and frown. "Wait, you said you were walking back to class. Where were you coming from?"

"Mr. B's office."

"Mr. B? Really?"

She shrugs. "He's been wanting me to come talk to him. You know. After everything. He probably has a quota of students he needs to 'help' every week, check them off his list of KPIs. We had a chat."

I feel my throat close up. "What did you talk about?"

"Not that it's any of your business, but I didn't tell him anything, if that's what you're asking. Some guy came by to talk to him, an old friend or whatever. So we stopped." She stands abruptly and brushes the dirt off her pants.

"Where are you going?" I ask.

"Inside." She turns to go, then pauses. "I won't tell Mak about this. Obviously."

I can't help a small smile. "Neither will I. Obviously."

She's about to walk through the door when I stop her. "Aishah."

"What?" She doesn't turn around.

"Why'd you decide to go back to school?"

She's quiet for a while. I can hear her breathing. "Because," she says finally. "Because it makes sense to be where I belong."

After she leaves, I sit for a long time, staring up at the boughs of the frangipani tree. It's not a Hallmark movie scene. But it's the closest we've come to a real conversation since everything broke. And I talked through it all. Maybe this was a good idea after all.

Fatihah

"This is not a good idea."

My parents try to tell me this, over and over. But I don't really listen. I want to go back. Why not? Why be scared? It already happened. It's not like it will happen again. At least I don't think so. Or maybe it will. Who cares? The damage is done. I was scared of being the new girl, but now it's even worse. Now I'm the first screamer. The one who started it. Patient zero.

Zero, ha, that's me. That's me, all right.

"Are you sure you are well enough?" Umi pats my knee while she talks. My mother is a toucher. She is always touching things— the wall, the back of a chair as she walks by, the jar of Sambal Nyet on the table, me. It is as if she wants to make sure we are all real.

"I'm fine," I say. This is not all the way true. My throat hurts and my head feels a little heavy. But so what? "I want to go to school," I say.

My father grunts. That's what he does. He doesn't talk much. My mother, she's the talker. The talker and the toucher. What does that make him? The grunter, I guess.

"What for?" Umi asks. This time she touches my hair. "Why not stay home for a few more days? Just rest?"

"It's been enough days," I say. We don't have Netflix, and Umi and Ayah set the internet to go off at six p.m. When it is on, they put parental controls on everything. If I told people this, they'd probably think I'm seven, not fifteen. "I want to go back."

Umi's hand is on my back now. Slow pats, up and down. "I know you miss your friends," she says. "But maybe—"

"I want to go back to school," I say again. "Please," I add. I forgot. You have to be polite, don't you? Especially to your parents. Umi says this all the time. Sometimes I forget. But if I forget too much, Ayah reminds me. With the feather duster.

I see Umi glance at Ayah. She's asking him what to do, but with her eyes. Not her mouth. He just grunts. I wonder how she knows what he means.

Umi sighs. "All right," she says. "But not on the bus. I don't want anything to happen to you in your current state. I'll ask your uncle to drive you."

My body goes all stiff. I don't mean for it to. It just happens. "Pak Su?"

Umi nods. "He lives near us, and St. Bernadette's is right near his office. Right, Yang?"

Ayah grunts. He is scrolling on his phone, down, down, down.

"I'll call Pak Su," Umi says. She sounds more sure this time. More convinced. "That will do wonders. Don't you think so?"

"Sure," I say. "Sure." It doesn't matter what I say. They're not listening. Sometimes people do this, you know. They ask you a question, but it is not a question. They just want to tell themselves you agree. Makes them feel better.

It's like when they asked me that time if I wanted to change schools. It didn't matter if I said yes or no. Only that they asked. That's the thing they want to remember. "But we asked you."

But they were probably right. That time anyway. Nobody at that old school misses me.

Nobody wants the girl who sees things in the shadows.

Rachel

I move through the day with mechanical precision, blank and efficient and immersing myself fully in the work presented to me. I do not want to think about yesterday, about how easily my tongue became hers, my mood shifted to her will.

You are becoming your character, I tell myself fiercely. *This is what the best actors do.* And I don't let myself think about how much she is becoming me.

"Are you okay?" Dahlia is looking at me, one eyebrow raised. "You're acting weird. Again." Dahlia has been shooting barbs at me any chance she gets, her way of paying me back for our little altercation yesterday. With every verbal blow she lands, I feel something inside me bubbling up, as if the girl with the pink lipstick is just waiting to be unleashed.

"What? Of course I'm okay. Why wouldn't I be okay?" I snatch my hand out of my pocket. Pink-lipstick-girl moves my mouth. "Mind your business." I concentrate on my notes, trying to ignore the fact that my hand trembles so that my writing goes this way and that. Who cares? Who the hell cares about handwriting anyway?

She holds up her hands, her top lip curling in disdain. "Relax, Speed Racer. I'm only asking because you've been clicking that damn pen at, like, the same bpm as Eminem's speed raps, so can you just, like, chill a bit? It's really distracting."

She turns back around, and I blink, first at the back of her head, and then at the black ballpoint pen in my hand. Have I been clicking it? I don't even remember.

The teachers are watching me, I know they are. Sometimes I catch sight of Mrs. Dev across a room, and she's just sitting and looking at me over the top of those glasses, like she's searching me for something. But she doesn't tell me what it is, and she doesn't call me in to see her again.

They are just waiting for you to mess up again, the Mother in my head tells me. *Because you will. And they know it.*

The girl in the pink lipstick rears her head. *Shut up,* she says. And Mother does.

Once the bell rings, I head to the assembly hall for Community Day practice. I am already thinking of where I can go to rehearse, where I can sneak to in time to run through my lines. As usual I'm early. I am chronically early for everything. Nobody is here but me, not yet anyway. I am suddenly overcome by a wave of exhaustion. I lie down carefully on the floor by the stairs that lead up to the stage, where I can't be seen if you walk past the hall, and I rest my cheek against the cool concrete. I think about pink lipstick and dry leaves and facial masks. *You look like you have lost your mind,* the Mother in my head hisses. *Where is your sense of propriety? You are embarrassing me.* But I don't care. Her voice sounds very, very far away today, far enough away to ignore. I think of the real Mother, of how she would react if she ever found out about the acting, or the C, or the homework I've been ignoring, and my stomach clenches in protest. I groan.

"Are you all right?"

The voice is deep and familiar. I open my eyes, and the man who told me to call him Uncle is staring at me with what can only be described as a look of deep concern. I struggle to sit up, my cheeks burning from the embarrassment of both being caught lying down and the memory of the last time we met and my own appalling rudeness. I shake my head when he offers me a hand. "No thank you." If the earth would swallow me up right now, I'd be extremely grateful.

I guess he notices. "Don't worry about it," he says. "Can't tell you the number of times I've wanted to drop everything and lie down quietly in the middle of the day." He looks around as if to check if anyone's listening, then leans forward slightly, dropping his voice. "One time, I told my secretary to block my time because I had some very important work to do. But I didn't. I locked myself in the boardroom and took a nap under the table."

Uncle looks so pleased with himself that it strangles a laugh out of me.

He grins. "There you go. That's better." He sits down carefully on one of the steps. I wonder if he worries about messing up his immaculate black pinstripe trousers, or scuffing his buttery leather shoes. "Isn't practice supposed to start already?"

"Soon," I say, checking my watch. "You're early."

"So are you," he says.

I shrug. "My mother says on time is ten minutes early."

He smiles. "I feel like I know at least a few people at the office who could benefit from this wisdom." He stretches out his legs and sighs. "You're wonderful on the piano. How long have you been playing?"

"Since I was, like, five?" I think of dangling my legs and practicing scales and arpeggios as Mother sat beside me, wooden ruler in hand, ready to rap my knuckles if I made a mistake. "My mother says I always had musical inclinations. She says it felt like it would be a waste of talent to wait until I was older to start. In fact, it's one of her everlasting regrets that she didn't start me on it at four."

"But do you enjoy it?"

I blink. "Pardon?"

"Do you actually enjoy playing the piano?" He is looking at me with warmth in his eyes, and it feels new and strange to have anyone—much less an adult—listen to me with this much attention, this much interest. I am unsettled by it. I reach my hand into my pinafore pocket, let my fingers cradle the smooth plastic of the lipstick tube that lies there. I wonder what the pink-lipstick-girl would say.

"I mean, Mother says—"

"You talk about your mother a lot, what she says and what she thinks. I was just wondering what you think. How you feel. Is music something you like to do?"

"I . . . um . . ." Nobody has asked me this before. And it sounds ridiculous, but I'm not sure I've ever thought about all the things I do in terms of whether or not I actually enjoy doing them. I do them because Mother tells me to do them. Isn't that enough? I bite my lip. The Mother in my head hisses, *He knows nothing. Nothing about you, and nothing about us.*

"It's okay if you aren't sure right now," Uncle tells me gently. "I didn't mean anything by it. I'm just an old man who likes to ramble. Don't mind me."

"I—" Before I can say anything, Cik Diana walks in, beaming, the other member of our trio in tow.

"Hello, everyone!" she trills. "Are we ready to begin practice?"

And we nod, and everything goes back to normal, and I try to forget that my world just shifted slightly on its axis.

Khadijah

I am going to the library, and it is my first debate team practice, and I might vomit. In fact, I am concentrating so hard on not vomiting that I almost knock over a cleaner just outside the library doors. I want to say sorry, but nothing comes. I can only put my hands together in a gesture of apology and hope she understands. But the old lady says nothing. She doesn't even look at me. She merely continues to sweep, sweep, sweep away at the leaves scattered all over the pavement.

I pause to take a breath. I tried to collect myself before practice. Went to pray Isyak at the school's surau, hoping the act of wuduu' and worship would help me calm down. But it clearly didn't work as well as I'd hoped. *Get a grip, Khadijah, get a grip.* Then I push the doors open and walk inside, the sound of the old lady's sweeping ringing in my ears long after she's out of sight.

The girls are in the back room. Clare the librarian calls this the "reference room." This means it's got a couple of ancient computers that take half an hour to boot up. The only books here are dusty, chunky tomes on things like world cultures and history. It's practically guaranteed that nobody will bother us.

All I want to do is learn more about Julianna.

And yet here I am.

I sit at a corner of the large table. I'm clutching my backpack to my chest like a shield. If I cover my chest, maybe they won't realize how much it's heaving up and down, how hard my heart is beating. On my left are the two other alternates. Form-three kids, fifteen-year-old babies. Puan Ani always chooses alternates from form three. "It's good practice," she says. "Gets them used to competitions, gives them a feel for what it's like." It's only me she ever let on the team right away.

The kids introduce themselves to me. I tap my name tag to show them what to call me. Their names are Anu and Erni. Once the pleasantries are over, they talk to each other in hushed whispers. Every once in a while I think I catch them glancing at me. I can't tell if they're impressed or horrified by my presence. I am confident I will never be able to tell them apart.

Across from me sit the three main debaters. Two of them, Rania and Felicia, I already know. They're fellow fourth formers who used to be alternates back when I was on the team. They are openly curious, but friendly.

The third is Siti.

Siti and I debated together last year. She was first speaker. I was third. Our second speaker, Louise, is now living the life in California. Her dad moved them all over there after he got some fancy Silicon Valley tech job. There are three important things to know about Siti. One: she is nowhere near as good a debater as she thinks she is. Two: she knows I am every bit as good as she wishes she were. Three: this is why she hates me.

I shrink farther behind my backpack. I wish Sumi and Flo were here. I wish I'd stop feeling the urge to pee. I wish I'd figured out anything else. Anything besides the note I hastily shoved into Mrs. Beatrice's hands.

She actually smiled. Complimented me on my "commitment to the school."

Puan Ani bustles in, her arms full of books. I've never been so glad to see a teacher in my life. "Hello, hello! Are you ready to begin, girls? Sorry I'm late. Bloody 3 Cempaka took too long with their quiz. Anyway, I'm here now. We can begin." She sets down her things. She is breathless and smiling. "Now, you all remember Khadijah, of course. Khadijah will be helping us with strategy and research, and I'm sure we're all very glad to have her."

She looks encouragingly around the table. There is a murmuring of "Yes" in varying levels of enthusiasm. Siti crosses her arms and keeps her mouth firmly shut.

Puan Ani clears her throat. "Now, girls. I know it's a little unusual to add what is essentially a third alternate at this point in competition season. But nationals are very important this year, and Mrs. Beatrice felt strongly that Khadijah should be part of the team, given the role she's played in it in years past. It's hardly her fault that . . . circumstances . . . meant she wasn't able to be as active this year."

I feel my entire body clench. Did she really have to bring up circumstances?

Rania smiles a wide, friendly smile. "I, for one, am really glad you're here," she tells me. "I think we can use all the help we can get."

"Yeah, I hear St. Gabriel's is going to nationals too," Felicia says. "And those boys are so absolutely full of themselves. Perasan nak mampus. I would love it if we beat them. In debate or otherwise," she adds, smirking.

Across the table Siti's lips curve into a grin. I am immediately on alert. This grin is not friendly. This grin is not welcoming. This grin is dangerous. "Oh yes, Puan Ani," she says, her voice dripping with sincerity. "As the leader of this team"—her eyes flash to me at this—"I'm happy to have Khadijah on board as a researcher." Does she think I don't notice that emphasis? "And of course we must all be very careful not to bring up the incident. We wouldn't want Khadijah to feel uncomfortable, after all."

I can feel my heart pounding in my ears. I've often thought about how many people know, how many people look at me and think, *There's that girl. You know,* that *one.* Maybe they all do.

"That's the spirit, Siti!" Puan Ani looks pleased at how well her team is getting along. How considerate everyone is being to poor, broken, silent Khadijah. I think I may throw up right here all over this table. "What a lovely way to welcome someone back to the team. I am quite confident that we'll be ready to take on any opponent now!"

"Of course!" Siti is smiling again. *A snake,* I think. *A snake locked on its prey.* "And especially now that we have our strongest lineup possible. Not a single weak link. Not even one." She stares right at me as she says it. "All of us know what to do now, and we're confident enough to speak up when we need to. Isn't that right, girls?"

There are nods and murmurs of assent. Nobody catches on to the fact that Siti is talking to me. That she's calling me weak. That she's sneering at me for not speaking.

"All right, then," Puan Ani says pleasantly, as if nothing has happened. "The topic for the next round is 'Nature is more important than nurture,' and today and tomorrow we will work on our points for the government before moving on to the opposition."

Across the table Siti makes a big show of pushing her notebook toward me. "Here, Khadijah," she says, smiling sweetly. "You can take a look at my notes to see what we've already talked about."

I nod and skim the notes quickly. Siti still has the habit of dotting her *i*'s with little hearts. Everything else is easy enough to understand. I hand the notebook back and let the wave of chatter wash over me until Puan Ani says, "Does that sound good, Khadijah?"

I jump at the sound of my name and look at her questioningly.

"I said, does that sound good?" she asks again. But I can't indicate if it does or doesn't. Because I have no idea what she's talking about.

"I don't think she was listening, Cikgu," Siti supplies. Her top lip curls back ever so slightly. Under her breath she adds, "And if she's not listening and she's not talking, what good is she to us?"

"Siti, quiet," Puan Ani says.

"I was just saying," Rania says quickly as Siti's face darkens, "that since it's my first time on the actual team, I was wondering if you'd be willing to take a look at my speeches once I'm done with them, Khadijah? I'd appreciate any notes to make my arguments airtight, you know?"

"Me too," Felicia says, nodding earnestly. "We just really want to do our best. Could you help us?"

Everyone is looking at me again. But at least this time their eyes are beseeching and not cold. I nod, and the girls grin as if I've just given them the best present in the world.

"Excellent," Puan Ani says, gathering her books and papers together. "I look forward to taking a look at those first drafts tomorrow. Siti, it might be a good idea for you to do the same and have Khadijah check your speech as well."

Siti looks like she would rather eat glass.

"Good job today, girls." Puan Ani stands. "We'll reconvene here again tomorrow, same time. Remember, that debate coach I was talking about will come by in the next couple of days to begin working with you. And, Khadijah—" She smiles at me kindly. "It's good to have you back, in whatever capacity. See you, girls."

Siti waits until Puan Ani is actually gone before turning to me. Scorn is written all over her face. "Just in case it isn't clear," she says. "Just in case it isn't obvious to you, we really don't need you here." She's pronouncing each word so clearly, so crisply, it feels like I'm being slapped. "We're focused on winning and bringing that national title back for St. Bernadette's, and we can't afford to be your trauma dumping ground or therapy group or whatever it is you're using us for. Go to therapy, or find some other avenue to work through your issues, and leave us out of it." After this long speech she flips her long, straight ponytail over her shoulder and walks off.

The other girls exchange glances. Erni hesitates before placing a hand gently on my arm. It's only then that I realize I'm trembling. "Are you okay, Kak Khadijah?" Her concern seems genuine.

I'm not sure if I am. But conveying that takes words. I just shrug.

"She didn't mean it—" Felicia begins.

"Yes she did," Anu says quietly, arms crossed, lips tight. "She always does. She can be nice when she wants to be, but when she doesn't, Kak Siti is mean."

"She just cares a lot about winning," Felicia says. "Don't we all?"

"Ya," Rania says. "We just aren't bitches about it. Don't worry about her, okay, Khadijah? We're on your side. We'll try to keep her in check. And I, for one, am really glad you're here to help us out."

"Me too" echoes around the table. For the first time this

whole session, I smile at everyone and mean it.

We leave the library together. In the afternoon light the walls of St. Bernadette's seem to glow. But I can't shake the feeling that there's something sinister just beneath. Something menacing. The way an anglerfish dangles a light to attract prey before crunching them in those sharp, sharp teeth. The girls are talking, and the day is still bright, and leaves crunch underfoot.

Crunching leaves . . .

I frown. Didn't the cleaner earlier sweep up the leaves on the pavement? And yet here they are, so many that you can barely see the pavement at all.

I shake my head quickly. *So what, Khad? The wind probably blew down more leaves,* I tell myself. *Stop being so paranoid.*

But as I walk toward the canteen to meet Sumi and Flo, it's hard not to notice that there isn't even the hint of a breeze in the air. There is no wind, none at all.

I find my friends in the canteen, their heads close together. Sumi's back is to me, but I can see Flo's face. It's uncharacteristically serious. I wave, but she doesn't seem to notice me. As I get closer, I can hear them talking. Arguing? Flo throws her hands up and says, "You can't say that! You know we have to do whatever we can. You know she's not herself right now. We talked about this."

Me. They're talking about me.

Sumi rubs her face with one hand. Even from the back I can picture her expression. How tired, how frustrated she is. "This isn't what I signed up for," she says. It's only seven words, but each one sticks in my chest like a poisoned dart. "I just want us to go back to how we used to—"

"Khad!" Flo finally spots me and waves me over. Sumi turns, and for a split second I see the complete dismay on her face. Just for a second. Then she pastes on her usual grin and offers up a fist for me to bump.

"What's up, karipap?" she says.

I move my mouth into an approximation of a smile. I don't know what to do, how to feel. I guess my mood is obvious. Flo and Sumi exchange glances.

"Have we got news for you," Sumi says, leaning closer, dropping her voice into a conspiratorial whisper.

I can't help it. I move back almost instinctively. Something flickers behind Sumi's eyes, but she says nothing.

I look at Flo, a question in my raised eyebrows.

"She's back," Flo says. "The first screamer is back."

And they keep talking. Excited, energized. It's a new lead. A chance to get the story from patient zero herself. But from somewhere in the school, the sound of sweeping begins once more. And for a long time it's all I can hear.

Rachel

I am still thinking about that conversation with Uncle when I get home, thinking about the strange feeling of having someone care enough to ask questions and then actually show interest in my answers. There was an accident on the road, and traffic moved an inch at a time; it was almost dark by the time Pakcik Zakaria dropped me off, and I am exhausted. Too exhausted to eat, even. I wave away Kak Tini's attempts to serve me dinner and head straight for the shower.

Afterward, in my comfiest baggy T-shirt and softest sweatpants, hair still wet, I sit at my desk. I take all my assignments from my backpack and line them up neatly on my desk, perfectly straight, one after the other. All the teachers say some version of the same thing as they pile on the work. "We won't go easy on you this year. Now is the time to buckle down and put in the work. St. Bernadette's has a reputation to uphold. Make your parents proud. Think of your future."

I will myself to pick up my pen and begin, each bit of homework a paving stone for the path my mother wants me to take toward a future she determines for me. I think about the girl with the pink lipstick, about what she would say, what she would do. What future she imagines for herself, for me, for us.

There's a sound outside, a movement, and then a soft knock that startles me out of my thoughts. The homework lies untouched on my desk; my hair is almost dry. How long have I been sitting here? "Come in," I call out, knowing it's not Mother, who comes into my room without knocking anytime she pleases, to see if I'm working, if I'm being her good, obedient Rachel.

The door opens slowly, and Kak Tini pokes her head inside. "Rachel nak buah?" she asks, gesturing to the plate she holds in one hand, filled with grapes and carefully sliced apples and orange wedges.

I manage a small smile. "Okay," I say. Then I turn my attention back to my notes. The plate is set gently on the table beside me. "Terima kasih, Kak," I say, my thanks muffled by the grape I've just stuffed into my mouth. I chew and chew and chew, until suddenly I realize that the soft sweetness of the grape is no longer soft and sweet at all; it is sharp-edged and paper thin, and when I spit it out, it isn't grape that I spit out, but one leaf, and then another, and then another, my mouth full of them, brown and dry, and I am engulfed by their musty, dank smell, and it feels as if I am being buried alive, and the leaves will not stop coming out of my mouth, and I choke and splutter and cough and wonder if this is how I will die—

And then a hand is shaking me, shaking me hard, and I

finally open my eyes and realize it was nothing but a dream, just a ridiculous, terrible dream, and the hand belongs to Kak Tini, half sobbing in panic as she yells, "Rachel! Rachel, bangun! Rachel! Stop, Rachel!"

I am at my desk, my head pounding, my skin damp with sweat. I am meant to be writing an essay, I remember, the thoughts coming as slow as snails. I am supposed to be analyzing a novel for Bahasa Melayu. I look around and realize that my notebook and the novel are both on the floor. Everything that was on my desk is on the floor. And my hands, I am realizing, are sore. I have been thrashing and flailing in my sleep.

"Rachel?" Kak Tini says, her eyes worried.

For a while all I can do is stare at her. Then I reach into my mouth and feel, almost tearing away at the insides, convinced that leaves still lurk in its depths, until Kak Tini squeals, "Stop, Rachel, stop!"

I pull my hands away and focus on trying to slow my breathing. "Sorry," I say, panting. "Sorry, Kak Tini."

She takes a step away from me, as if I scare her. "I will get you some water," she says, then walks quickly out of the room, glancing back every so often like I'm going to chase her down.

The only sound in the room is my own hoarse breathing.

Fatihah

Being back is . . . It's, well . . . How do I describe it? That one word, you know. Ala. You know. What was it? Words are hard, these days. Everything is hard, these days. I'm so tired. It is hard to sleep.

What was I talking about?

Weird. That's it. That's the word. "Weird."

There's no big welcome or anything. No happy smiles. No friend who comes running over, says, *I'm so glad you're back! I missed you!* But that's understandable, right? I was the new girl. I'm still the new girl. I came to this school three weeks ago. Not even a month. Come all the way here, and what do I do? Scream.

But I can feel them staring at me, you know. All those eyeballs looking my way. I don't like it. I just don't. I liked the way it was before. Nobody noticing me. Forgetting I was there. It's nicer than it sounds. Peaceful. That's what it was like, last time. At the other school. Before they knew what I could see.

Now people look. And they come close. They ask questions.

Things like, *How are you?* And, *How are you feeling?* It's very polite. There must be feather dusters at their houses, too. But behind the nice, proper questions, I can hear the real ones. The ones like *What happened?* And *What did it feel like?* And *Was it scary?*

I don't know why they don't ask. I would answer. Like this:

What happened? I was sitting at my desk, like normal. I was trying to finish my math work. My desk is in the back corner. A wall on one side, a wall behind me. I like it there. It's quiet. The teacher was explaining something. No, I don't remember her name. I'm bad at names. And remembering. Anyway, she was explaining something. Talking a lot. Talk, talk, talk. It was hard to pay attention. I was getting sleepy. I always get sleepy after recess. But then I looked up and I saw it. The shadow. All big and black, near the ceiling. I stared at it for a long time. I thought maybe I could see a face. I'm not sure now, though. It felt like we were having a staring contest. I didn't want to know what would happen if I lost. So I kept staring. And it got bigger and bigger. I wanted to yell at my classmates, you know. All those other girls doing math. I wanted to ask them, *Don't you see it? Don't you see it?* How could they not see? But I guess it knew what I was thinking. Because when I opened my mouth, it jumped down at me, all of a sudden. And then all I did was scream. But I scratched, too. That teacher said. He showed me. Long, red scar down his arm. My fault. Like a cat, you know. A cat that got cornered.

I didn't remember all this for a while. Then it started coming back to me in little bitty bits. I put them together like puzzle pieces. I'm good at puzzles. Very good. I can sit for a long time, just figuring out how all the shapes fit together. Patience, that's what it is. Sabar. Sabar itu separuh daripada iman. Patience is half of faith. My mother taught me that.

What did it feel like? Cold.

Was it scary? Um. Hmm. Maybe if you're not used to it, I guess. But I am. Because I've seen this shadow before.

All the girls, they like to talk. I hear them talk all the time. About the scary things in the corridors. About the third stall in the bathroom. About the wailing woman you hear deep in the night. But they tell them like stories. All cartoony. Big vampire fangs and blood on the walls. The school has ghosts, but, well, nobody understands. They're not ghosts, not really. The school remembers. It's all there in its bones. Deep in the stones. Buried inside the concrete. All the things it's seen, everything. Over a hundred years of it. When the girls talk about seeing ghosts, that's what they're seeing. The school's memories.

But not the shadow. The shadow is different. It follows me. Been following me since the old school. Made people think I was cuckoo. Gila, they called me, the crazy, crazy girl with the shadows in her head. I thought it would go away. But I move, and it moves with me. It must be true, then. Crazy girl, crazy girl. Only crazy girls try to outrun their shadow.

Anyway, nobody asks. But that's what I'd say. If they did.

Rachel

When I wake up, my throat is bone-dry and scratchy, as if I have spent all night swallowing sandpaper.

Or dry leaves.

I get up and shower and go through all the motions of getting ready for school. I make sure all my books are packed, then quickly shove my homework out of sight behind them, trying to ignore the blank spaces where answers are supposed to be. They'll forgive me, I tell myself. They will. It's a onetime thing. I'll catch up in no time. I'm Rachel Lian.

I make my bed, and then I make it again, checking to see that each corner is absolutely perfect, that my pillows are fluffed just so. I tidy everything on my desk, line each thing up in its exact spot.

Before I leave, I carefully tie my hair back into its usual ponytail, making sure my part is perfectly centered. I check my reflection in the mirror. The shadows under my eyes are as dark as bruises, as though I've been punched. But otherwise I look fine. Neat and tidy, and above all, normal. Absolutely normal. Normalcy, I tell myself, is how I will chase away the shadows of the night before. Normalcy is how I will get back to my life, my real life as Rachel Lian. As me.

But something about the way I look in the mirror makes me uneasy. As if I am wearing a uniform that's a size too small, or two left shoes, or there is a tag somewhere in my top that is making me itch, that I just can't find. I look and look and look, but I can't figure out what it is that's making me fidget. Until at last I untie my hair and part it into two low pigtails. I rummage around in my desk drawer and finally find it, a ribbon that came wrapped around a gift box on my last birthday. I thought I would be getting a phone. Mother gave me tickets to a recital instead, telling me I could really learn a lot from the pianist if I simply watched carefully and tried harder.

Carefully I snip the ribbon in half. Then I tie each half into a bow around each pigtail.

I look into the mirror once more, and immediately I'm flooded with relief. *This looks right,* I think. *This looks like me.* And I go to school with a lighter heart, the darkness of the night forgotten, the bitter taste of leaves on my tongue a ghost of a memory, as if it had happened to somebody else.

The feeling of relief is only intensified when I reach St. Bernadette's. I move from the freezing air-conditioning of the car's back seat and slip into the school's warmth, and it is as if I am being hugged. *A building cannot hug you,* the Mother in my head says, and she sounds almost angry as she says it. *A building cannot love you.* But St. Bernadette's loves me. I know it does. I can feel it.

"Have a good day, Rachel," Pakcik Zakaria tells me.

"I will," I say. Of course I will. I am here, where I belong.

. . .

"What's wrong with you?" Dahlia asks in class, her nose wrinkled, her eyebrow raised, and my lips curve into a knowing smile. I know now. I know how unimportant she is, how insignificant, how beneath me. It's not that I'm better than she is. It's that she doesn't actually matter. And when I see the look in her eyes change, I know she knows this too.

But somehow, even with this confidence, this sense that I am where I am supposed to be, something odd happens. The day keeps slipping away from me. I blink, and it's second period; I look down, and my book is filled with notes that I don't remember writing, in handwriting that doesn't even look like mine. I blink, and Mrs. Dev is lecturing me about an assignment I can't turn in, that I never even attempted to do. I blink again, and we're coming back to class after recess, my breath tasting of noodle soup that I don't remember eating. I blink once more, and I'm halfway down the stairs, backpack on my shoulder, heading to . . . heading to . . .

I pause, midstep. Girls flow around me, going up, going down, but the usual after-school chaos is a lot more subdued now that so many aren't here.

Where am I going?

The answer takes some time to appear. Practice. Community Day practice. Of course, that's where I'm going.

I walk to the assembly hall slowly, my white ribbons fluttering in the breeze. My calm confidence of the day is quickly dissipating; I feel unmoored, as if I've been cast out to sea before I was ready.

What happened to me today? Why don't I remember?

. . .

I am early, as usual. But not the earliest. Uncle sits on the steps of the stage, leaning back on his elbow, one hand flicking through his phone. He looks up as I enter, and his face creases into a smile. "Hello, hello," he says. "Just you and me, of course."

"You're earlier than me this time," I say.

He nods, his face serious, his eyes twinkling. "Someone much smarter than me told me that on time is ten minutes early."

I glance at my watch. "But this is twenty-two minutes early."

"Even better." He grins. "Especially if it gives me more time to chat with my young friend."

I put my bag down and sit cross-legged on the floor, facing him. There is something calming about his presence. Maybe it's just nice to be around an adult who treats me like a person, who isn't expecting something from me, who isn't disappointed in me, who seems happy just to talk to me.

"You look nice today," he says, gesturing toward my hair. "I like the hairdo."

"Thank you," I say. I can feel heat creeping into my cheeks. I don't often get compliments; I get compliments about my looks even less. "Thank you," I say again, awkward and unsure, and he laughs.

"You're welcome." He leans forward as if to get a closer look. "And is that . . . lipstick you're wearing?"

I freeze.

He doesn't seem to notice. "It looks great—beautiful,

actually—but I'm not sure your teachers would approve."

Lipstick? I have lipstick on? I reach up to touch my mouth, then snatch my hand away as if it might burn me. "Excuse me," I mumble, getting quickly to my feet. "I need to go to the bathroom."

Uncle gets up too, his face a mask of concern. "Are you all right?" he asks. "Do you need help?" It's hard not to contrast how much he cares with how little my mother does.

"I'm fine," I say. "Excuse me," I say again.

Two girls are leaving the bathroom as I enter; they stop chattering for just a moment as they pass. I can't interpret the look I see in their eyes, but I know well what it means when girls begin whispering as soon as you turn your back.

In the mirror my face is pale, my mouth bright pink.

When did I put the lipstick on?

I take a tissue out of my pocket and rub and rub and rub until my lips are raw. My hands are trembling, and the lipstick smears all over. It looks like I'm some kind of monster. I stare at myself in the mirror. "Who are you?" I whisper.

The girl in the mirror reaches out a hand to caress my face. Her fingers are cold, and I can feel an answering trail of goose bumps all along my arms.

"Pay attention," she says.

I shut my eyes. When I open them again, the reflection in the mirror is just me. But written in bright pink lipstick on the mirror are two words.

SAVE US

Khadijah

The first screamer is back. The first screamer walks among us. Just another girl in a sea of girls in school uniforms, giggling behind their books in class, lining up for food in the canteen. She started all of this, all the anxiety and the fear. And now she is here.

And I have to find her.

My head whirls and whirls around these same thoughts all day. The girls around me take notes; I draw complicated diagrams with intersecting lines between FIRST SCREAMER and JULIANNA, mapping out everything I've learned and need to learn. I am feverish, frantic. There must be a connection. There must be. But she hasn't disappeared, the first screamer. Not yet. Will she? If I figure all of this out, can I stop it from happening to her? To Aishah?

The problem, I think as the girls recite surahs around me, *is that there is still so little I know about Julianna.* Everything has been a dead end. Google searches. Sasha A. Mr. B.

My pen stops beside his name. I click my pen top thoughtfully, over and over. This is an old, old school, one with a fine reputation. Teachers often stay a long time at schools like this.

There have to be more of them. Of course there are. More teachers who stuck around. Who remember what happened nine years ago. Who wouldn't mind talking to me.

I click my pen one last time, a triumphant, loud click.

"Yes, Khadijah?" the teacher says. "You have something to add?" She doesn't look particularly hopeful. I shake my head. "Of course not," she murmurs.

I don't care. She's only been here for three years at most. She's not who I need. From the corner of my eye I see Sumi and Flo trying to get my attention. Trying to see what I'm doing, to ask me what's up. But I pretend I don't see them. Pretend I don't feel the sting when I think about the me they want me to be. The me I can't get back.

Instead I pore over my notes, ignore everything else that's happening around me, and start making plans.

After school, armed with my stolen copy of *The Beacon*, I begin my quest.

First I comb through the pages of teachers, staring at each face. It's hot out; sweat traces cool trails from beneath my hijab and stings my eyes. There were a lot of older teachers back then, teachers on the brink of retirement, maybe. Few look familiar. I'm starting to get frustrated. Nine years wasn't that long ago. Surely somebody had to have stuck around. Somebody besides Mr. B.

When I finally emerge from its pages, I have two names, a headache, and a mind hell-bent on finding both teachers. Yes, I'm supposed to be at the library with my team instead of hiding here just behind the shrubbery of Brede's House. I chose this spot specifically because nobody—well, "nobody" meaning "Sumi or Flo"—would think to look for me here. But also because it's outside. At least there's some space here. Some distance from the stone walls that seem to listen, the shadows that seem to cling a little too close.

I get up to leave. Then pause. And turn back.

I would swear I heard something. Something coming from the building behind me. And as I peer at the peeling façade, I'm almost certain I see something move behind the streaky glass above. Watching me.

I blink.

Whatever it is, it's gone. And I have no time to dwell on the Brede's House ghost, or whatever that might have been. I have a mission to fulfill.

The first name is a dud; she's pregnant and out on maternity leave. Someone is always out on maternity leave here. This means there's only one name left.

I walk into the teacher's room and stride over to her desk. Then I pause, unsure. I didn't actually think about what to do beyond this point. But it's too late. She looks up.

"Yes?" she asks, frowning slightly and looking over the top of her glasses.

She wears her regulation black name tag pinned slightly crookedly to her long-sleeved top. White letters spell out her name. MRS. DEV.

"Well, girl?" She sighs, already impatient, already weary. "What is it? Spit it out, mm?"

I place *The Beacon* carefully on her desk. Flip open the page. Point out Julianna. There is still a circle around her face from when I was in Mr. B's room. I jab at the photo. Use my finger to underline her name. *Tell me about Julianna Chin.*

It's so small, so minuscule. I might not have noticed if I weren't watching so intently. But as she realizes who it is she's looking at, I see her face change. Just a little.

"Mm, yes. This girl." She busies herself with a stack of filled-out worksheets. Grabs a red pen from a holder shaped like a sloth. Her tone is suspiciously nonchalant. "Used to be a student here, I believe. Why, mm?"

I grab my notebook and pen. Write, *Tell me what happened to her.*

Mrs. Dev reads my note, then looks up at me. Understanding dawns. "Ah, so you're that one. The girl who doesn't talk."

I nod.

"Well, girl who doesn't talk—" I tap my name tag, and her eyes flick over to my name. "Khadijah. I'm not sure why you ask, but I teach multiple classes a year, each with almost forty students. I can barely remember who I might have interacted with last year, much less from as long ago as this."

I scribble furiously, my writing barely readable. *She disappeared. What happened?*

Mrs. Dev shrugs. She will not look me in the eye. "Mm. I suppose she might have run away? You teenage girls, you are such a mystery to me. Now, please, Khadijah. I am very busy."

My trembling fingers make it harder and harder to write the

words. *Why didn't the school tell us that girls have screamed before?*

"Screaming, what screaming?" Mrs. Dev mumbles. She is focused entirely on the papers on her desk. "How many days already with no screaming, so why must we still talk about it? Mm? Focus on your work, Khadijah. You are still a student, you know. Still a young girl."

I write, *The last time, the screaming came first. What if another missing girl is what comes next?*

Mrs. Dev pushes the note back toward me without looking.

I can feel my cheeks turn red hot. From anger. From frustration. I take the note back. Write, *DON'T YOU CARE ENOUGH TO STOP THAT FROM HAPPENING??*

But she keeps refusing to look. Refusing to answer. Refusing to take me seriously. Rage rises up my throat. I rip the page from my notebook. Take a pin off the bulletin board that leans against the side of her desk. And I jam it through the note, right through the center of the worksheet she's marking.

She whips her head up to look at me. Glasses askew, cheeks aflame. "Look, girl," she says quietly, evenly. "All you're going to do is get us both into trouble. I told them I wouldn't talk, and I won't, so please just leave me alone."

And with that she gets up and walks away. Quick, mincing steps down the narrow path between desks, as if she's worried I'll chase her.

But as I walk slowly over to the library where I was supposed to be all along, I'm just left wondering, *Who's "them"?*

Rachel

"Next."

All of us who signed up for the forensics tournament are gathered here in the assembly hall, orators and actors and debaters. The teachers want us to show them what we are working on right here, on this stage, in front of them and all the girls who signed up this year, in whatever event.

"This is not an audition," Puan Ani is quick to tell us. "Everyone who signed up is allowed to participate! So don't be nervous. We just want to make sure you are well prepared, and give you tips on how to improve, if you need them. After all—" She stops and smiles at us. There is lipstick on her teeth. "After all, St. Bernadette's has a reputation to maintain, yes?"

I reach into my pocket, just to touch the tube of lipstick, make sure it's still there. I try to ignore how my fingers tremble. I try not to think about words in pink on a mirror, or about how I both want to slip into her and am incredibly scared to allow her back in. *You need this, Rachel. You've been looking forward to this for so long. It's your chance to prove yourself to everyone, to become the Rachel Lian you truly want to be. And maybe, just maybe, if you do it right, she'll be satisfied, and she'll stop trying to take over. Maybe all she wants is one shot to shine in front of an audience, to be seen. Maybe that is what will save us.*

Onstage the girls working on original oratory are rehearsing their speeches.

"And with that, I rest my case." The speaker bows theatrically, and there's a smattering of applause.

Each minute that goes by feels like a boulder on my back. I can feel myself hunching over more and more, sitting cross-legged on the cold, hard hall floor, as if I'm trying to fold my body up and make myself disappear. *Save us. Save us. Save us.*

Next an acting duet takes the stage to do a scene from P. G. Wodehouse, which I only recognize because it is from one of Mother's approved books. She'll never know how many romance e-books I download to read on my laptop. I don't think Bridgerton is really the class of British literature she has in mind. I don't think I'm what she had in mind either. Maybe whatever break with reality my mind is going through is the direct result of my own disobedience. I have tainted the altar of achievement with my deviance; I must suffer.

"Righto, Jeeves," one of the girls onstage says. I am so anxious that I think I may vomit right here in the middle of the assembly hall.

There is a sharp, familiar clack, clack, clack then that makes me raise my head. I know this sound; it's the sound of expensive leather shoes, so different from the soft shuffle and thud of our canvas school shoes, or the comfortable flats most of our teachers live in. It's Uncle.

For a second I feel disoriented, breathless, panicky. The world tilts slightly. Am I at forensics tryouts or at music practice? Am I where I'm supposed to be? Have I dropped another ball?

"Oh, Datuk Shah!" Puan Ani stands, and I am almost certain she blushes. Through the fog that envelopes my brain, I manage to think, *Gross.* "You're here to work with the debaters today? Sekejap, I'm so sorry. I didn't realize you were already here. Let me just—"

"No, no, you're busy." His smile comes so easily. Uncle is like this, charming people off their feet left and right. "I can make my own way there."

"Oh, we cannot have that." Puan Ani looks around, flustered, until her eyes land on me. "Rachel!"

I can feel all the heads in the hall swivel in my direction, all the girls, and the teachers, and this man, and my ears start to burn. I wanted their attention but not like this, not as Rachel the prefect, Rachel the teacher's pet, Rachel with all the As and zero friends. I want them to see me as her, onstage, magnetic and bold.

"Rachel," Puan Ani says, tapping her foot impatiently. "Wake up, please. Can you escort Datuk Shah to the library? He kindly wants to spend some time helping the debate team."

My mouth moves before I can stop it. "But, Puan Ani," I say, "it's almost my turn."

Puan Ani's friendly smile morphs into a frown. "It's not like you to be so unhelpful, Rachel," she says.

My desperation almost makes me feverish. *I have to get away. I have to do this. I have to get onto that stage. I can't go with him.* And I don't know who is thinking all of this, whether it's me or whether it's the girl, with her bold pink lipstick, her bold, outspoken mouth. "But, Puan Ani—"

Uncle beams. "Oh, hello, Rachel!" His face when he sees me is open, friendly, delighted. He reaches out a hand to grasp mine, an approximation of a handshake. My vision blurs. "I don't need an escort, really, but I wouldn't mind some company. Maybe we can go over our—"

My hand is engulfed in his big one, and I'm trying to listen, I really am, but my throat is suddenly dry. All I can hear, echoing in my ears, is the sound of a broom against concrete. Sweep, sweep, sweep, so loud that it's almost deafening.

"It's absolutely necessary. Otherwise I'll be the one making us all look like fools!" He looks at me and winks, and behind him there is the girl in the pink lipstick just staring and staring and staring at me, but when she opens her mouth, there's no scream, only the sound of sweeping, and behind the girl blooms a huge, dark shadow, swelling and growing until it looks like it will swallow us all, the assembly hall, the school, the city, the world, until nothing is left but black, and I want to move, I want to run, but I can't, and I want to close my ears because the sound of the sweep, sweep, sweeping is so loud that it makes me grit my teeth in pain, and I want to speak, I want to ask for help, say, *Please do something; please save me,* but when I open my mouth, the shadow lunges at me and folds me into the darkness, and all I can do is

Scream.

Khadijah

We hear it. Of course we hear it. It breaks through the air as we're about to enter to the library—a heart-pounding series of screams. From the same person. Over and over and over.

It stops us in our tracks.

"It's happening again," Siti breathes. "Again."

"It's been, like, a week, right?" Rania whispers. "Why would it start again now?"

It's been nine days, actually, I think. But I don't speak up, and I don't correct her. My eyes dart here and there, trying to find the screamer.

"Where?" Erni says, scanning the school grounds. She squints her eyes against the sun. "Where's it coming from?"

"There," Rania says, pointing. We all see her at the same time. The girl being dragged out of the hall by Puan Ani, another teacher I can't make out, and a man I've never seen before. The girl is fighting and kicking so hard that we can see the dark blue shorts she wears under her pinafore. Hair is coming loose from the white ribbons that tie it back. Stray strands plaster against her neck and face. She is pale and sweaty. Her eyes are screwed shut, and her mouth is open, and her screams just won't stop.

My breath comes fast now, and my hands are clenched tight. *It's happening again*, I think desperately. *And I'm no closer to figuring out why.*

I need to find the first screamer.

"She's really making them work," Siti observes quietly, arms crossed. She's not even fazed anymore. It's as if this is just how it is now. This is who we are. Those hysterical girls from St. Bernadette's.

Beside me I feel Anu shiver. "I hope she's okay," she says quietly. "And I know this sounds really selfish or mean or whatever, but I really hope that if there's another one, that it isn't me."

I want to tell her that this is not selfish. It's smart. There is no shame in thinking of yourself. But my desire is not enough to move my tongue. And my thoughts are running on a single track: *First screamer, first screamer, first screamer, first screamer.*

Everyone else starts to head inside. But my body feels like it's been flooded with ants. I cannot just sit still. I cannot just be. I am about to make some excuse, about to leave, to find the girl I'm looking for. But Siti stops me.

"Just where do you think you're going?" she hisses.

I gesture vaguely outside.

"No." She tugs at my arm, hard, so hard that it jerks me back towards the door and over the threshhold. "Come on. The new coach is coming. A team member missing makes us all look bad."

She will not let me go. I follow and sit down in my usual

THE HYSTERICAL GIRLS OF ST. BERNADETTE'S

seat. My knees won't stop moving up and down, up and down.
I bite my lip. If only I could explain, let them know that I'm
trying to help them. That I'm saving us all.

"I wonder what he's like," Erni says across the table. I don't
need to ask who she means by "he." Puan Ani told us he'd be
here today. The debate coach. Someone to help us to victory. I
remember marveling at the idea that my teammates were still
thinking about victory at a time like this.

"I hear he's actually a member of the parents' association,"
Anu says. "You know. The PIBG. They told me he—"

But we never find out what Anu was about to say. Because
Puan Ani bustles up right at that moment with a man. The man.
The same man we saw earlier, helping the screamer. He's dressed
in a sharp black suit and pale blue shirt, no tie. His hair is thick
and threaded with gray. His eyes flit across all of us, keen and
missing nothing. Despite the fact that we saw him handling a
screamer just moments ago, he looks spotless. Flawless. Puan
Ani, on the other hand, is disheveled, her hijab knocked askew.

"Girls," Puan Ani says breathlessly. "I'm so sorry we are
late. We were . . . er . . . unavoidably detained. This is Encik
Shah—sorry, I mean 'Datuk Shah.' He's here to help us win the
debate this year. Datuk, these are my girls: our alternates, Anu
and Erni; our first speaker, Rania; our second speaker, Felicia;
and of course our third speaker, Siti." Siti simpers and actually
drops a curtsy. Even in my current stupor, this may be the most
embarrassing thing I've ever witnessed with my own two eyes.

"Nice to meet you girls." Datuk Shah grins, his teeth white

and even. This man knows he is charming. I want to leave. I am not sure I like him. "And who is this?"

Puan Ani puts a hand on my shoulder and smiles. "This is Khadijah. She's a bit like an assistant to me. She's a star member of the team."

He nods, all warmth and friendliness. Siti's face falls slightly at hearing Puan Ani call me a star.

"You don't have to call me 'Datuk,'" he tells us kindly. His voice is deep and commanding; I can believe he knows how to use it onstage. "I don't really care about titles. Just call me 'Uncle.' My daughter attended school here, and though I'm no longer on the board of the PIBG, I'm grateful for the education she received here and still am very much invested in the welfare of the school. And now that my niece is here, I have an excuse to come back and bother everyone again." He laughs easily at this. Everyone laughs along, buoyed by the sound. Everyone but me. "I used to be a debater myself," he continues. "And now I'm a lawyer. Which means I'm very used to convincing people I'm right. I look forward to helping the team win nationals this year."

"Wonderful!" Puan Ani actually claps her hands. My mind may be going a million miles an hour, but it has time to think, *This is the second-most-embarrassing thing I've ever seen.* "I cannot wait to see how you can help us. How would you like to start, Datuk? Or should I also call you 'Uncle'?" She giggles. She actually giggles.

My desire to not be here increases tenfold.

Uncle smiles and pretends he didn't hear that last part. "All right," he says, clapping his hands. "Let's see what you've got. Time to rehearse those speeches. First speaker?"

I hand Rania her marked-up speech. She takes a deep breath before launching into her arguments. I try to follow along, but I'm having trouble listening over the chanting in my head. *First screamer, first screamer, find the first screamer.* I am right by a window, and through the frosted glass I can hear sweeping. And with every minute that passes, it gets louder, and louder, and louder, and—

"What's the matter?" Felicia whispers. I look at her questioningly. "You keep looking at the window," she says.

Do I?

I look again, but all I see is a shadow. A dark mass, bent over, moving along to the sounds. The sweeper.

Then I look back at Felicia. I point to my ear and then to the window. *Don't you hear it?*

But all she does is look at me, her expression one of utter confusion.

"Does anyone else have any comments?" Puan Ani asks, and I jump. "Khadijah, are you all right? You seem very distracted."

I shake my head.

"Well, then." She gives me a warning glance. "Let's keep our focus on whoever is speaking, please, particularly when our guest is taking time out of his busy day to be here with us."

I nod. My fingers will not stop tapping complicated tattoos on my knees. As Felicia begins to speak, I look back at the window to see if the sweeper is still there.

But the shadow is gone.

. . .

It's Friday. School ends early on this day, and most of the girls have left by now, eager to get home, to start their weekends. Two blessed days without the threat of screaming hovering over their heads. *Yet they choose to come back, day after day, just like you do, Khad.* Maybe that's the mark of a Bernie. What was that line from *Alice in Wonderland?* "We're all mad here."

Thanks to some digging by Sumi, I know where the first screamer will be. Fatihah. That's her name. She's in chess club, and they're meeting today because there's a competition coming up. Just like for us. The club meets in a classroom in the form-four block just off the canteen. Up a flight of stairs and off to the right, where all the classes are lined along a dusty, dimly lit corridor with broken furniture piled at one end. St. Bernadette's is a premiere school, but that doesn't mean we're rich.

I wait out of sight by the stairs. I sit and watch all the kids coming down after their meeting, in giggling groups of two and three and four.

It's easy to spot Fatihah. She's the only one who comes down alone.

"Fatihah," I say. I am surprised by how easily it comes out. As if I never stopped talking at all. Maybe it's easier to speak to people who have gone through things. Who understand. Maybe it's easier to speak when there's a purpose, when I know that what I say matters, that people will listen.

She whirls around to face me, startled. Her eyes are wide in her thin face. Dark bags are smudged below them like bruises.

There's a haunted look in them that I recognize. It takes me a beat to understand that they remind me of Aishah. Maybe all the screamers are marked the same way. "Do I know you?" she asks. In her voice I can hear notes of anxiety and exhaustion.

"No," I say. "But I'd like to talk to you, if that's okay."

I can tell she wants to say no. I can also tell that Fatihah was raised to be good, to obey her elders, to listen.

So she says yes.

We sit in a quiet corner behind the library. There's a bench here, cigarette butts littering the drains. A spot for staff who don't want to corrupt us with their filthy habits. The school is quieting now. But I still don't want to take any chances that anyone will hear us. I don't want them to realize I'm talking again.

Fatihah sits and waits patiently. I thought she'd be a fidgeter. But she sits perfectly still.

"I wanted to ask you," I say, "about the screaming." I don't see any point in beating around the bush.

Fatihah smiles. "Why?" she whispers.

"Because my sister was one of them," I say. "And I want to know how and why it happened to her."

"But it's over now," she says. "For her, anyway. And for me. Why does it still matter? Why do we have to talk about it?"

"Because," I snap, and then I pause to try to collect myself. "Because it happened, and pretending it didn't doesn't help, and because if we can figure out the how and the why, we can stop it from happening again. That's why."

Fatihah smiles again. Why does she keep smiling? "I just

don't want to talk about it anymore," she says dreamily.

I take a deep breath. "Please," I say. "Please, can you tell me what happened to you?"

When Fatihah speaks again, it's slow, and soft, and stilted. As if she has trouble formulating her thoughts into sentences. "It was only a week," she begins. "Only a week since I came. I didn't really know anyone yet. I still got nervous every day to come to school. Still get nervous," she says, correcting herself. Again with that smile, that small crooked smile. "Still no friends, really. Not then. Not now also." A giggle, born more out of habit than mirth. "The counselor made me go see him. Mr. Bakri? He said it was to say welcome. 'Selamat datang, Fatihah,' he said. He said I wouldn't have trouble making friends. He doesn't know me very well." Another little laugh. "In class I started getting dizzy. Pening. Whole room spinning, whewwww." She makes twirling motions with her fingers so I can see. "Made me hold on to my desk hard. So hard. Like I was going to fall over sideways." She grips the bench till her knuckles go white, as if to demonstrate.

Following along with her train of thought is like trailing a frog jumping from lily pad to lily pad. It's making my head hurt.

There is a pause.

"Then I saw it," she says.

"Saw what?"

"Something dark. A black shape on the ceiling. A shadow."

I stare at her. "What was it?" I ask.

"Jinn? Jembalang? Mana aku nak tau." She giggles again. I'm

starting to recognize it for what it is, a nervous tic, like biting your nails or picking your scabs. "It got bigger and bigger. Like it was going to swallow up the whole room. And I was scared. So I did what my mama taught me. I said Ayat Kursi. Wanted to keep it away. Next thing, I was in the sickroom. They told me I was screaming." She shrugs her thin shoulders. "Maybe it was the first time some of them heard my voice."

"And then lots of people started screaming after you," I say.

Fatihah nods. "Ya. That hantu got a lot of us that day. Busy boy." She laughs.

"You really believe it was a hantu?"

Fatihah stands abruptly. "You asked me," she says. "That's what happened."

"I know I asked." I reach out to touch her sleeve. "Thank you for telling me."

She nods, then hesitantly she asks, "Your sister, is she okay?"

I think about Aishah. "Not really," I answer honestly. "But I hope she will be soon."

"Okay." She picks up her navy-blue backpack. "I'm going home now." Her smile fades. "My uncle. He's waiting for me."

"Thanks for talking to me."

"That's okay." She grins at me. "Watch out for the hantu. Don't let it get you too."

"I won't," I say softly as I watch her walk away. "I won't."

Fatihah

Was that normal? That wasn't normal, was it? How can I tell?
How can anyone?

It's not every day a girl talks to me. Asks me questions. Like
I'm interesting. Worth knowing about. I wonder if she would
like to be friends. It would be nice. She's older than me, though.
I think. But that doesn't mean anything. Right?

I walk down a corridor. I am trying to get out. I am trying
to go home. My uncle sits in his car. Waiting for me. It's a big
car. It's not meant for just two people. I'm not meant for that
car. But every day I sit in it anyway. Every single day. Even when
I don't want to.

I walk down a corridor. Is this where I'm meant to be? Is
this the way out? I keep walking, but the corridor keeps going.
My uncle will be mad. I walk faster. I don't like when people are
mad. They yell. Sometimes there's a feather duster.

I walk down a corridor. I still walk down a corridor. Is it the
same corridor? I stop. I am confused. Which way is out?

My head hurts. It aches a lot more nowadays than it used to.

After the screaming. And it's still there, you know. The shadow. Hanging out right on the edge of my eyeballs. I keep trying to catch it, get a proper look. But I turn my head and it's gone again.

Jinn, jembalang, hantu. That's what I told that girl. What was her name? I forgot. Already. I'm forgetting a lot these days. It's the headaches. Maybe I should tell Umi. Maybe we should go to the doctor. Dr. Leong, who's been seeing me since I was two. He's a longer drive away, now that we moved. Maybe Umi will take me to someone new. I wonder if they have lollipops? Dr. Leong always had lollipops. Even when Umi said I was too old for lollipops, Dr. Leong always gave me lollipops.

I walk down a corridor. My head. My head really hurts. Somebody nearby is sweeping and sweeping. The noise makes me itchy. My head hurts and the shadow is staring at me and I want to go home.

I walk down a corridor. I follow the noise. This time the corridor lets me out. There's an aunty with a broom right there. In front of this old building. It has a fancy window, colored glass all mucky with dirt. Umi would tell me to wipe that up. Make it shine. We don't hide such pretty things. Show them off. Show them off to everybody. Let them see, let them touch. Let them do whatever they want.

Sweep, sweep, sweep, sweep, sweep.

Maybe if I ask, the aunty will stop sweeping for a while. Maybe. Just so the ache in my head will stop.

"Aunty," I say. "Aunty." But the aunty won't look at me.

Why won't she look at me? The shadow is coming closer this time. It's not at the edges anymore. It's creeping in. My head hurts. "Aunty," I say again. Sweep, sweep, sweep. Why is it so loud? Why won't she look at me? My head. "Aunty!" I shout it this time. Is that rude? *Ayah will get the feather duster if you're rude again, Fatihah. Don't be naughty. Listen to me, good girl. Do what I tell you. Good girl. Good, good girl.* My head hurts. Sweep, sweep, sweep, sweep, sweep.

Then it stops.

The lady hunched over the broom stops. And she looks at me. Dark eyes in a wrinkled face. And my head hurts. And the shadow. The shadow. The shadow is everywhere. The shadow is everything. She is looking at me. She keeps looking at me. *Show it off, sayang. Let me see how pretty it is.* Sweep, sweep, sweep, sweep, sweep. I want to go home.

I want to go

I want to

Khadijah

I scan the list over and over again. It's in Flo's writing, so neat, so careful. I say the names to myself, one by one. As if I'm committing them to memory.

"I've been looking and looking," Flo says, stretched out on the living room floor. "But as far as I can tell, it's really hard to figure out anything these girls have in common."

"Different ages, different classes, different races, different religions." Sumi grabs a cashew from the pack of mixed nuts she took from the kitchen, and pops it into her mouth. "Nice of . . . whatever it is that's making these kids scream to think of diversity, I guess."

I barely hear them. I chew on my lip, staring at each name. There is a connection here, something that ties them all together. But what? What is it that I'm not seeing?

I sigh aloud. I am almost positive I see them shoot one of those glances at each other. Those "talk about Khad without talking about Khad" glances. The ones I hate.

"I know it's frustrating," Flo says gently. "But we're doing our best. We'll try to figure it out."

I gesture to the list. Jab at the names. I underline Aishah's name three times. Surely they see. Surely they understand how important this is.

Flo licks her lips. "But, Khad. I know you were wondering about Julianna, but these girls, they're all fine. Some of them are at home still, sure, but they'd be staying home if they were, like, recovering from a cold, too. Nobody is disappearing. We're always here for you, you know that, but . . ." Her voice trails off.

"What we're saying," Sumi says, "is that maybe we're taking things a little too far? And I'll admit, part of it is my fault. I shouldn't have suggested breaking into Mrs. Beatrice's office. You know how I get carried away. But hey, you're back on the debate team! Maybe now we can let all of this go, get back to, like, normal life. All of us. You included. We can just go back to how it used to be! Like the old days."

I clench and unclench my fists on my lap. Is that what Sumi wanted for me all along? To forget everything that happened to me all those months ago? A return to normal, a more acceptable, less broken version of myself?

Flo coughs. "Sumi, maybe we—"

But before we can continue, my mother comes out of her room. Her face is strange, and I look at it and immediately think, *Something is wrong.*

And I am right.

"I just got a message from St. Bernadette's," she says. Her voice sounds so unlike her. So serious, so somber. "A girl has gone missing. A girl from your school. Her uncle was waiting to take her home, and she just . . . never came out." She clears her throat. "A Nur Fatihah something. Do you know her?"

Fatihah?

Fatihah is missing?

Julianna Chin, I think. *Julianna Chin, the first screamer who went to school as usual and then never came home again.* Sumi and Flo shoot stricken, panicky looks at each other as if I can't see them. I bend down low, trying my best to catch my breath. *Fatihah,* I think. Then, *Julianna.* And then, *Aishah, Aishah, Aishah,* and suddenly it's all I can think about.

Sumi and Flo rub slow, comforting circles on my back. Trying to calm me down. Trying to keep me tethered to this world. Terrified I'll break down.

In the background I hear my mother's voice, tinged with panic. "Khadijah? Khadijah? Are you all right?"

"You were right," Sumi breathes out beside me. "You were right all along."

I was. But I wish I weren't.

Rachel

Mother takes my screaming personally. "How could you let this happen?" she asks. "Now you will always be associated with . . . with . . . whatever this is!" I see the weekend stretch endlessly before me, full of cold recrimination. Not for the first time, I long for St. Bernadette's and the warm embrace of its old stone walls.

"I didn't mean to," I tell her. I take a sip of water, grateful for its cool relief. My throat is still parched and sore from yesterday. They told me that I screamed for almost half an hour, that I kicked so hard, I broke a chair. "I couldn't stop myself." I feel bone-dry and fragile, like if she touches me, I might shatter into a million tiny pieces and tell her everything—about the scream and the girl and the acting. All of it, everything, all at once.

Mother sniffs. "Ridiculous supernatural nonsense."

From the look on her face, I am fairly certain she doesn't believe a word I say. Mother doesn't believe in lots of things: ghosts, superstition, luck, most parts of organized religion. Me.

She sits down on the edge of my bed and sighs as she smooths the hair away from my forehead. "Are you feeling better?" she asks, and my heart goes all light and bouncy at this touch, this rare show of tenderness.

"Better," I say, smiling at her. This is it. This is the moment to speak, to tell her everything. Everything. "A little shaken up. And my legs are still all wobbly, but I—"

"Rachel," Mother interrupts me, then stops. Then just looks at me, as if she's trying to figure out what to say.

"What?" For some reason my heart is in my throat.

She coughs. "A girl from your school is missing."

"What?" My brain stops working; it's like all I can do is repeat myself. None of Mother's words make sense to me.

"I received this message yesterday, but I thought it was best to let you…recover. But yes. Someone is missing." She taps on the phone, squints at the screen. "Nur Fatihah. Do you know this girl?"

I shake my head. The shock has erased my ability to process. "When?" I manage to choke out.

"Yesterday afternoon," she says. "Her uncle was waiting to drive her home, but she never came out of the school."

"But where could she have gone? Who could have taken her?"

Mother shrugs. "Who knows? Probably she ran away. Some family trouble, or maybe she had a boyfriend. You know how some girls are." She sniffs dismissively. "I am only telling you because they might talk about it at school. But there does not seem to be any immediate danger. So you can go on Monday, as usual." It's not a question. I look down and realize I'm holding on to my blanket so tightly that my knuckles are all white.

"What?" It's my third time saying it, but I can't think of anything else.

Mother clicks her tongue, and I automatically feel small, like she is Pavlov and I am nothing but a dog. "Stop saying 'what, what, what.' Say 'pardon.'"

My throat feels so dry that it's hard to get a word out. "Pardon," I say.

"Well." She stands up and begins rearranging some of the books on my shelf. She can't stand it if they're not organized right. "If you are feeling better, then you can go back to school. No sense in missing out on any lessons, or those extra classes. Yes?"

I nod. Mostly it's because I'm trying not to speak, because if I speak, I might cry, and I know Mother would hate that most of all.

After she leaves, I lie in my bed staring at the white ceiling overhead. A girl is gone, has simply vanished from the safe confines of St. Bernadette's; and I have screamed my head off for no discernible reason; and my mother simply does not care. About any of it.

She doesn't mean to be like this, I tell myself. She has no idea how she makes me feel. And I bet she'd be upset if she knew. This is just the skin my mother had to grow to survive after my father left us for some other woman he had already gotten pregnant, skin thick and hard enough to withstand other people's gossip and disdain and, worst of all, their pity.

"We never show people what we are going through, or our weaknesses," she would tell me after playground fights or hard falls. "How you present yourself—that is everything. If you cry, they say, 'Look, see. This woman is so emotional.' They use it as an excuse to say you deserve less. To say you ARE less. So you don't give them any excuse." She used to wipe away my tears; then she would hand me tissues to wipe them myself; then she expected me to have my own tissues, to be prepared; then she expected me to stop showing my tears at all. This is the gift she is trying to give me: skin so hard that nothing can ever hurt you. She did what she had to do. I know that. I owe her everything.

But in the dark like this, with wet cheeks from the tears I can't show her, I sometimes wish she would just understand. *The way Uncle did,* I think, and it's like the twist of a knife in my chest, the idea that someone who is almost a stranger can care more than my own mother.

I close my eyes, but sleep refuses to come. I think about Mother, about the girl in the pink lipstick, about screaming, about how it feels to have a body you have no control over. A body that everyone seems to see as a vessel, to use for their own personal ends. I am almost convinced that if someone were to tap my chest, it would sound hollow. Nothing inside, ready to be filled with whatever you wish.

There is a quiet knock on the door. I peel my eyes open to see Kak Tini standing by my bed, her face worried, tender. A hand reaches out to touch my cheek.

"Rachel okay?" she asks.

It's her usual question, the one she asks me every day. Somehow it makes me want to cry even harder.

"Rachel okay," I say back. We both know it's a lie.

Khadijah

"You need to tell the police, obviously." Flo paces around my room. She's nibbling away at her bottom lip. A thing she only does when she's anxious. "Or Mrs. Beatrice. Or somebody. Somebody who will know what to do."

Sumi stares at Flo as if she's suddenly said she'd like to move to Timbuktu and join a cult. "You cannot be serious."

"What?" Flo frowns as she perches on the edge of my mattress-less bed frame. "This isn't just about us playing detective anymore. There's an actual emergency now, and actual detectives involved to find an actual missing person. Shouldn't we be helping them?"

Sumi nibbles at her nails as she thinks, a sure sign that she's conflicted. "Technically ya, okay, I see what you're saying," she says slowly. "But takkan you want to put Khad through that again?" She glances over at me. "Don't you remember what happened last time?"

Last time.

I remember last time.

Last time, Sumi and Flo sat outside every interview room waiting for me. Making sure there was a steady supply of snacks and stupid, mindless conversation. Rubbing my hands that were perpetually cold even when the air-conditioning was turned off at my request. They were there the day I stopped talking. And instead of trying to cajole or demand or force the words out of me, they just kept talking to fill the silence. Never leaving me alone. Making sure I knew that they were still there no matter what. That they'd wait for me to come back.

Trauma can be so selfish. Because it never occurred to me that they were affected too. It's only now that I ask myself, *What toll did this take on them?*

Flo bites her lip. "I remember," she says. "And it sucked, and it was hard. But this . . . this could really help us find out what's going on, right? And more important, this could be the difference between Fatihah turning up dead or alive, you know?"

Sumi shrugs. "She probably just ran away or something, right? Why must we talk about life and death suddenly?"

"Because I don't think this is the kind of thing we should hang on 'maybe'!" Flo flings back. She looks over at me. "What was she like? When you talked to her? Did she seem okay?"

"She told us already," Sumi says. "Remember? Anxious, jumpy, weird."

I didn't say "weird." I said she unsettled me.

"You see?" Flo says. "That might be a clue to something—"

"The girl was talking about hantu. About spirits. About

being haunted." Sumi crosses her arms, defiant, stubborn. "She sounds like she was unstable."

Something about this makes me fidgety, restless. How many times have we heard this? How many times have we dismissed a girl because she acts in ways that make us uncomfortable? Make us question ourselves? How many times might Sumi have thought this about me, said these same words behind my back?

"All the more reason to tell the police about it," Flo returns. "Maybe it'll help them. Besides, you're the one who says you want everything to go back to normal. Isn't this the fastest way to get there?"

She looks at me. "What do you think, Khad?" she asks, and I know what she wants. She wants me to open my mouth. Say I'll do it. March right up to the teachers and the police and tell them all about it, everything I know. She wants me to speak up, say something, use my voice.

But I don't know if I can.

So I sit there silently. Hating her for expecting this much out of me. Hating myself for being such a coward.

"I'm not saying you have to decide now," Flo says. I can hear her wrestling to keep the disappointment from bleeding into her words. "I'm just saying, think about it."

I nod. It's all I can do.

Later that night my laptop pings.

Sasha A
What did u do

Khadijah Rahmat

What do you mean? What are you
talking about?

Sasha A

You've been asking questions, I know u
have

Snooping around

And now a girl has disappeared? Again?

That's not a coincidence

Khadijah Rahmat

I didn't do anything. This isn't my fault

Sasha A

Like hell it isn't

That's not just some random girl

That's my baby cousin

She's only 15

And now she's GONE

My fingers are trembling now. It's hard to think of the right words. Harder still to type them.

Khadijah Rahmat

I'm sorry to hear that
But that still doesn't make any of this my
fault

Sasha A

All I can say is

You better hope she's had enough now

Khadijah Rahmat
She?

Sasha A
When I mentioned it, the other girls
laughed and made fun of me
But even when it happened, I thought
Well there it is. There's the sacrifice
The school demanded one girl
She short-listed her picks—the screamers
Then she narrowed them down to the per-
fect one
Once she got what she was after, the
screaming stopped

I'm just staring at the screen now. I cannot untangle my confusion from my frustration from a strange, rising fear. I can only watch as Sasha A keeps typing.

Sasha A
It was really just a theory
Just something I randomly thought of
But when Julianna disappeared and the
screaming stopped, I knew
I knew I was right
After all, you stop eating when you're full,
right?

St. Bernadette's ate her fill, and then she
was satisfied

I squeeze my eyes shut. She's just some rando on the internet, right? Sumi and Flo said so. They said I shouldn't believe her. They said I should stop taking her word as gospel.

Sasha A
You made her angry
You started asking questions

Don't believe her, Khad. Don't believe her.

Sasha A
Your sister's a screamer too right?
Better hope St. Bernadette's is full

Rachel

As I stride up the hill toward St. Bernadette's, I review the decisions I made over the weekend. One: This is clearly some kind of mental breakdown I'm going through, and the screaming has to be the byproduct of too much stress. I have been so concerned about juggling all these different activities, about lying to my mother. Two: Therefore the only solution here is to juggle less, to get rid of the one activity that has been taking up too much of my time and my brain.

To stop solo acting. At least for now. At least until I can get a handle on things—my grades, my relationships with my teachers, making sure my mother doesn't find out. I need to stop until I can get a handle on myself.

I tell myself that this is the right thing to do, that I need to set aside these childish ideas of dreams and focus on being the daughter my mother wants me to be. This is for my own good.

But deep, deep down, so deep that I can almost ignore it altogether, I know it's because I am afraid of who I have become. Who I have let in. And maybe if I stop for a little while, maybe if I stop opening the door for her, she'll stop coming in. She'll give up. She'll go away.

It's worth a try.

There are strange people loitering beside the fence when I walk up the hill to St. Bernadette's this morning. They come up to girls that pass. The strangers have their phones in their hands and these big fake smiles pasted onto their faces.

"Excuse me, girls. Excuse me. Would you be interested in talking to us about what's happening in your school?"

I try hard to walk past without making any eye contact, but one man spots me before I can make it.

"Hi!" he says. He starts walking beside me. "Would you mind having a little chat with me about all this screaming happening at St. Bernadette's?"

"No, thank you," I say. I am polite. Mother says you must always be polite. *Without your manners what are you, Rachel?* But I also start walking a little faster.

He matches his pace to mine. He does not seem to hear me. Maybe saying anything at all was my mistake. The Mother in my head clicks her tongue in grave disappointment. *Stupid Rachel. You encouraged him. You gave him a reason to keep going.* "What's the atmosphere like in school right now? Do your teachers talk about this stuff with you?"

I keep my eyes up at St. Bernadette's, at its familiar arches and wide doorways and slatted windows, at the cross on the gable, at the school motto spelled out in brass letters across one of its walls: SIMPLE IN VIRTUE, STEADFAST IN DUTY.

HANNA ALKAF

"What a school," the reporter says next to me, just under his breath. "It gives me the creeps. A line of girls just getting swallowed up in it, one by one."

Swallowed up? I think. Is that how they see us? Is that what St. Bernadette's looks like to outsiders? It seems so strange, so alien to me; even now, the school calls out to me like it knows I need someplace safe. Someplace to belong. Maybe we all just see what we want to see. Maybe nobody will ever understand this but us.

The reporter tries his hardest to sneak in a couple of questions just as we reach the gates. "What do you think happened to those girls? Do you worry whether it could happen to you?"

Even if he paid me, I wouldn't want to answer any of these.

"No, thank you," I say again. It doesn't make any sense, but I just want to get away.

I quickly walk past Pakcik Saiful, the school security guard, who glares at the reporter and says, "No trespassing" in his grumpiest voice, then smiles his most reassuring smile at me as I walk into the hall. I've never been so grateful to see him in my life.

Everyone is surprised to see me back at school, absolutely everyone. The teachers look at each other when they think I don't see them, girls whisper to each other in my wake, and Dahlia gives the most over-the-top gasp when I walk into the classroom, as if I am a ghost.

"Sorry," she says as I take my seat. "It's just that we didn't think you'd be back already. Like, everyone else who screams is gone for, like, a few days. Minimum. Like, if I were you, I'd be milking that shit for weeks." She leans over to stare at my face. "Are you sure you're okay?"

"I'm fine," I say. I want to swat her away like a fly.

"No offense," she says. "But you don't look fine. You know?"

"I said I'm fine," I snap, and she shrugs.

"Suka hati kau lah."

She turns around. I stare at her back for a while, the way her hair meets the nape of her neck. I wonder how much of that was me and how much of it was the girl with the pink lipstick, the girl I allowed to take over my life. I have a sudden urge to pull on Dahlia's ponytail, to make her turn around and look at me, to tell her everything like we're old friends. How I barely slept last night. How I worried and worried about my mental breakdown, about how I feared I was losing my mind. How, when I did sleep, my dreams were full of strange, dark shadows. How when I told my mother, she just laughed. *Dreams cannot hurt you, Rachel,* she said. *Silly girl,* she said. How even the Mother in my head is silent, because real or imaginary, Mother simply doesn't like when things don't work the way they're supposed to, when they fail, when they break.

I could do it. I could tell Dahlia all of this, and maybe she would feel sorry and sad for me, and maybe that would make me feel better. Or at least make me feel a little more human.

Or maybe it will just confirm what she already suspects, that I'm weird, strange, crazy Rachel Lian.

"Rachel!"

The sound of my name gives me such a shock that I bang my elbow on the corner of my desk. "Ow," I say. Then, "Yes, Cikgu?"

"You are dreaming, girl," Mrs. Dev says gently. "I have been calling you for the past five minutes."

"Oh."

"Mr. Bakri wishes to see you," she continues, and sure enough, there he is by the door, waving at me.

"Oh," I say again. "Um. Why?"

"I assume this is something the two of you can discuss yourselves," she says drily. "Perhaps without having to involve the rest of us, mm? I have a class to teach, after all."

I step outside, trying to ignore the eyes of the other girls. Mr. B waits for me in the corridor, in the space between the double doors so fewer people can see us. "Sorry to drag you out of class, Rachel," he says. "But I wanted to check up on you. I check up on all the girls, you know. The um. The affected ones."

"Oh," I say. It seems like that's all I can say today. Thinking feels like trying to squeeze more toothpaste out of an empty tube. "Okay."

"Would you mind coming to my office during last period?" he asks. "I'll get your teacher's permission."

It doesn't feel like a question. It feels like a command. "Um."

"Just for a little chat," he says. He tries so hard to be sincere. "It might help, you know. To have someone to talk to."

How does he know? How does he know that's what I've

been thinking? For a second, right there on the edge of my vision, I can see shadows moving.

I close my eyes.

"Rachel?" I open them again, and Mr. B is staring at me, his face all confused. "You okay?"

"Yes," I say. "Fine."

"So last period, ya?" He grins. "I'll see you then?"

"Sure," I say. The shadows flicker like they're trying to get my attention. "Sure."

"Good. Now get back to class."

"Okay." *I am a robot,* I think as I move back to my desk. All stiff limbs and one-word answers. Beep, boop, beep, boop. An alien life-form, jumping at shadows that aren't there.

"What was that about?" Dahlia whispers, and I shrug.

"Nothing," I say. "Nothing important."

I am summoned during last period by a prefect I recognize, a form-four girl named Aimi, who appears exactly five minutes after class begins. Everything about Aimi is soft: the curves of her body, the way she knocks on the door, the way she walks into the room, the way she speaks to the teacher. "Encik Bakri nak jumpa Rachel."

"Rachel," the teacher says. "Go and see Encik Bakri in the counseling room, please."

I try to draw the line in my head from Top Student Rachel Lian to Screaming Rachel Lian in Need of Counseling, and fail. "Okay," I say.

"Make sure to find out what you missed from your friends later." I wonder if she's joking.

Aimi has trotted off back to her class, so I make my way to Mr. B's office on my own. It's a narrow sliver of a room just off the library, with a black plate on it that proclaims COUNSELING ROOM in white letters.

I knock, then open the door when I hear his cheery "Come in!"

I've never actually been in here before. I don't know what I expected, but somehow it's a letdown—piles of papers and books neatly stacked on the desk, a gray file cabinet, chairs for visitors, and a standing fan that hums loudly in the corner as it oscillates slowly from left to right and back again. On the wall, a poster that's peeling off at the corners says, LET'S TALK ABOUT IT.

"Welcome to my humble abode!" Mr. B says. He is exactly the type of person who would say things like this. "Sit, sit, make yourself comfortable."

I sit on one of the chairs in front of his desk, one of the white plastic ones we usually use for events in the assembly hall. I guess it was too much to get him his own chairs.

"Now, Rachel." Mr. B rests his elbows on his desk and brings his palms together. "I know you must be going through a very tough time right now."

How does he know? I wonder. How does anyone know, who hasn't experienced this for themselves?

"And yes, I know what you must be thinking," he continues with a soft chuckle. "How can I possibly understand, right?

How can I have any idea what this experience has been like for you?"

He must see the shock in my eyes, because he grins.

"Rachel, every student I've talked to who is going through what you're going through says the same thing. And I understand that, I really do. Which is why I'm proposing this." He takes out his phone with a flourish and taps on the WhatsApp icon. "Ta-da!"

I frown. "You're . . . buying an IKEA sofa secondhand to . . . help us?"

"What? No." He quickly fumbles with his phone, all flustered. "That's my chat with a Carousell seller. Need a sofa for my apartment. I just moved, you know. . . . No. I mean . . ." He clears his throat. "I mean, I'm starting a support group for all the girls who have been affected by . . . recent incidents. Part of that will include in-person meet-ups, but since many students have not yet returned to school after what happened to them, I got permission from parents to add their daughters' cell phone numbers to this group. I'll lead you all through a series of daily exercises and discussions that can help you with your trauma! You see?" His face is glowing. "Finally get to put that training to good use," he says, and chuckles.

It's nice that he's enjoying this so much, I guess. "Great," I say. "Your mother agreed that it was fine."

I nod. Of course she did. It's like having Kak Tini around. Mother likes when someone else cleans up the messes she doesn't want to bother with.

The door creaks, long and loud, as a gust of wind slowly pushes it open. Mr. B mops his face with a handkerchief and sighs. "Hang on. Let me just close that. I take confidentiality very seriously, you know, very seriously indeed." He gets up to fiddle with the door. It seems to be stuck; for some reason, he can't get it to close. The door has a windowpane in its center. I see myself reflected in the glass, except it isn't me at all. It's the girl, with her pink lipstick and the white ribbons in her hair. And even though I jump slightly—I cannot help it—even though I can feel my chest heaving up and down, up and down, the girl in the reflection does not move. She just stares at me.

I feel myself going pale.

"Hello? Rachel?" Mr. B coughs, and I drag my eyes away from the girl and back to his face. I'm sweating. "This was just a little introductory thing, so you're not blindsided by being added to the group," he says.

"Um." I don't want to look at the window. I don't want to know if she's still there.

Mr. B is looking at me like I'm supposed to say something.

"Can I go now?" I ask.

It's not what he expected. He looks like a deflated balloon. "Sure," he says. "You can go."

I glance at the window as I leave. The girl is no longer there. But when I walk through the doorway, I'm hit by an icy cold blast, one that leaves goose bumps all over my skin. And a shadow trails me all the way back to class, a shadow that I try to pretend I don't notice.

Khadijah

When I walk into school on Monday, I am more afraid than ever.

The sun shines weakly through gathering storm clouds. Against the gloom, St. Bernadette's looms threateningly. I can feel her rage in the slant of her arches. In the glimmer of her windows. In the darkness of unlit doorways. In the screeches of the monkeys swinging restlessly on the trees beyond her fences.

One of her own has disappeared. Again. And St. Bernadette's is angry.

Or.

Or.

And here my brain stutters before it completes the thought: Or maybe she is angry because there are too many people in her way. Asking questions. Stopping her from doing what she wants to do.

Sasha A's message drifts into my head. *St. Bernadette's ate her fill, and then she was satisfied.*

Is she satisfied yet?

I shake my head as if this will dislodge my thoughts. Make

them go away. Like with an Etch a Sketch. It is ridiculous to think of a school, a bunch of bricks and wood and concrete, as some kind of living entity. Ridiculous to think of it swallowing girls whole. Like some kind of cartoon ogre.

St. Bernadette's has always been the one place where I feel safe. The one place where I feel like I belong.

But still. Today it takes a lot of courage to step through those gates.

Why Julianna? Why Fatihah? In what world did these two have anything in common? I keep trying to find the answers. And it feels like the school is furious at me for not being able to.

That feeling, that unshakeable sense that St. Bernadette's is seething, stays with me all day. Through classes where I pay no attention. Through a recess where I don't eat. Sumi and Flo sense my mood and try to fill my silences with endless desperate banter. All this does is make me feel even more distant from them.

After school I wave away their offers of company. I check that Aishah is in the band room, frowning as she concentrates on her notes. Making beautiful music. *Strange,* I think. *Strange how beauty can still exist even in darkness.* Then I head straight to the library. Straight to debate practice. Along the way I put out one hand and glide it across the school's walls. Concrete and brick, weathered and immovable. *Why are you so angry? Is it me you're angry at?* And then, *What have you done?*

I am the first one to arrive. There are other girls there who are not my teammates, girls busy whispering, talking, laughing. It might sound strange, that they can still laugh when one of us is missing. But perhaps that's part of our resilience. Perhaps girls just do whatever they can to get by. To survive.

I make my way right to the shelf. Run my fingers gently over the row of yearbooks. Choose the one from the year when Julianna first entered St. Bernadette's. Flip through the pages to find her. She is here, all her thirteen-year-old awkwardness forever trapped on the page. Like a butterfly pinned to a wall. Her smile is all braces and light. It beams up at me from her class picture. From her sports house. From drama club. I cannot help feeling that she holds the key to the screaming girls. To Fatihah's disappearance. To all of it.

I flip through the next year's issue, and the next. I watch her grow older, one grainy image at a time. See her lose the braces. See her evolving hairstyles as she tries to settle on a look. See her adopt the white ribbons that would appear in every picture from then on. See her begin to discover the stage, and her place on it. See her with the pink lipstick slicked on under the bright stage lights, every trace of awkwardness gone. I trace the curve of her smile. In this photo she is performing in a class play. Dressed in a batik baju kurung, ponytail held back by one white ribbon. She is fifteen and as vibrant as a flower in full bloom. She doesn't even know what is coming.

I shuffle through the pages, desperate to drink in more of her. As if I can absorb the real Julianna through the pages and years. As if, if I truly understand who she is, I can understand how she disappeared. *Where are you?* I think as the pages turn. *Who are you?*

I stop. Julianna stares up at me from the page. Cheek to cheek with a woman who could only be her mother. They have the same smile, the same set to their chin. There are other photos, other girls with their mothers. They do not interest me. I see only her.

The headline of the article reads ST. BERNADETTE'S: A LEGACY OF EXCELLENCE. I skim the introduction long enough to understand that it's about girls whose mothers, grandmothers, aunts also went to St. Bernadette's.

Julianna's mother was a Bernie? I frown as I begin to read more closely.

Julianna Chin says she always knew she was going to attend St. Bernadette's, long before she was the right age for it. "My mother made it very clear," she laughs. "She always told me she spent some of the best years of her life here."

"Not that the years right now aren't great also," her mother, Joanna Lim, quickly says. "But there is something about the experience of being at St. Bernadette's that will stay with you for the rest of your life."

There is something unbearably sad about this last line. I wonder what she'd say if someone asked her about St. Bernadette's now. I wonder if she regrets sending Julianna here.

And then realization dawns, and I think, *Why wonder, when you can just ask?*

Rachel

Mother says I must go straight back to my old routines, that nothing will conjure normalcy like returning to life as I knew it. "You must show them how resilient you are," she says. "That you will not break under some nonsensical screaming."

So I try it. I tell Mother I will attend my "extra classes" as usual today, because not going would mean admitting there are no extra classes, and admitting there are no extra classes means admitting that I lied, and admitting that I lied means having to explain why. And somehow, at the end of the day, I still do not want to disappoint her.

You already have, the Mother in my head hisses, and I let her. It's what I deserve.

I wander around the school until I find somewhere quiet that isn't Brede's House. *Not Brede's House. Anywhere but Brede's House, Rachel.*

I settle on an empty classroom in the form-five block. I plunk myself down heavily on a wooden chair and lean back, closing my eyes and letting the sounds of St. Bernadette's swirl around me. It is not loud; people are more scared now, more subdued, as if too much life will attract the darkness that swallowed up the disappearing girl. But there is still something about the school that makes me feel protected. Safe.

In the quiet I can admit to myself what I will not say aloud, that screaming terrified me, yes, and sometimes I am still scared to close my eyes because of the darkness that awaits behind the lids. But also, screaming made me feel . . . powerful. Liberated. In that moment, I had a voice, and I used it, and everyone, everyone heard me.

They heard me.

Nobody ever seems to hear me.

The Mother in my head stirs. *Perhaps you simply say nothing worth hearing,* she breathes into my ear.

Normally I would ignore her, tell her to be quiet. Or I would let her get to me, cast a black pall over the rest of my day. But today is different. Today I get angry instead. I feel the anger creeping through my body, that unfamiliar heat of rage, that eagerness to lash out, prove her wrong. Acting was my chance. My shot at being seen, being heard. Rachel Lian reborn. Surely I will not let some figment of my imagination wrestle that from me. Surely I can stay in control.

I do my best, then. I stand up and say the words, try to summon her again, but it's me saying them, me, regular plain old Rachel Lian, not the incandescent flame of a woman with her pink lipstick and her flashing eyes. I hold the imaginary wineglass, but it's just my hand awkwardly cupping the air; I trail the glass through the air, and it's as if I'm a child mimicking an adult's movements, something I've seen on TV, stiff and exaggerated and wrong, just all wrong.

I made her leave, and now she's well and truly gone, and the loss makes me buckle onto my chair, my body heavy with despair. I slink down low, my head resting on the hard back, my butt just barely balanced on the edge of the seat, my legs stretched all the way out. Like I'm about to melt into the floor. I am exhausted. If she won't come, if I can't become her at will, then what has all this been for? How can I be free?

I ignore the tears that trickle down my cheeks from behind my closed eyes. Outside, I hear a mishmash of yells layering and crisscrossing over each other.

"Five, six, seven, eight!"

"Kiri, kiri, kiri, kanan, kiri . . ."

"Pass the ball, PASS THE BALL!"

And through them all, just on the edge of my hearing, but slowly getting louder and louder, is the sound of a broom against concrete.

The sound of sweeping.

Suddenly I realize my teeth are chattering. Cold air mists against my cheeks, sends shivers down my neck.

I open my eyes, and the girl's face hovers above me, inches away from mine, eyes rimmed in black smeared by tears, staring straight at me, tendrils of hair and white ribbon caressing my skin, me but not me, her but not her. The girl opens her pink-painted mouth, and I brace myself for the scream. But there is none. Instead she says, *When will you start paying attention?*

And then I fall from the chair to the floor, and *Save us, save us, SAVE US* is roaring in my ears, and I yelp as sharp pain shoots up my hip, and she's gone.

I sit there, and I cry, and cry, and cry, for all the things I let go, and the things that need saving, and for the fact that I cannot even save myself.

Khadijah

Flo sends the link that night. There's a voice note after. Flo hates having to type long messages; she records them instead. Her voice on the phone is tinny, breathless. "That's her cake business," she says. "My mama pulled it up as soon as I asked. She said Julianna's mom used to be super active in the alumni group, but, like, after it happened, she refused to talk to any of them, left the group, unfriended everyone on every social media. Mama says it was like she was trying to forget that St. Bernadette's ever existed." Then, in a follow-up message, "But she did say the cakes are really good."

I click on the link. It's an Instagram account. Joanna's Sweet Bakes. Picture after picture of gorgeous, intricate, delicate cakes. *WhatsApp to order*, the link at the top says.

I check the prices. I check whatever money I have in the hollow book I use as a piggy bank.

Just enough.

I click over to WhatsApp. Carefully I type, I would like to order a cake.

"What are you doing?" Mak asks me. "No phones. It's dinnertime." I set my phone carefully down on the dinner table and shrug. Across from me Aishah stares at her plate of rice and beef rendang as if it's worms.

We are all pushing food around on our plates, trying to make it look like we're eating, when Mak's phone pings.

"No phones. It's dinnertime," Aishah deadpans.

Mak ignores her. Reads the text message aloud. Her voice shakes, and she doesn't try to hide it. She's in WhatsApp groups for both our classes. I guess the teachers blasted it out through those groups. "Anyone with any information on Lavinia Darshini from 5 Cempaka, please contact the school immediately."

Another missing girl.

"That does it," Mak says firmly. The fear in her voice is real. "I will not let you walk into that school until we know exactly what's going on. I simply cannot—Khadijah!"

My phone vibrates urgently. I get up from my seat at the dining table and walk into my room.

Behind me my mother keeps yelling, "Khadijah! Sit down! I am not done talking to you!"

I close my door so I can't hear her.

It's Flo again. **Was she one of them?** she asks.

I walk over to my desk. It's hard to pick the piece of paper up with trembling fingers. But somehow I manage. Slowly I run my finger down the list. My heart is beating fast.

My finger stops.

Lavinia, 5 Cempaka.

Yes, I type back. Yes, she was one of them.

Sumi types. Pauses. Then types again. So it's confirmed. Once is a coincidence, twice is a pattern. Screamers are disappearing.

So now they believe me. There is both validation in that and a certain bitter aftertaste.

I sit heavily down on my chair. I don't like it in here. My room is mostly fine during the day, when the sun streams through the windows. But as soon as the shadows start growing long, I find it harder and harder to breathe within its confines. Even with the mattress gone, even though I burned the clothes I wore and the sheets I slept in, the night taints every inch of this room with memories that no amount of scrubbing can get rid of.

Sumi's words play in my head, over and over. *So it's confirmed. You were right all along.* Why are words so often not enough? Why must we buy belief with bodies? And how many bodies does it take?

They made me do this too, back then. Barter myself for their support, their protection, their action.

"It's not your job to protect me," Aishah told me. Could've fooled me.

My whole life it's been, "Hold your sister's hand." And, "Watch out for your adik." And, "Let your sister go first. You're older, after all." And, "Why did you let her do that? Weren't you watching out for her? That's what big sisters are supposed to do."

That's why, when our brand-new stepfather-to-be was introduced to us for the first time, when Mak smiled a big, desperate, please-like-each-other smile at us and told us that this was the man she was going to marry, I felt myself begin to sweat.

That's why, when I saw the way he looked at Aishah anytime our mother wasn't looking, and he smiled like a tiger with its sights on a young deer, I felt my whole body clench.

That's why I tried to tell my mother. About the way his gaze would wander lazily along our young bodies, lingering where he liked. And that's why it shattered me when she dismissed me. Or worse, laughed me away. "He is a good man," she said.

They all are, until they're not. Until they're caught.

That's why I talked less and less. Talk, I discovered, did nothing in a world that expects its girls to be silent and biddable. Only victimhood could give me any currency. Only victimhood would help me protect my sister. And so, when I sensed he was about to pounce, I lay awake, wary and watchful, praying it would be me and not Aishah, knowing full well I was the only one who could use my voice to shut him down and keep him away from my sister.

That's why it was almost a relief, when that door slowly swung open. When his silhouette was all I could see. That's why I gritted my teeth and bore his weight, hating every inch of him, letting him believe he was safe, that I was safe. Before I clawed at his back and made him scream his evil to the world.

I fight, remember? This is what I do. Did.

That's why I endured it all when they made me tell my story over and over and over again, my mother pale and wan but never leaving my side. For weeks and weeks and weeks. Until he was locked up and I lost my will to speak at all. Because they stopped seeing me as anything but a victim. Because all anyone ever asked me about was my pain. My body for their belief, a complete transaction.

That's why I will do this now. Buy a cake I have no intention of eating. Face a missing girl's mother. Ask questions. Raise my voice if I must. My sister will not be that body. My sister will not pay for their belief. I will not allow it.

That's why.

Because that's what big sisters are supposed to do.

Rachel

Save us, I think. *Save us, save us, save us.* Why is the pink-lipstick-girl asking for my help? What danger is she in? And why me? Why won't she just leave me alone?

Do I want her to?

What good am I to anyone else when I can't even save myself?

I roll over in my bed so that I'm staring up at the ceiling. I am a screamer, and soon, maybe, I will disappear. It's easy to see that this is the pattern. One may have been a coincidence, but two? That's a pattern. But if I tell Mother this, if I ask to stay home, I know what she will say. Mother will say, *This is not an excuse to neglect your studies.* Mother will say, *Don't be lazy.* Mother will say, *Is this how you repay me for everything I have done for you?*

Part of me doesn't want to be next. But another, smaller part, one that I try hard not to acknowledge, wonders if it might be nice to be removed from your old life, to never again have to think about all those things that make you anxious or frustrated or scared.

I wonder if the other screamers feel like this. I wonder if they're haunted by things that aren't there, things that ask to be saved. I wonder if—

My phone pings.

There it is. I've been added to a new WhatsApp group, St. Bernadette's Post-Incident Support Group.

There is a long list of phone numbers, all the numbers he's added one by one. Then a message:

~Mr B

Welcome, all students, to your support group! We at St. Bernadette's understand you must be going through a difficult time. Please use this space to discuss your thoughts and feelings. This space is moderated by myself, Encik Bakri (otherwise known as Mr. B 👀), along with Puan Fatimah and Mrs. Sumathi. We are always here for you at any time!!!

This welcome message has big good-morning-meme-forwarded-by-your-elderly-uncle energy.

~Mr B

Every day, I will post discussion questions at 5pm that you are free to think about and answer at your leisure. Do note that we will periodically be required to report the activities of this group to your parents! But also know that we are all here to help you however we can!!

Any hope that I had for this group fizzles out instantly. Well, that was short-lived. The minute you tell me that Mother may see what I say in here is the minute I choose to say nothing at all.

~Mr B
Remember, we are here to support you, and to help you support each other!!! Take care, until we chat again tomorrow!!!

Absolutely not.

I tuck my phone under my pillow and roll onto my side. There is no way I'm taking part in these weird group-counseling sessions, not if the moderators are going to hover over us the whole time, taking note of what we say, reporting it to our parents. To Mother. I imagine saying how I really feel, what I really think, and how she would react. I wonder if the rest of the screamers have to hide from their loved ones this way. Or if they're honest and open and accepted and loved through it all. I wonder if they have nightmares, or if the shadows move for them in unsettling ways now, the way they do for me. I wonder if they are haunted like me, if anyone asks for their help to be saved, if they know what that means, if they know what to do. I wonder if they think about if we'll always be known as the screamers, all of us, for our entire lives.

All of us.

All the screamers.

I sit bolt upright.

I don't have to wonder. They're all right here. All I have to do is . . . ask.

I think about what it would be like to feel less alone, to talk to people who understand me, who might know the answers to my questions. What it would feel like to have a friend. I wonder if banishing my loneliness would mean banishing my ghosts. I wonder if these girls can save me, the way my nightmares ask to be saved.

If only. If only I could just talk to these girls without hesitation, ask them things without fear that one of the teachers is writing down everything we say for Mother's intense, prying eyes. If only the teachers weren't there at all.

Like, for example, if we had our own WhatsApp group.

Khadijah

They're all there on Tuesday morning. Brand-new security guards, patrolling around inside, outside, all over. Their uniforms are so crisp, so clean that they practically creak as they move. Cars drop girls off right in front of the gate, so they can go straight inside; the ones who do walk up the hill do so in silence. Everyone ignores the reporters who still wait to lay siege upon us. Who come rushing at us with their voice recorders, their phones, their eager questions. There are more and more articles about us now. Us freaks, us weirdos. The hysterical, disappearing girls of St. Bernadette's.

Mak bites her lip as she guides the car slowly to the gate. "I hope this is the right thing to do," she mutters. "I hope you both stay safe." Aishah and I say nothing back. I wonder what my sister is thinking.

When we exit the car, a guard directs us straight inside. "Tak payah main-main," he tells us, stone-faced. "Just move straight through the gates and to the hall, please."

I want to tell them, *You cannot protect us.*

And so we move. The girls who aren't silent talk only in hushed whispers. As if they're in a sacred space. Or as if they're scared to awaken a beast. We walk through the open maw of the archway that takes us into the hall, and I think, *We are walking straight into the monster's mouth.*

When the bell rings, I see the guards close the gates. The wrought-iron clang echoes in my ears. I think about the screaming. I wonder, *Are you locking the danger out? Or locking it in with us?*

Assembly is short today. They send us off to our classrooms, where the gaps are big again. The disappearances have scared more people away. We all sit huddled together in the middle of the room. Waiting for first period to start. For our teachers to pretend anyone still cares about learning anything at all.

"I wonder where everyone else is," Balqis says. She is munching on kuih keria from a plastic bag. I think it would take an actual earthquake to shake up Balqis.

Farah looks at her as if she's begun speaking in tongues. "Are you serious?" she asks.

"End-of-year exams kan starting soon," Balqis says, dusting crumbs off her baju kurung. "Aren't they worried about studying?"

"I think they might be more worried about, like, being kidnapped," Sumi says from beside me. "Since girls are, you know, actually disappearing? My ma was not pleased that I told her I was still coming to school, let me tell you. She said I'm not so big that she can't still whack me with the broom handle."

Like Mak, I think. The fight for us to go to school gets more intense with every passing day.

"What is this?" she asked us despairingly this morning. "What are you doing? Are you punishing me, is that it? Am I being punished for marrying him, for putting you in danger without even realizing what I was doing? For not listening to you the first time? Because trust me, I am punishing myself enough. Every damn day." She raked a hand through her hair. We sat in silence, Aishah and I, just watching her. "When will you learn, Khadijah, that you don't have to throw yourself into the path of danger just to prove some ridiculous point?"

She gave in, in the end. Maybe she recognized that we would have come anyway. But I pondered all the way to school, *Am I punishing my mother?* She did everything right: stood by my side, made sure my attacker got his due, apologized over and over for bringing him into our home. She couldn't have known. I know this. I know it deep down in my bones. She couldn't have known what he really was.

But part of me is still angry. Angry about the times I spoke and wasn't heard. Angry about what it took for her to believe me. And my anger is a wall that keeps her firmly on one side and me on the other.

"Then how'd you manage to come?" Zulaikha asks Sumi.

Sumi grins. "I may not be too big, but I'm definitely too fast for her. I just ran and got the bus before she could stop me."

"You're gonna pay for that later, lor," Flo says.

Sumi shrugs. "So what? At least I'm here."

"My mother asked, kenapa nak kena datang? 'Why do you wanna be there so bad?'" Zulaikha shrugs. "I said I dunno. Only that it feels better to be here, with everyone, than at home. Then she said, 'It's like this school is possessing you.'" She laughs. "Imagine being possessed by St. Bernadette's."

Imagine being eaten by her, I think, and shiver.

Puan Ramlah makes her way into the room, and we stand. We stragglers, we survivors. We sing-song our usual morning greeting.

"That's weird," Balqis says, frowning. "It's not English time right now."

Puan Ramlah sighs deeply at this. "Thank you, Balqis," she says pointedly. "No, it is not. But I'm here to make a few announcements. First of all, you'll notice many new guards patrolling the grounds. The school, thanks to a generous sponsorship by the PTA, has hired a security firm to keep an eye on students, since ensuring your safety is a top priority. Though, I'm sure the missing girls will be found soon enough." She pauses to sniff delicately into a lacy handkerchief. "Still. We don't want to take any chances. Students are not to go wandering off alone after school; guards are stationed where the school buses are, to make sure you get on board safely, and parents who pick you up themselves are now required to drive or walk up to the school gates to do it. You will not be allowed to leave unless it is with a parent or guardian." She consults a sheet of notes in front of her. "Otherwise, we will try to make sure your days proceed with as little disruption as possible, and this includes learning and cocurricular activities as usual. Any questions?"

Jacintha raises her hand.

"Yes, Jacintha?"

"Puan Ramlah, what do you think happened to those girls?"

I'm not sure this is the kind of question Puan Ramlah expected. She stares at Jacintha for a while as if she's having trouble slotting the right words into place.

We wait.

In the end she just shrugs her shoulders. "I don't know," she says simply. "I don't know, but I am scared and worried for you all, and I want you to stay safe. So please, just do as we ask. I don't want to lose a single one of you."

It's the most honest anyone has been with us in weeks.

In the library my teammates thrust their speeches at me. I am supposed to be going over them as Uncle works with everyone on their delivery. I'm to check the speeches for gaps or inconsistencies. Help make them airtight, perfect. But the words blur together in incomprehensible blobs.

"Good work, everyone," he says finally. I glance up. I have not heard a word of what any of them have said. "Go ahead and get home now. Have a good rest. You've earned it."

Siti pauses. "But, Uncle," she says. "There's still, like, twenty minutes of practice."

He smiles, displaying those white teeth. You'd expect such a groomed man to have perfectly straight teeth. But his are crooked. It almost makes him better-looking. "I know Puan Ani said practice should be two hours. But you've done some

THE HYSTERICAL GIRLS OF ST. BERNADETTE'S

great work already, and I believe in rest and not pushing your-selves too much. We want victory, but not at the expense of your health and well-being."

I blink. It feels like a long time since someone prioritized us over our utility. And it is a relief, such a relief that I can stop pretending to be useful.

Siti bites her lip. "O . . . kay," she says, gathering her things slowly. The others share none of her reticence; they're already done packing up.

"Bye!" they say, waving cheerily on the way out.

"Stay a minute, Khadijah," Uncle says.

I blink again. And nod. What does he want with me? What have I done? I am suddenly acutely aware that I am alone. With a man.

My brain stutters to a stop. A man. I try to concentrate on each breath, taking air in slowly through my nose, blowing it out slowly through my mouth. *You're okay, Khad. You're okay.*

"I just wanted to talk to you," Uncle says. His voice is warm, gentle. "Is everything all right? You seem particularly distracted today."

I nod. *Fine, I am fine, just fine. Please let me leave.*

"I know about your . . . situation." He is trying too hard to be delicate. "Puan Ani informed me. I don't know all the details, of course, and I don't need to know. That's your business to share as you wish." He pauses. "But I hope you know that there are people around to support you, if you need it. All you have to do is reach out." And then he does it. He places a warm hand on my cold, trembling one. And immediately I snatch my hand back and recoil, standing so quickly that my chair makes a loud, ugly scraping sound that shatters the quiet of the library.

A look crosses Uncle's face then. Surprise, and something else. Frustration, maybe. Or anger.

"Sorry," he says quickly. "Sorry. I shouldn't have done that."

I nod, holding my hand against my chest as if I've been burned. Then I shove everything into my backpack—notebook, papers, everything—and run out of the library. I don't look back. I wonder how long I will run away from people who try to help me. How many more times I will disappoint them.

Rachel

At school Mr. B corners me somewhere between assembly hall and class. "So you're part of the group now, right?" he asks me.

There is a glass-covered noticeboard next to us, filled with official school announcements and flyers and hand-drawn posters. Out of the corner of my eye, I see the reflection. With its white ribbons, it looks like it could be me. But it is watchful and wary, and it moves in unsettling ways, and I know it's her. "Um. Yes," I say. I am trying my hardest to ignore her, but the prickling feeling at the back of my neck lets me know I'm being watched, and it's hard to keep my eyes from darting in her direction.

Mr. B notices my restless eyes and immediately gets them wrong. "Don't worry about that," he says. "If your teacher starts scolding you for being late, you can just tell her I was talking to you."

"Right," I say. The girl in the reflection cocks her head all the way to one side, as if she has no bones, or as if she doesn't mind breaking them. Her lips are painted with a fresh coat of glossy, eye-searing pink. I can feel cold sweat on my forehead. This may be the first time in my academic career when I can swear that I don't care about being late at all.

"Anyway, do you think it's going well? The group chat, I mean? People don't seem to be participating as much as I'd like."

"Um." My lips are dry and my mind is blank. *The girl,* I think. *The girl, the girl, the girl.*

Luckily, Mr. B doesn't seem to need me to participate in this conversation. He frowns. "I wonder what else I can do to help you feel, you know, more comfortable. What do you think? Any ideas?"

I shrug. "Not really, sir."

He sighs. "Ah well. I'll just keep trying, then. Hopefully at least a few of you find these resources helpful." He looks so let down that I think I almost feel some sympathy for him. Almost.

Until I glance at the noticeboard and see the girl just staring at me with those tormented eyes, and then I don't think about Mr. B at all.

For the rest of the day, all I do is struggle. The girl waits for me in every shiny surface, watching me. I shut my eyes in the bathroom, look straight down at my desk instead of out the window. I skip the canteen during recess and sit beneath the frangipani trees on my own, thankful for once to have no friends, so that I don't have to explain my sudden fear of spoons.

By the time I slide into the back seat of the car and say an absent-minded hello to Pakcik Zakaria, my head is buzzing with thoughts. How am I supposed to save "us"? Who is it that she wants me to save? Am I going crazy? How do I make this stop? Round and round and round go my thoughts, all the way home, while I check every mirror to make sure she doesn't follow us there.

"Rachel?"

I look up, surprised. We're already home, and Pakcik Zakaria is twisted in his seat, staring at me, his brow furrowed. "Rachel okay ke? Kita dah sampai rumah ni."

"Oh." I shake my head. *Wake up, Rachel, wake up.* "Terima kasih, Pakcik Zakaria."

He accepts my thanks with a nod, but his face still has concern written all over it. Pakcik Zakaria has daughters of his own, I remember then, little daughters in St. Bernadette's primary school, little daughters who could grow up to become screamers like me. "Rachel—"

"I'm okay," I say quickly. "Don't worry about me. And don't mention anything to Mother. Okay?"

He hesitates.

"Please."

"Okay," he says quietly. "Okay, Rachel."

The girl doesn't follow me home, but that doesn't mean I don't stay vigilant. I keep watching for her out of the corner of my eye, as if she'll reappear at any time. I walk through the house holding my breath, like she is waiting for me just around every corner, in every reflection, in every shadow. But she isn't there. She really isn't there.

"What are you looking for?" Mother asks me, irritation

bleeding into her voice. She is wearing a pristine tracksuit that doesn't look like it's ever been used for more than walking around malls sipping on Starbucks. She has a tai chi class this evening in the park with her friends. "Cannot sit still, like ants are biting your backside."

"Nothing," I mutter. "Nothing."

"No homework today?"

"No," I say, thinking of the stack of worksheets and pages of neglected assignments I still need to work through, stuffed at the bottom of my backpack. The Mother in my head tweaks viciously at my chest, sets off my guilt. "I mean yes."

Mother frowns. "Which is it? Yes or no?"

"I have homework," I say.

"Then go do it, Rachel. Why are you just wandering around the house like this?"

"Okay," I say.

"I will be going out for dinner after tai chi with Aunty Helen and Aunty Lydia," she says. "Kak Tini will set your dinner out as usual."

"Okay," I say again. "I'll just . . . go get some water."

In the kitchen, as I stand at the filter watching my glass slowly fill to the top, Kak Tini comes over and rubs my arm gently. My breakdown from the other day doesn't seem to have fazed her.

"Rachel okay?" she asks softly, just as she always does. Just as Pakcik Zakaria did.

There are suddenly tears in my eyes. "Rachel okay, je Kak

THE HYSTERICAL GIRLS OF ST. BERNADETTE'S

Tini." I nod, trying to smile so she doesn't notice the tears.

Her voice is gentle. Kak Tini has always been the most sooth-ing, restful person. "If you need anything, you tell me. Okay?"

"Okay, Kak Tini," I say.

I open my chemistry book and take out the assignment that was due three days ago, and I do nothing but stare at one spot on my desk where the whorls in the wood veneer look just like eyes and a nose.

The solution is right there. I know it is. At any time, I could just do it, add all those numbers to a new group. I could talk to them, ask them if this is happening to them, too. We could figure it out together. Even if they're not hearing and seeing the same things, maybe just talking to people who understand, who have screamed too, will help me fix my broken brain, exorcise the ghosts it absorbed through the cracks. And it makes sense, right? Here is a group of people who share one singular experi-ence, one thing nobody else can possibly understand. Isn't that the basis of friendship? Common ground?

I open the original group, the Mr. B pet project, and scroll through. After a string of lukewarm messages saying hello and hi and a round of introductions—Hi, I'm Rachel from 5 Melati. Nice to meet you, everybody—the chat has remained mostly silent, the pings coming from Mr. B himself, desperate to get everyone to participate. He asks questions, reacts overly enthu-siastically to every little reply, uses far too many emojis, and tells us he has special office hours for anyone in the group to drop by whenever we like. I wonder if anyone does.

Part of me takes the silence as a sign that nobody wants to talk, that they just want to move on with their lives. Part of me takes it as a sign that they, like me, want to talk somewhere where they won't be observed like lab rats, and then snitched on to their parents.

They won't be your friends, you know, the Mother in my head hisses, spiteful, nasty. Just as in real life, she doesn't like it when I ignore her. And she gets meaner when I do. *No matter how much common ground you share, why would they be friends with you?* I think about all the years I've spent on my own, trying to get close to people and failing, not really understanding what it is that makes them fit together like that, feeling like a puzzle piece that got put into the wrong box.

"That's not the point," I say aloud, gritting my teeth. "It's not about friendship. It's about finding out what's happening, so I can make this girl stop haunting me."

Your lies are getting better, the Mother in my head observes. *You have even gotten good at lying to yourself.*

Shut up, I think. *Shut up, shut up, shut up.* Quickly I take my phone from where it's charging on my bedside table. I open WhatsApp, take a deep breath, and start a new group. Carefully I add each number, double-checking each time not to add anyone else, anybody who might not understand us.

Group subject, WhatsApp asks me.

I pause to think about this. Then, slowly, I type it in: St. Bernie's Screamers.

I tap on Create, then shove my phone under the pillow. I

don't want to wait and see how many people will join. What they might say. And I can't seen to muster up the courage to type anything first.

Typical, the Mother in my head sneers. *Typical, fearful Rachel.*

I close my eyes and pretend I don't hear her.

Khadijah

The girls went to an actual debate this morning. I saw them off, standing awkwardly beside the car while they all piled in. Siti claiming the front seat, of course. Everyone else crowded into the back, sweating in their navy blazers. It was a big debate this time. Zone finals. The whole team looked slightly queasy with nerves. Except Siti, who unfortunately still looked fabulous.

"We'll let you know how it goes!" Puan Ani called cheerily from her open window. "Wish us luck!"

I raised my hand in a tentative little wave. The guards opened the gate to let them out. The few optimistic reporters who remained swarmed to them like maggots on fresh meat. They were looking for distraught parents, a crying teacher or two. The disappointment when they saw the team in the car was palpable. They want missing girls, not obviously there girls.

I chew on my lip now and wonder how it went. It was not their first debate since the screaming began. But it was their first since the girls started disappearing.

I wonder how that made the debaters feel.

But I do not wonder for long. My mother believes I have debate practice. She thinks this is why I will be home late. My friends, on the other hand, know there is no debate practice today. There never is on a competition day. The girls are meant to rest. My friends think I have gone home.

"Bye!" they called, and waved merrily on the way to the bus stop.

And I waved back. Goodbye, goodbye, goodbye. For at least a couple of hours, everyone will believe that I am where they think I am supposed to be, and nobody will realize they are wrong.

Which is what I want.

I should feel guilty. Guilty for fooling everyone. But I don't. Not even for deceiving Sumi and Flo, who have been nothing but loyal. Who have gone along with every one of my whims and plans. Even when they don't necessarily believe what I believe. Even when they think I should just go back to "normal."

Before I leave, I walk past the music room. I peek into the windows. Wince slightly at the bursts of discordant sounds. Aishah is there, glaring ferociously at her sheet music. She always looks angry when she's concentrating. She holds her flute, poised and ready. I feel a pang of guilt. I do not want to leave her here by herself. I do not want to leave her at the mercy of St. Bernadette's appetite. But I need answers. I say a quick doa. Beg the Almighty for assistance. Plead with the school itself: *Please, just leave her alone. Let her be.*

As I walk outside, I feel my steps slow down. As if the school is tugging at me. Invisible hands, begging me not to leave. Begging me to stay here, where I belong. Where I am safe.

Or so it would have me believe.

I grit my teeth and put one foot in front of the other. Step by step by step. Until I am beyond the gates. Until I am released. Until my feet suddenly grow lighter. Until I am running, putting St. Bernadette's far behind me, until it is nothing but a shadow in the distance.

I slow down as I get closer. The message came in this morning. **Your cake is ready!** We set a place to meet. The parking lot of a café I knew I could walk to from school. I am sweating beneath my white hijab. I'm not sure whether it's from heat or nerves.

I pat my pocket to make sure my wallet is there, fat with notes from my piggy bank. Fish my phone out of where I hid it, deep in the recesses of my backpack. Away from the prying eyes of prefects and teachers. She usually asks for a deposit, but I told her I'd pay the total upon collection. **I'm a student,** I explained, **and this cake is a surprise for my mother.** She relented. Of course she did. She was a mother too. Is a mother still.

I'm here, I type carefully.

The answer is almost immediate. **Me too! I'm parked in front of the mural.**

I glance all around the parking lot. The café and lot are both full; this is a hip place, and parking in the center of the city is a highly-sought-after commodity. The mural she's talking about covers an entire wall. A scene of Kuala Lumpur's shop houses as they used to be. Brightly painted buildings, wooden shutters, hand-painted signs advertising the wares. A little girl peeks out of an open upstairs window, her cheeks painted a rosy red. I stare at her and wonder if she is real. If she knows her body is on display for the world to see. If anyone even asked.

A deep blue car idles in one space, the only one that's running. That must be her. Sure enough, the driver's door swings open and she steps out. Black leggings, long pink T-shirt. Sensible white sneakers. The kind that make it feel like you're walking on clouds. The kind that cost a lot of money. "Hiiiiii!" She waves, and I wave back. "Let me just get your cake!"

She opens up the back door. Draws out a small white box. I stand and fiddle with my wallet. It's dawning on me now that I'm going to have to talk. To ask. It would be so much easier if Sumi and Flo were here. But I was so sure. I knew I wanted to do this on my own. Knew they'd tell me it was a bad idea.

"Are you Joanna?" I ask. My voice feels foreign in my throat. An alien thing, waiting to choke me with my own words.

"That's me," she says. Joanna Lim. Julianna's mother. "Ta-da!" She presents the box to me with a flourish. "Go on, check and see if everything is okay. I want to make sure you're satisfied."

I set the box on the car. Open it up carefully. The cake isn't too big. About six inches across. It's all I could afford. Delicate piped flowers climb up along its dusty-pink sides. In swirly writing on top, in a pale green, it just says, *HAPPY*.

"I was confused at first," she tells me, smiling. "I thought for sure you'd made a mistake. Surely it should say 'happy birthday,' or 'happy retirement' or something, you know?"

"It's my wish for her," I say aloud. "For us."

She nods. "It's a good wish."

I hand over the cash silently. Watch her count it. "It's all there," she says. She notices me surreptitiously wipe the sweat from my forehead. I can feel it pooling underneath my hijab. "Poor thing," she says sympathetically. "What time is it? Goodness, you must have had to rush here after school finished just to meet me. You must have really wanted this cake!"

I nod. Here it is. Here is my chance. "My school is not too far," I say carefully. "I go to St. Bernadette's."

I watch her busy hands go still. Her expression go guarded. Her eyes go dark. "Oh really?" she murmurs. "You're right, that's not too far at all."

"Ya." I nod earnestly. "I just had to walk through the alley, then cross a couple of streets over, and then—"

"I'm quite familiar with St. Bernadette's and where it is, thank you," she says. Her voice has gotten all tight. Like she's forcing it out of her.

"Oh, you are?" *That's it, Khad. Play it oblivious. Play it naïve. Play it like you haven't picked up every hint she's dropped that this makes her uncomfortable.* "You have a daughter there or something? What's her name? Maybe I know her!"

Joanna Lim is breathing heavily now. In through her nose, out through her mouth. I know the drill. I have done it a million times. "I used to," she says. "But not anymore."

Without meaning to, I find myself leaning forward. Trying to get closer. Eager to hear more. "What happened?" I ask her softly.

Something flashes in her eyes. She straightens up to look at me. "What do you mean, 'What happened?'" she asks. *Oh no. Oh no, oh no, oh no.* Too late I realize I have done this all wrong. "You're one of them, aren't you?" Joanna Lim practically snarls. "One of those brats who find out about my Julianna and decide they need to investigate. Find the truth behind the ghost story you've turned her into." She jabs me in the chest, and I think my panic may choke me. "Julianna is not some urban legend. Some scary story for you to tell in the dark. She is my daughter. My daughter." Her face crumples for a moment before she collects herself. "I told the school then, and I am telling you now. I never want to have anything to do with St. Bernadette's again. Especially after what they did. You go back and let your little friends know."

"What did they do?" I blurt out. "What did St. Bernadette's do?"

I don't know why she answers. She doesn't have to. Maybe she sees the desperation in my eyes. Maybe she feels bad for me. Maybe she wants me to know how angry she is. Whatever the reason, she does answer.

"Nothing," she tells me, almost spitting it out. "Absolutely nothing. No investigation, no comments for the press, no allowing anyone to talk to me, Julianna's own mother, about what happened the day she disappeared. Nothing." She opens the car door with so much force, I think she may pull it off. "And that is what that school is to me now. Nothing." She looks at me one last time before putting on her sunglasses. But not so quickly that I don't see the way her eyes glisten with tears. "Enjoy your cake," she says. The car door slams, and she peels out of the parking lot with a squeal of tires. Like she can't get out of here fast enough.

I stand there, cake box in my hands. I am shaking so much, I am sure I am destroying Joanna Lim's work.

Why would everyone involved with the school not want to work with Joanna? A grieving mother and her questions? Unless . . .

Unless they knew nobody would like the answers.

Rachel

I don't stay away from my phone for long. At some point my curiosity gets the better of me, and I fish it out from behind my pillow and watch as the other screamers enter the group, one by one by one.

My finger hovers over the send button, hesitant, unsure. I thought about this moment throughout the entire school day. I've spent ages crafting this message, thinking about every word, spending whole class periods writing and rewriting versions of it on lined sheets of paper I slipped into the pages of my moral studies notebook, versions I read over and over and over again.

Hi, everyone. My name is Rachel Lian from 5 Melati. And just like you, I am a screamer.

I'm sorry for adding you to this group without asking, and you are obviously free to leave anytime you want. But ever since I screamed, I've been feeling strange and lonely, like nobody understands. Only, that isn't true, right? Because everyone here understands. And I thought we could help each other, and maybe not feel so alone.

It's perfect, I think. The right tone, the right message. Appealing to their emotions, and our common struggles. Nothing in here suggests that I have any kind of ulterior motive, that I'm here to sift through these girls until I find my own personal nightmare. Because that's why I'm doing this, right? That's the whole point. And I pretend I don't feel an excited little pang at the idea of maybe making some friends after all.

Nobody will answer, the Mother in my head sneers. *Nobody will want to talk to you. Why should they?*

That thought makes me pause. The Mother in my head is far too good at this, far too adept at unearthing the most sensitive parts of me, the things I keep hidden away, and then pressing down until it hurts.

I take a deep breath and hit send, and wait, and wait, and wait. The pause is too long. With each passing second I feel myself sinking deeper and deeper into the quicksand of my own anxiety. *What are they thinking? Are they annoyed? Are they laughing at me? Will anyone respond?*

And then I see it, the little status message at the top of the window that says someone is typing.

A ping.

~NN

What is this? What is this group for?

I chew on my thumbnail, a habit I can't shake when I'm nervous. I know this may be a sticking point for some people. Who likes the idea of being added to some random chat? I could be anyone—an MLM shill, a hacker, a pedophile.

This is a group for the screamers. A private group, one our parents can't access unless you choose to share things here with them.

I don't know if this is a good idea . . . My mom doesn't like me talking about this

That's okay. You can leave if you want. I don't want to get anyone into trouble.

The silence is longer this time, stretching on and on and on. I don't have any nail left to chew on my right thumb, so I start on my left. The Mother in my ear whispers, *That's it. They're leaving. They won't come back. You'll be alone again, just like you always have been, just like you always will be.*

Ping. Another message.

~Selena.Marie
I'm so glad you did this. I have been dying to talk to you guys, really talk to you guys, but that other group . . . it just didn't feel right, you know?

It's like this opens the floodgates, and they all come rushing through, message after message, confession after confession. They come so fast, it's almost impossible to keep up, and I have to keep scrolling back to make sure I don't miss any. My lips hurt, and I wonder why until I realize it's because I'm not used to smiling so wide, so much.

~Nik Luvs U
OMG I'm so happy this exists

> **~jamie khoo**
> I'm so glad you all understand.

~Arissa.Aziz
Do you have trouble sleeping too?

> **~Bhavani**
> Do you have nightmares too?

~NN
You too?

> **~Sheila.Victor**
> Me too.

~Liyana Banana
Me too.

> **~Ranjeetha P**
> Me too.

Maybe, I think, *maybe understanding "save us" begins with trying my hardest to save myself.* The Mother in my head is silent; the grin on my face is wide. I type a reply and hit send before I even realize that I'm doing it.

~Rachel Lian
Me too.

Khadijah

"Would you stop fidgeting?" Siti hisses. "Everyone's going to be looking at us in a minute."

I can't believe the school has decided to go through with this. A banner that hangs over the stage reads ST. BER-NADETTE'S: STRONGER TOGETHER in big bold letters. A young teacher whose name I can never remember bustles around and tells people what to do. She tells us that this win—our win—is a big boost for "the entire school community." St. Bernadette's being declared zone champions is "a perfect way to cap off our Community Day celebration." I can't bring myself to believe that anyone cares this much about the debate team.

After yesterday I'm having trouble believing anyone cares that much about us girls in general.

I walked all the way back to school with the cake in my hand. I forgot it was there at all. Tossed it into a trash can when I finally realized. I couldn't even think about eating it without feeling like throwing up.

"Where'd you go?" Aishah asked, already waiting at our usual spot for Mak to turn up.

I didn't answer. I didn't want to tell her I'd been out chasing ghosts.

Why would the school not help Joanna? Not let teachers speak about the screamers? About Julianna?

What is it that they don't want us to discover?

Now we are herded through the proceedings like sheep. Lined up outside the assembly hall, waiting to hear our names called. They made us practice walking across the stage, shaking the hand of some teacher standing in for the true VIP. Receiving a blank piece of paper rolled up into a scroll to make it look like our certificates. *Why am I even here?* I think. *I am not really part of this team.* The debater who doesn't even speak.

Now Felicia squirms uncomfortably in her blazer. "I can't help it," she whispers back to Siti. "That's why I'm fidgeting. Because they're going to be looking."

"This is weird," Rania mutters, tugging at her tie as if it chokes her. "Why are we bothering with all this? Those girls are gone. Shouldn't everyone be figuring out where they are? How to get them back?"

They don't want to, I think. They're bothering with all of this so they don't have to bother with all of that. With those messy, emotional, hysterical girls. I dig my nails hard into my palms, leave perfect half-moon indents in the sweaty flesh.

"You all need to shut up." Siti looks poised and perfect, as always. "Just sit back and enjoy this. We worked our asses off. We earned it."

Did we? Does it matter? We all continue to pretend it does. One by one, teachers take to the stage to talk about how wonderful we are. What a great job we did. First Puan Ani. Then Mrs. Beatrice, who paints a glowing picture of the honor and glory we've brought to the school. She keeps saying "in these trying times."

Onstage the teachers nod approvingly. They've even got Uncle up there. Discreetly looking at his watch between polite claps. He's probably dying to get out of here. I remember the look on Julianna's mother's face as she told me how the school turned its back on her. These trying times. I don't think we are trying nearly hard enough.

From the audience Sumi and Flo wave wildly in my direction. I avert my eyes, stare straight ahead. I have not told them about my side quest. That I lied to them. It makes me squirmy and restless. I think this is the first time I've ever lied to them about something like this. Something that matters.

"St. Bernadette's is proud of you," Mrs. Beatrice intones grandly. Then she eyes the crowd. They get the hint. Scattered applause breaks out in the hall. "And to show our gratitude for all the effort you have put in, as well as to raise your fighting spirit for the competition ahead, the Parent-Teacher Association, together with all of us here, has some tokens of appreciation for you."

Another round of polite applause. The blazer is itchy. I want to take it off. I want to tear off my own skin. Something is not right here, here in the blazer, here in the school, here inside me, in my own flesh.

Mrs. Beatrice makes her way to the side of the stage. Gestures to Uncle to come with her. Beside them is a small table covered in lace and a row of shiny wooden plaques. I guess we won't just be getting certificates.

"Girls, make your way to the stage when we call your name, please, to receive your token of appreciation from our esteemed guest, Datuk Shah," Puan Ani says into the mic.

I am finding it hard to breathe now. I spend a lot of time making sure nobody notices me. Nobody looks my way. And now all eyes are about to be on me. I don't like it.

"Siti Amira binti Luqman."

Siti walks across the stage. Crisp, confident steps. Ponytail swinging from side to side. She takes a plaque, smiles dazzlingly at Uncle and Mrs. Beatrice. It's almost like she doesn't want to get off the stage.

"Felicia Lee."

My stomach does another backflip.

"Rania binti Ahmad Afif."

I think I may throw up.

"Anusyia Anne Raj."

Oh no. Oh no, oh no, oh no.

"Nur Khadijah binti Rahmat."

I stand on legs that feel like jelly. Is it my imagination, or does a murmur move through the crowd, like a breeze rifling through trees? The speaker who doesn't speak. I look down at my feet, so alien as they move across the stage, and I focus again on the hole above my little toe. I can see the sock peeking through. I should have worn different shoes.

"Congratulations!" a voice says. I'm here, I've arrived, I did it, it's almost over. "Job well done." A hand grasps mine and shakes it heartily.

I look up.

And I freeze.

Behind Uncle and his wide grin, behind Mrs. Beatrice and her tight-lipped smile, a shadow looms; a dark, inky-black specter that blooms and swells before my eyes and pulses as if it's breathing. As if it's alive.

As if it's hungry.

"Khadijah?" I hear a voice say, but it sounds very far away, like I'm underwater and I'm drowning and someone is trying to call me back to land. "Khadijah?" But I can't move, I can't move at all, and someone somewhere has begun sweeping, sweeping, sweeping so that the sound is all that fills my ears.

The specter hovers, as if it's waiting.

I hold my breath, as if I'm waiting too.

And then it lunges.

And before I know it, I throw my head back. And I begin to scream.

Khadijah

This proves to be Mak's last straw.

Now both Aishah and I are stuck at home. And this time Mak actually takes time off from work. To be with us, she says. To take care of us. No matter where we go, she's there. Eating toast while standing at the kitchen counter. Poking her head into our bedrooms to check on what we're doing. Taking Zoom calls in the living room while K-dramas play on mute on the TV. Forcing us to go on a walk "for our mental health."

"I am not leaving," she tells us adamantly. "Not until I know what's going on over at that school, and not until I'm one hundred percent sure you're both okay."

I pretend I am annoyed by this. I pretend not to care. But as we walk through the neighborhood, the evening sun filtering golden yellow through the trees, I realize that it feels . . . nice. It feels like it used to. Before everything.

Flo and Sumi send me message after message in the group chat. Before school starts. When they get home. The messages are about everything and nothing. I just woke up and the drool stain on my pillow kind of looks like a whale, Sumi says at 5:48 a.m., or OMG. Khad, I saw Faris today and he looked SO CUTE!!!!! from Flo at 3:22 p.m. My phone pings and pings. They tell me about the homework I'll have to do. Or little bits of gossip from school. Anything to keep me tethered to them and to St. Bernadette's and to reality. It doesn't matter if I reply or not. They send them anyway.

Aishah slips out into the living room at night when Mak is asleep. She talks without expecting an answer. When she's done talking she simply sits beside me, her hand holding mine. A month ago I might have pulled away. Today I don't.

"What was it like for you?" she asks. I tell her what I remember of the before (not much) and the after (a sore throat, a circle of concerned faces surrounding me, Mrs. Beatrice's stale breath in my face).

"So you don't remember anything either," she says. It's not a question.

I think about this. "I remember being scared," I say finally.

Aishah nods. "Me too."

"But it's not just that," I say. I try to gather my thoughts, to snatch at the shards of memory floating at the edge of my brain before they disappear again. "It's not just that I was scared. It's that the fear was familiar."

There is a silence. I hear Aishah let out a slow breath. "Because your body remembered," she says.

I nod. "I guess so."

She pauses before she asks her next question. As if she knows it's a risk she's taking. "When are you going to start talking to her again?"

I don't answer. Mostly because I don't know.

"I think maybe you've punished her enough, you know," she says. Then she is quiet. And then she falls asleep on the other end of the sofa, our legs all scrunched up so we both fit, toes touching under the blanket.

My phone pings. I check the time. 10:37 p.m. Sumi or Flo, I think. Again.

Only it isn't.

It's a new group that I've been added to. *St. Bernie's Screamers*, it says across the top.

What is this?

I check the list of group members. It's a long string of numbers unfamiliar to me. Except for one.

"What is this?" I say aloud.

Aishah stirs. "What?"

I say nothing. Just shove my screen in her face.

She squints. "Oh. Did you just get added to it?"

I nod. "When did they add you?"

"A couple of days ago." She yawns. Stretches like a cat. "Some girl started it. So we could all talk without teachers spying on us, or whatever. You can read her message at the top, look."

I tap on the pinned message in the chat.

~Rachel Lian
Hi, everyone. My name is Rachel Lian
from 5 Melati. And just like you, I am a
screamer. . . .

"Everyone seems nice." Aishah is still talking. "I haven't said much, though. You know how really big group chats make me anxious."

This is an understatement. The first thing Aishah does in every group chat she gets added to is go into the settings and hit "mute forever."

"I'm not exactly a joiner either," I mutter. But the screamers all being in one place piques my curiosity. And, I slowly realize, having them all here, learning their stories, gives me a chance to find the common thread I've been looking for. Gives me the chance to figure it all out. Gives me the chance to save Aishah, to save them all.

Save us all, I guess. Since I'm one of them now.

I'm about to type something when another message comes through. From an unknown number.

"Who's that?" Aishah asks, leaning on my arm, still peering at my screen. I shake her off.

Hi. This is Rachel. I'm sorry for adding you to the group without introducing myself first. It's just a place to find people to talk to who have gone through the same thing. But I just wanted you to know that you can leave at any time if it makes you uncomfortable.

"Are you going to say something back?" Aishah asks.

"Stop looking at my messages," I tell her. I wait for her to huff back under her blanket before composing my reply.

That's fine. My name is Khadijah. And I'm happy to be here.

I will figure out what's going on, I think. *I will save us. I will save us all.*

Rachel

The last screamer asks strange, direct questions, questions that everybody else has been avoiding, questions nobody really wants to ask or knows how to answer.

Has anybody ever called you a freak?

Do you think our families think we're weird or broken? Not that they'd say that to our faces. Or I hope they wouldn't. I'm sorry if that happened to you though.

What do you think the other girls think about us? Do you think they are scared of us?

She tells us her name is Khadijah and that she's a fourth former. I think about her questions all through the day, which I'm forced to spend in school because Mother signed me up for some motivational workshop for form-five students. "Something to help you focus on what matters," she'd told me. As the speaker stands on stage, flipping through slides and gesticulating wildly as he talks, I stare at the bored faces around me. *Do you think I'm a freak? Are you scared of me?* From my seat in the hall I stare at the tops of the frangipani trees outside, not even bothering to pretend that I care what the over-enthusiastic speaker is saying. Something—someone—whispers in my ear, *Are you paying attention yet?* I blink, unsure if I'm hearing things, and the white frangipani flowers aren't flowers anymore; they're ribbons, white ribbons, tied neatly around every branch, fluttering in the wind like cobwebs or ghosts. I blink again, and they're flowers once more.

The Mother in my head smirks. *Of course they are.*

The workshop ends at twelve thirty p.m., an excruciating four hours of speeches, games, and a visualization segment where we were meant to picture our parents dead so it would, I don't know, make us realize how much they deserved our good grades now, while they were still alive, I guess. Mother, the real Mother, is not home when Pakcik Zakaria drops me off; she probably told me why, but I've forgotten. *Do you think our families think we're broken?* I manage to choke down about a third of the bowl of steaming-hot fried rice Kak Tini sets before me, and ignore her gentle tutting as she clears it away.

Among the chatter in the group, Khadijah asks us a new question.

How did it happen for you guys?

I think about the way I hesitate, waiting for the right moment to bring it up, still so afraid nobody will answer if I haven't laid the right foundation, if they don't like me enough. Khadijah asks so easily. As if typing it isn't awkward for her, as if her thoughts don't need to be erased and rephrased and worked over a hundred times before she reveals them. Is it so easy for everyone else?

The answers trickle in, some as single sentences, some as long paragraphs.

> **~Sheila.Victor**
> I was walking back from the bath-
> room . . .

~NN
I was onstage getting an award . . .

> **~Mel =^.^=**
> I was just in class . . .

~FazNFurious
I was on the field playing netball . . .

So many stories, so many screams. I type my own: I was in the assembly hall, about to perform onstage, when it happened.

Khadijah immediately replies, Hey, it happened onstage for me too! Stage buddies!

It surprises a small smile out of me. *Stage buddies,* I think. *We're stage buddies.* Then another message comes in, not in the group, but from one person.

~Khad
I have a question for you

I check the number, and sure enough, it's Khadijah. What could she possibly want from me?

Rachel Lian
What is it?

~Khad
Now that we're all gathered in one group
thanks to you, I was wondering if we should
put a buddy system in place.
You know. Keep an eye on each other,
protect each other. Make sure none of us is
ever alone.
Some of the girls are saying they might
want to go back to school.
I think it would help. Safety in numbers and
all that
Whatever's happening to screamers, whatever's taking us, it would be a lot harder if
we stuck together

    I don't ask why she says "whatever's taking us," and not
"whoever."

~Rachel Lian
I don't know. I'm not sure it would work.

~Khad
It's worth a try, right?
And it's better than sitting around and be-
ing scared
Alone

~Rachel Lian
I'm alone anyway. I don't think anybody
would want to buddy up with me.

I blink, surprised at this rush of honesty. It's only one line, but it's certainly more than I meant to reveal to this complete stranger, this person with whom I don't think I have anything in common besides a scream.

Khadijah's response is typical; no thoughts, no hesitation.

~Khad
I'll be your buddy.

Khadijah

The WhatsApp group changes everything. Screaming made me feel untethered. Like I was removed from my body, my thoughts, my life for a second, and then put back with everything not quite in the right place. Realizing there are people out there who get it, who've been through the same thing and understand how I feel, changes everything. Yes, I have Sumi, and I have Flo, and yet neither of them truly knows what it's like. Neither of them has been here.

Of course there are people who leave the chat group. Aishah does. She says she can't stand any of it. The constant pinging. The anxiety of trying to keep up with a massive chat. The daily reminders of what happened to us. She has no desire to talk about her feelings over and over again with people she doesn't really know.

"I just want to move on and forget it happened," she tells me.

Is what I'm doing not moving on? I wonder. But I don't care. For the first time in a while, I belong somewhere again. And it feels right. And I will save them all.

Starting with the buddy system. They liked that idea a lot. Girls have been talking about going back, about feeling better in school. We know that screamers have disappeared. None of us seems to care. **I want to go back**, the messages say, over and over. **I want to go back to St. Bernadette's.**

I was worried about overstepping. It wasn't my group to take over, after all. And that Rachel girl, she didn't seem too enthusiastic at first. But then she said that thing about being alone, and it sparked something. **I'll be your buddy,** I said. I didn't even need to think about it.

She is strange, Rachel. Strange and stiff and stilted. Like she's just learning to be around people. But who am I to judge? How am I supposed to know what traumas a person has suffered? How can I, of all people, determine what is normal and what isn't?

Rachel is your buddy now, I tell myself. *And you have to protect her. That's what buddies do.*

I'm coming to school tomorrow, I text her. **I'll come and find you. So we can stick together outside of classes.**

~Rachel Lian
Are you sure that's okay?

I feel a pang of irritation. This girl is so timid. So unsure.

~Khad
Why wouldn't it be?

~Rachel Lian
No reason, I guess. See you tomorrow.

Now to tell my mother I want to go back to school. When she's already told us both multiple times that we need to stay home "until they figure this all out."

I sigh. I'm sure this will go well.

I find Mak outside. She is digging away at the stubborn ground with a trowel. "I'm going to plant vegetables here," she tells me, not looking up. Her face is streaked with sweat and dirt. "Chilis, brinjals, lady's-fingers, daun kari. We'll save so much money. And I think it would be nice, watching something grow and knowing it was your hard work that did it. Don't you think so?"

She doesn't expect me to answer. Why should she? I haven't answered for weeks, and I don't plan on starting now.

Instead I shove a note into her hand. She unfolds it, reads it aloud.

"I want to go back to school." She snaps her head up to glare at me. "Absolutely not. I am not letting you out of my sight, young lady. Neither you nor your sister will be going to school until they figure out what's going on." She places the note very deliberately on the ground. Turns her attention back to the dirt with renewed vigor. "It's the only way I can protect you."

I feel the familiar anger moving in my chest, the old resentment. Who is she to talk of protection? Who is she to decide what keeps us safe? She didn't do it before, did she? Not until I gave her something to believe in, something she couldn't deny. Not until I paid the price.

I snatch the note from where she's set it down. Shove it back into her hands. Jab at the words.

She grabs me by the wrist. Her grip is so tight, it pinches. I try not to wince at the feel of her skin. "Why?" she asks. She won't let go. "Why do you have to go back? Don't you see how dangerous it is?"

I don't explain. Don't tell her how I need to find out what's happening. How I need to protect Aishah. Make it all go back to normal. I say nothing at all, and it makes her furious.

"When will you stop this?" she asks me, trembling, her eyes glassy with tears. "When will you start talking to me? Start telling me what's going on in that head of yours?" Her voice breaks. "When will you forgive me?"

My throat aches. I know if I speak now, my words will turn into tears. I have shed a lot of tears, these past months. I do not want to cry anymore. I just watch my mother, until her shoulders eventually stop shuddering. Until she stops sobbing.

From the open doors Aishah watches us. Wary. "If she's going back to school, then so am I," she says.

"Do what you want," my mother says, her voice thick with stale tears. She takes her trowel. The air fills with the steady sounds of metal on dirt.

I wake from a fitful sleep, full of the girl, and white ribbons, and dry leaves, and screams.

~Khad
I'm coming to school tomorrow. I'll come
and find you.

She will come and find me, I think. *She will come and find me, and I won't be alone. I'm not going to be alone anymore.* The invisible bands wrapped around my chest loosen, and I feel like I'm finally able to breathe. Not alone, not alone anymore. She's coming to find me.

The Mother in my head reaches out a poisonous finger, unfurls a tendril of doubt. *But once she finds you, will she like what she sees?*

I dig a nail into my thigh, as if I can force the poison out. *Shut up. Shut up. Shut up.*

When I arrive at school, I position myself in the corridor by the stage, where I can see everyone milling through the gates, and I tell myself I'm doing it so I can go say hi as soon as she appears. I know what Khadijah looks like, from the photo in the little circle by her name on WhatsApp. I know the way her hijab is folded over her rounded cheeks, the way one side of her mouth lifts up a little higher than the other when she smiles. So it's easy to see when she arrives, flanked by her friends. (*Her real friends*, the Mother in my head says cruelly.) I watch as they enter the assembly hall, watch some more as they loiter by the doors waiting for assembly to start. Khadijah smiles as her friends talk, but her eyes wander like she's looking for something, or someone.

Me, I think. She's looking for me. And even knowing that, I can't make my feet walk over there. *No wonder you have no friends,* Mother's voice says.

The bell rings, and once again I am too late.

That feeling, that nagging sensation of *Too late, too late, too late, before it's too late,* hangs on to me all through the morning. I don't do any work; I don't take any notes. At this point I'm not sure the teachers even expect me to; they've stopped looking at me when they ask questions in class, stopped expecting me to raise my hand the way I used to. All I do is try to catch a glimpse of Khadijah. I take far more bathroom breaks than I usually do, just to see if I can get a peek into her classroom. ("You got diarrhea or what?" Dahlia asks me, and I do not care.) I am a stalker and I am a freak and I am unraveling bit by bit and I don't know why I'm so afraid to meet her.

I am walking to the bathroom again, neck craned in the direction of Khadijah's classroom, when I see Mrs. Dev striding purposefully toward me.

"Rachel!" she calls, paper in hand. "Rachel!"

I know she's about to ask me questions I can't bear to hear, that I have no answers for. I veer right down a corridor, go up a flight of stairs two at a time, then sprint across the entire form-five block. People turn to look as I streak past, but I don't look back, not even as I hear Mrs. Dev yell my name again, her voice getting farther and farther away. My heart beats loudly in my ears, and my breath is ragged, but I can't face her right now. I just can't. I go down corridors, take stairs, duck between buildings. I don't even know where I'm running to; I just run.

When I finally pause to catch my breath, sides aching, I look around and realize I'm where I least want to be. I'm standing in front of Brede's House. On the handle of one of the doors, something flutters in the wind.

A white ribbon.

From somewhere inside, behind those wooden doors, someone begins to sweep, sweep, sweep, and I forget everything then, all my pain, all my panic. All I feel is a sense of dread. *I cannot be here. I cannot. I cannot be here.*

I turn to go, but my feet won't move, and I look down and realize that my wrists are wrapped in white ribbons bound so tight that they bite into my skin, and they're holding me fast and pulling me back, and instead of walking away from Brede's House, I find myself being dragged slowly backward, and I know the doors are open, I can feel it, but I cannot bring myself to turn around, cannot bring myself to know what awaits me in the shadows and whether it's wearing bright pink lipstick, and all I can do is mutter, "No, no, no, no, no" over and over again as tears stream down my face.

And then there is a hand on my shoulder, and it's Mrs Dev, and her expression is one of anxiety with just a hint of terror. "Rachel?" she says. "Are you all right?"

I look down at my wrists, and the ribbons are no longer there.

"I'm all right, Mrs. Dev," I say, trying my best to stop trembling, rubbing the red marks on my wrists where white ribbons used to be.

Khadijah

"I'm so glad you're okay!" Flo wraps me in a giant hug the minute I get out of the car.

Sumi reaches over her head for a high five. "We were worried about you," she says quietly, and I smile.

After the screaming, it does feel good to be here in this familiar place. Here between Flo and Sumi. Letting them bicker over my head like they always do. I try to hold on to this feeling as we walk into school. I keep an eye on Aishah as I go. She's with her own friends. But I told her to stay close to me. If she had to come, I can at least make sure she stays around people. Stays safe.

St. Bernadette's stands with its gates wide open. Not like a mouth but like arms waiting to embrace me. The morning sun caresses the warm beige walls and makes them glow. Every step I take on the well-worn tiles beats out a comforting rhythm: *I am back, I am back, I am back.*

"What's with you?" Sumi asks when we're in the hall waiting for assembly. We're early, for once. A miracle.

I look at her questioningly.

"You keep looking around like you're searching for someone."

Flo takes a little mirror out of her backpack. She's been fidgeting with her hair every five minutes. "Ugh, I should never have gotten bangs. They're so hard to maintain."

I shrug.

Understanding dawns on Flo's face. "Aishah's right there, you know."

Sumi gives my shoulder a squeeze. "She's fine as long as she stays with her friends. Just make sure she knows not to wander off on her own."

I nod. I haven't really talked to Sumi and Flo about Rachel. I should, I guess. But I haven't. I'm not sure what to say. I told them about the group chat, obviously. What a huge help it's been for me. How nice it was to talk to people who understand. And they've both made supportive noises. Said all the right things about how nice it is that I have this, and what a good idea to let us all share our experiences. But there's a weird undercurrent beneath it all. A feeling I can't quite place.

But I can't think about this right now. I can't. I have more important things to do.

By the time the bell rings, I still haven't found Rachel. Why didn't we make more concrete plans? It's not like we can bring phones to school, not like we can text each other a place to meet. Classes go on as usual. Sumi and Flo go on as usual. The world goes on as usual. But I go about my day like there's an itch just beneath my skin that I can't seem to get rid of.

When the recess bell rings, we head to the canteen. We're walking and they're chatting. And then somehow I drop my water bottle and it rolls away and I click my tongue in irritation because nothing is going my way.

I wave at them to go ahead.

"We'll save you a spot," Flo says, squeezing my arm. "Before all the tables are gone and we have to eat by the drains or something."

They run off, and I go hunt for my bottle. But as I'm searching the ground for it, a shadow falls across my path.

There is a girl standing there, my bottle in her hand. A girl with blunt bangs and hair in two pigtails, tied with white ribbons. A girl with a pale, pale face, and dark shadows like bruises under her eyes. A girl who looks vaguely familiar. I glance at her name tag. RACHEL.

Rachel.

"Hi, Khadijah?" she says softly. She keeps fiddling with her wrists. Looks at me, then looks away. My name hangs in the air, shaky and uncertain. I realize then that the last time I saw her was when she screamed. Being taken out of the hall, white ribbons blowing behind her in the wind. Face contorted, sweaty.

I nod. Then I reach out and tug at her sleeve. Gesture at her to follow me.

She is so hesitant, so unsure. "Okay," she says.

We walk in silence to the canteen. I keep an eye out for Aishah, my body tense. It's only when I see her that I let myself relax. There's an audible exhale, and Rachel looks at me questioningly. But I don't tell her anything. I don't speak. I should probably have mentioned that to her in our chats.

The table Sumi and Flo have found is in the back corner, by the stairs leading up to the music and art rooms. They chose this one on purpose. If I position myself just right, nobody can see or hear me talk. As we approach, their faces turn from wide, eager smiles to confusion.

Sumi quirks an eyebrow at me. "Khad?"

"I'm Rachel." Rachel smiles, just a little, tentative. Worried. "Khadijah told me I could hang out with you guys. Is that okay?"

There is a silence. Sumi and Flo look at each other, then at me. I know what they're thinking. We've never let anyone new into this group, ever. It's always been just the three of us. Khad, Sumi, Flo. They're going to have so many questions. So many questions.

"Khad told you that?" Flo asks. "Our Khad?"

"Well." Rachel glances at me. Her expression is slightly confused. "Not in so many words."

"Yeah," Sumi mutters. "Khad doesn't really have many of those to spare."

"She doesn't talk," Flo explains to Rachel. "Not right now."

"Oh." Rachel rocks slightly on her heels. She is more confused than ever, I know. I'm so sweaty. I wish I hadn't dragged her into this. I wish I had explained better. "Is it some kind of illness? Or did something happen?"

"A lot happened," Sumi says. "But it isn't our story to tell. Still . . ." She glances over at me, and there's no denying how annoyed she is. "Still, if she told you to come eat with us, well, then . . ."

"I don't have to," Rachel says quickly. "I could just—"

I grab her wrist before she can turn away. Gritting my teeth against the feel of her skin against mine. She winces as if this pains her just as much as it pains me, and I let go.

Flo and Sumi stare at us, and then at each other.

"Sit," Flo says finally. "Eat with us."

"You're sure?" Rachel asks. "I can . . . I can just contact you later, Khadijah. When you're free."

"We're sure," Flo says. "Did you hurt your hand or something? You keep rubbing it."

Rachel automatically puts her hands behind her back. "I'm okay," she says. "Only . . . I don't want to butt in or anything."

"Oh no," Sumi says. "You're not butting in. Not at all." Even the way she breathes betrays her anger.

Rachel must sense the tension. It's impossible not to. "I'm just going to go buy a drink," she says. "I'll be right back."

"Can't wait," Sumi says.

I watch as Rachel walks away. Her back is perfectly straight, not one hair in her pigtails out of place, the ribbons tied in perfect bows.

I turn back to two stone-faced girls staring right at me.

"You want to tell us what this is all about?" Sumi asks, arms folded.

I shrug. I'm trying to project nonchalance. Trying to no-big-deal my way out of this. But it doesn't work.

"Why would you invite someone new into the gang without telling us first?" Flo asks quietly.

I take my notebook and pen out of my pocket. Scribble furiously. *I'm not inviting her into the gang. I'm inviting her to recess.*

"Still." Sumi regards me, arms still crossed. "It's just a little weird that you wouldn't at least let us know."

She's a screamer, like me, I write. *Only, she doesn't have friends like I do. Friends like you guys. People who can watch out for her. And we're disappearing, us screamers. So I thought she could use one.* I can feel tiny prickles of irritation start to needle at my skin. They were so quick to judge. So quick to jump to conclusions. So quick to prioritize their own feelings, their own hurt, over anyone else's. *We're allowed to have other friends, right?*

There is a silence.

Flo sighs. "Sure, Khad. Of course we are. It's no big deal. We can handle a new person at the table, no problem. Right, Sumi?"

But as Rachel sits back down with a glass of iced Milo, Sumi says nothing at all. Not one word.

Rachel

"Hi," I say when I get there with the Milo I never intended to buy. The canteen aunty filled the cup too sloppily; Milo drips down one side, making my hands sticky, uncomfortable. "I'm back," I say awkwardly, as if it isn't obvious.

"Hooray," the girl named Sumi mutters under her breath, and I can feel a knot in my chest.

I am trying for normalcy, trying to forget the strange ordeal from earlier, trying to remember how to be a person. I sit and open my container. Kak Tini has packed me egg sandwiches. Will the smell of eggs annoy anyone? Will I make a mess and spill egg all over myself? Across from me Khadijah and Flo are eating from the same pack of nasi lemak, and Sumi is eating a piece of the canteen's famous fried chicken, still steaming in its little plastic bag.

"Are you not that hungry?" I ask Khadijah, who stares at me. Right. She doesn't talk. I point at the packet, being sure to angle myself so she doesn't see my wrist. "You're sharing the nasi lemak?"

"Oh." Flo laughs. "I love nasi lemak, but spicy stuff does

baaaaad things to my tummy, so Khad eats all the sambal and the pedas parts, and I eat everything else."

"Oh." I smile, a small little smile. There is something so comfortable about it, two friends eating out of the same pack. I can't help the little pinch of envy I feel somewhere in my belly. "Okay."

I take a bite out of my egg sandwich. I wonder if it would be weird to ask anyone else if they want some. Is that what people do? I wish I didn't feel so awkward. I wish I didn't feel like the episode from earlier clings to my skin, like I am tainted by my hauntings. Like everyone can see that something is wrong with me, that I'm a freak, a weirdo.

"Sumi, on the other hand," Flo continues, "doesn't share her food at all. Not even if you ask nicely. Not even if you're starving."

"I'm a growing girl." Sumi shrugs, taking another bite of her chicken. "And you, madam, are in no danger of starving."

"You sound like you've been friends for a long time," I say, nibbling at my bread. *Save us,* a voice whispers in my ear. *Small bites, Rachel, and don't look at the shadows. Don't notice how oddly they move.*

"Since primary school," Sumi says.

"Too long," Flo says at almost the same time.

Sumi sets down her chicken and leans her chin on one hand to stare directly at me. "And how about you?" she asks. "How long have you been friends with Khad?"

It feels like the air around us suddenly changes. I put down my sandwich and will my fingers to stop trembling. "We've only been talking for a little while," I say quietly.

Khadijah shoots Sumi a warning glance.

"I'm being nice, what," Sumi tells her. "I'm just making conversation. Getting to know your friend." She turns back to me. "So what is it you two talk about?"

My throat suddenly feels really dry. "Just . . . stuff. All kinds of things."

"The screaming?" she asks. Her eyes are so sharp; it's like she's trying to look right into my brain to see my thoughts for herself.

"Sure," I say. "That."

"That's great," Flo says quickly. "It's nice that you have things in common. You'll have to forgive us if we act a bit weird, Rachel. It's just been so long since we added anyone new to the group—"

"We're not adding anyone new, though, right?" Sumi cuts in, then takes a sip from her water bottle. Its contents must be cold; it leaves a perfect circle of moisture on the table. "That's what Khad said. 'I'm not inviting her to the gang. One meal does not a gang invite make.'" The last sentences have a mocking lilt to them. I wonder if it's me she's making fun of.

Flo frowns at Sumi, and Khadijah turns red. "Rachel, that's not what she meant," Flo says.

"It's okay," I say, standing up quickly, fumbling to close the lid on my food container. "It's almost time for the bell anyway. I should go. Prefect stuff."

I just want to get away.

At home later I mull this interaction over and over again in my head. I didn't like the way it made me feel, obviously. Or how Khadijah had put me in such an impossible situation. Not telling her friends, not telling me that she doesn't even talk. But there was something oddly comforting about it all the same. *They care about her,* the Mother in my head tells me. *They care about her in a way that nobody has ever cared about you.*

Mother means it as an insult, as a way to hurt me, but I smile because what she says is true. It was nice to be around a relationship so non-transactional, so clearly based on love and companionship and camaraderie. Even the bits that made me feel bad or small—I could see that those came from concern and jealousy, the kind of jealousy you can feel only if you really care about a person.

I'm not sure anybody has ever felt that jealousy about me. I imagine myself becoming one of them, one of the gang. Khadijah—no, what did her friends call her?—Khad, Sumi, Flo, Rachel. A foursome. We'd have inside jokes and whispered conversations that nobody else would be allowed to hear; we'd exchange secrets and fight each other's battles. They'd help me figure out what "save us" means, put ointment on my sore wrists. I think of one packet of nasi lemak shared between two people and wonder at the intimacy of it all.

My phone vibrates. Khadijah—Khad—she must have sent this as soon as she got home.

~Khad
That wasn't so bad, was it.

It's not a question. *Typical Khad,* I think, as if I'm already one of the gang.

> **~Rachel Lian**
> I've had warmer welcomes.

~Khad
Where? Antarctica?

I snort.

> **~Rachel Lian**
> Don't worry about it. I'm fine.

~Khad
Are you sure?
Was there something else wrong today?
Besides my friends

There's a long pause, and then messages start coming in one after another, as if she finally worked up the courage to let it all out.

~Khad
I know it's our first time meeting each other
I should have mentioned the no talking
thing
I know it's weird
I'm sorry

I set the phone down and inhale sharply. I'm not used to receiving apologies, and I'm not sure how to respond.

It's a solid minute before I pick up my phone again and start
to type.

> **~Rachel Lian**
> I can deal with weirdness
> I've got some of my own that I'm not
> sure I'm handling half as well

~Khad
Like what?

I chew on my hangnail before I type it out.

> **~Rachel Lian**
>
> I've been having these nightmares.

~Khad
All of us are having them. You're not alone.

> **~Rachel Lian**
> I don't think anyone else is having them
> quite the way I am.

I pause and stare out the window for a long time, trying to
find the right words, the strength to type them out.

> **~Rachel Lian**
> I was in solo acting. You know, for the
> forensics tournament? I signed up, and

I started practicing. And it was cool at
first, becoming this character.
But it got weird

~Khad

What do you mean?

~Rachel Lian

I mean
I mean that I didn't just start acting as
her. I started . . . becoming her
Or she started becoming me
Taking over
Saying things I would never say
I thought it was the stress. Trying to
juggle everything, you know? I told
myself I'd quit solo acting, that I'd stop
giving her access to me
I don't know what to do.
She keeps telling me to "save us."
I just want her to leave me alone.

~Khad

Save who?

~Rachel Lian

I DON'T KNOW.

~Khad

Then why don't we find out?

I bite my lip hard and taste blood on my tongue.

~Rachel Lian

What if that just makes her angry?

It used to be just at school. But now she follows me home too. And she's getting bolder with her moves

I see her everywhere. In my dreams. In every reflection. White ribbons and pink lipstick

A longer pause this time. *Khadijah is typing . . .* the message at the top of my WhatsApp reads. Then the app message goes away. Then appears again.

Khad

What does that mean? White ribbons and pink lipstick?

I blink.

~Rachel Lian

It's what she makes me wear. What she likes, I guess

White ribbons in my hair, and bright pink lipstick

I know it doesn't really make sense, but I guess nightmares don't have to have any rhyme or reason

Hello??

Are you still there??

I knew it. I knew I shouldn't have said anything.

~Rachel Lian

I bet you think I'm crazy now

~Khad

I don't think you're crazy

I think I have to show you something

TUESDAY
26 DAYS AFTER

Khadijah

I need to help her. I need to help Rachel Lian.

Part of it is that I recognize myself in her. The nightmares. The burden of seeing monsters everywhere. The haunted look in her eyes. There's a special trick your mind plays on you when you've been through horrors. It trains you to watch out for them. To see them lurking in the shadows. It thinks it protects you by giving you this power. It doesn't realize how much this costs you.

Rachel, I know, is bearing this cost now. Only, I am not sure she can. I can see the cracks she's trying to hide, the ways she is breaking.

And maybe I am the only one who can help her.

But there is another, larger part to this story. The part that made me sit bolt upright last night. Full-on Eminem style: palms sweaty, knees weak, arms heavy. I didn't vomit, but I felt it rising in my throat. Because as soon as she said it, as soon as I read about white ribbons and pink lipstick, I thought, *Julianna Chin.*

Is that what I have been missing? Is it St. Bernadette's who is hunting screamers, or is it Julianna?

The thought makes me breathless. I have to sit down. This whole time I've assumed Julianna is still alive somewhere. Taken. But what if she isn't? What if she's dead?

I take in air in quick, shallow gulps. My chest heaves up and down, up and down. What if this is her ghost, or spirit, whatever you want to call it? And if it's her, what does she want? Why is she doing this?

When will she stop?

I know I sound like I've lost my mind. I know. I try to tell myself to calm down. To be rational.

But I can't get Julianna Chin out of my mind.

I have to talk to Rachel. I have to show her everything I know.

After school Rachel takes me to a secret spot. A quiet corner behind the library that I've never even noticed before.

I open my backpack and draw out the copy of *The Beacon* that I stole. I open it up to Julianna's class photo.

"What's this?" Rachel asks, face creased in confusion.

I point at Julianna's face. At the ribbons in Rachel's hair.

"I tried not to put them on this morning," she tells me through gritted teeth. "But she made me." Rachel still looks confused.

I flip over to the pictures from *The Wizard of Oz*. There she is onstage, lips bright pink, white ribbons tied in perfect bows.

It's her, I want to yell. *It's you.*

Rachel reaches out to touch the picture. Julianna's face is animated, her mouth open, her expression radiant. "Is that her?" she whispers.

I take out my notebook. Write furiously. *She was a screamer nine years ago. And then she disappeared.* I point straight at Rachel. Straight at her heart. And then I write, *And now I think she is you.*

She is trembling. "But why?"

I don't know. I guess we need to find out what she wants.

"We know what she wants." Rachel licks her dry lips. Takes a deep, steadying breath. As if she's trying to shore herself up. "She wants me to 'save us.' But I don't know from what." She bends over the page again. Studies the pictures as if she's trying to drink them in, commit them to memory. "She looks so happy," she says softly. "I get it, you know. That's how I felt too, when I was still acting. Before . . . everything."

Maybe that's why she chose you. Because you understood.

Rachel pauses, eyes glued to the pictures again. "Who is that?" She points at a figure hovering toward the very left of the picture. A man, watching from backstage, arms crossed. It's Julianna who's firmly in focus, so he's fuzzy and grainy. But he looks vaguely familiar.

"I know him," Rachel says, frowning. "I think that's Uncle."

Uncle? The same uncle who coaches us in debate?

"That's him," she says, nodding firmly. "That's definitely him. We've been practicing together for Community Day. I didn't know he's been around that long. But I guess he did mention he had a daughter here a while ago. And now his niece goes here or something."

I flip the page to the behind-the-scenes photos. I've been so busy searching for Julianna that I didn't notice him at all. But among the shining, excited faces, there he is. Arm around one of the girls, mugging for the camera. There's a caption. *Sasha Alaina Shah, 4 Melati, backstage with her father. St. Bernadette's is so grateful to Datuk Shah for taking the time to help out the drama team this year!*

My fingers trace the words. Sasha Alaina Shah.

Sasha A?

Given our last conversation, I'm not sure Sasha A still wants to talk to me at all. But I have to try. I have to. I have to know what really happened.

For Aishah. For Julianna.

For me.

So the first thing I do when I get home is head straight for the laptop.

Khadijah Rahmat

Hey

I'm really sorry to bother you

I know you're probably still upset with me

Sasha A

Obviously.

What do u want

> **Khadijah Rahmat**
> I just had one question
> Were you in drama club with Julianna?

Sasha A
God you really won't let this go
Obsessing over a missing girl is really freak-
ing unhealthy okay
Seek HELP

> **Khadijah Rahmat**
> Please
> Could you just answer the question?
> I promise I won't bug you again
> I swear

Sasha A
You are SO weird
But yes, if u must know
My dad really wanted me to get involved.
He volunteered to coach the team
He loves acting and debate and all that stuff
That's why he was helping out I guess. Why
he's STILL helping out, even though he's not
technically a Bernie parent anymore

> **Khadijah Rahmat**
> Why didn't you tell me?

Sasha A
Unlike you my life does NOT revolve around

shit that happened YEARS ago

Now can you leave me and my family alone

God

You're lucky I didn't tell my dad about u

> **Khadijah Rahmat**
> What do you mean

Sasha A

You think living through ONE girl disappearing was easy?

He already felt guilty about Julianna. Now
we have to live through Fatihah too??

My fingers pause over the keyboard. *Guilty?*

> **Khadijah Rahmat**
> Why would he feel guilty?

Sasha A

He was the one who made us stay back for
rehearsals

Competition was coming up and we still
sucked

But Julianna wasn't there

Which was weird, because she wasn't usually late to things

> **Khadijah Rahmat**
> But how does that make what hap-
> pened his fault?

Sasha A
Well she wouldn't have been at school if he
hadn't made us stay, right?
He was so annoyed, he spent aaaaaages
looking all over school for her
And in the end it was all because she got
into trouble
She'd talked back to some teacher again.
Couldn't come to rehearsal until she got
done picking up trash and sweeping up
around Brede's House
But of course then she just . . . never came
at all

I stop. I can't keep typing; my fingers are shaking too much.

Sweeping. Julianna was sweeping the day she disappeared. I think of the harsh sweeping sounds that have been haunting me, and I'm suddenly cold.

Khadijah Rahmat
What teacher?

Sasha A
Can't remember his name, don't really give
a shit
It was one of those teachers that tries to be
cool and tells you to call him by an initial.
Like J or KZ or something. KZ! Your name is

Kamaruzzaman sir, u are fooling nobody
Now can you leave us alone?
We're done here

I reply, say I'm sorry. Tell her I'm going to stop, I really will. But my messages go unread. I'm fairly certain I've been blocked.

I lean back on the sofa, my head swimming. Mr. B. She had to be talking about Mr. B. I remember the way his demeanor changed when I brought up Julianna. How her mother told me the school had shut down any investigation. Closed its ranks tight, protected its lofty image. Was willing to close its eyes, to refuse truth. Was willing to sacrifice anything to maintain its reputation.

Even us.

Rachel

I am still thinking about Julianna, about missing girls, about white ribbons, about Khad and the screamers and how we can possibly save each other, when I walk into my room and see Mother sitting on my bed, crumpled pieces of paper spread out all around her—pages of my script, the quizzes and assignments with Cs and Ds that I hid all over my room, like a rat hoarding food. Books and clothes and random items are scattered all over the floor; my closet doors and desk drawers are open.

For a second I forget how to breathe.

"Rachel," Mother says, and I've never heard her voice sound like this before. "Rachel. Tell me what is happening."

"What do you mean?" I say. It is the silliest thing you can say in such circumstances. I know what she means. She's surrounded by what she means. But somehow I think that if I just ignore it, if I pretend it's not happening, then the world will adjust itself to fit.

Wrong, Rachel. Wrong, wrong, wrong, all wrong.

"What do I mean?" Mother asks me, her voice rising, her

tone incredulous. "You dare stand there and ask me what I mean? Look at this! Look at all this!" She takes a handful of papers and tosses them into the air. "What do you think I am talking about? What is this?" She points one indignant finger right at a page of my script as if she wants to stab it.

I stay quiet. She is doing that thing again, that thing where she asks questions when she already knows the answers. My answering her does nothing but add to my own suffering. Better to shut up. Better to wait and see where this is going.

"Acting, Rachel? Acting? We talked about this!" She gets up and begins to pace around the room, arms crossed tightly like she's trying to keep herself together. "Acting does nothing to help your future. Acting does nothing but distract you from your goals."

Your goals, I think. *Your goals, not mine.*

"Do you know how embarrassing it was?" she asks, her face tight. "Do you know how malu I was to pick up the call today and hear your teacher tell me how badly my daughter is doing at school? Top student, acting like this? Where am I supposed to put my face?"

I focus on the picture on my nightstand, a picture of Mother and me after my first piano recital. I am all dimpled smile and contentment, knowing that I did well, that I made her proud. I try to ignore the way her voice shakes and cracks.

"I already stopped," I say, my voice small. "I already quit."

"As you should. At least you still have that much sense." Mother is so angry, her nostrils are flared all the way out. "I don't know where you get this from, Rachel. The lying, the deceit. After everything I have done for you." She snorts. "Sometimes you are your father's daughter, one hundred percent."

And she stalks out of the room, leaving me to stare at the mess and wonder how I got here.

I don't know how long I stay here, on my knees, surrounded by the debris of my life. I don't think about Mother or her anger, about being my father's daughter. I hold the pages of my script, crumpled and torn, and I think about her, the her that I was onstage, bold and open and honest in her pink lipstick. My chest aches.

Eventually I stand up. The shadows are long now; it is almost night. I walk out of my room slowly. There is banging and sizzling coming from the kitchen, where Kak Tini makes our dinner silently, without her usual happy humming. Mother is sitting on the sofa with her legs crossed, reading a magazine. I can tell from the way she flips the pages that she's still angry.

"Mother," I say quietly.

Flip, flip, flip, so hard, so deliberate, as if with the edge of each paper she could slice into my skin.

"Mother," I say again.

"Mmm." She is all tight-lipped, as if saying anything more will somehow make things even worse.

"Mother, I need to go to school," I say.

Her eyes dart up at me. Perhaps she was expecting me to say sorry? I don't know.

"I left a book there," I tell her. "My biology textbook. I need it to finish my homework. So I don't get into any more trouble." The girl with the pink lipstick is the one who moves my lips, and I want to tell my mother so, but the girl holds me tightly so that I can't. I can only watch.

Mother frowns. "Pakcik Zakaria has already gone home," she says stiffly.

"I know." I look down at my toes. "Could you please drive me?" the girl with the pink lipstick asks.

Mother lets out a loud, noisy sigh. "So on top of everything else, you are careless now as well." She gets up and begins to gather her things, grabs the car keys from the hook on the wall. "Tini, saya keluar sekejap!" she yells.

Kak Tini yells back, "Okay, Puan!"

In the car I sit with my hands folded together, trying not to take up space, trying not to make even a single sound. My mother drives leaning forward, eyes on the road. Every once in a while she mutters something about "ungrateful daughters" and "all my sacrifices."

When we get to the school, Pakcik Saiful stares at us, confused.

"I forgot my book," I tell him as I exit the car. The shadows are longer still now; the day has been almost completely swallowed by night. He glances at my mother, who sits behind the wheel looking straight ahead of her, as if looking at me or him or St. Bernadette's disgusts her.

"Okay," he says, shrugging. "But hurry up. School is almost

empty already. Classes finished fifteen minutes ago."

I glance down at my watch. It is exactly seven p.m. "Okay," I say.

She wants me to hurry, the girl with the pink lips and the white ribbons. I can feel her urgency. But I walk slowly through St. Bernadette's. I let my feet take their time. I did leave my biology textbook here, I really did, and she knows it. But something in my chest also just aches to be here, on these grounds, where I feel safe. Where I feel even the smallest sense of belonging.

My head hurts. *I should have slept more,* I think. We should have tried harder, Khad and I, to figure this all out.

From somewhere in the school I hear the sound of sweeping. The cleaners, still so hard at work. Mother used to point at cleaners in malls, tell me, "You see, girl? You see? If you don't work hard, you'll end up like them." Is that bad? I ended up like me instead, and is that really better? "Your father's daughter," Mother said. What does that mean? What does that mean, anyway?

I turn the corner, and suddenly he's there, a familiar face, a familiar voice calling my name.

"Hey, Rachel, are you okay? What's wrong? What are you doing here?"

I stare at him, unblinking, uncomprehending, and when he reaches out a hand to grab my arm, I pull away and I run, and I run, and I run, and once again I don't know why I'm running or where I'm running to, but I do it anyway, until my feet finally slow down and my steps become more purposeful, more measured. I am here, here at St. Bernadette's where I belong, and even if I don't know what I'm doing, my feet do.

Sweep, sweep, sweep, sweep, sweep. I let my feet walk along to the rhythm. It's like a dance. I've never been good at dancing. Maybe Flo could teach me. Maybe Khad and I could learn together. *Khad,* I think. Khad, the possibility of making my first real friend. Khad is probably wondering right now why I am not replying to her messages. Mother would say, *You don't need friends to succeed, Rachel.* Mother would say, *The only person you can depend on is yourself.* Does Mother mean I cannot depend on her, too? Something is making us all disappear. Does Mother want me to disappear? Would she care if I did?

My feet stop. I didn't tell them to. Did she tell them to? The girl? Julianna? I look up, and I'm not in my classroom at all, not even close. I'm in front of Brede's House again. There is a cleaner there, bent over her broom, sweep, sweep, sweep, sweeping up the leaves that fall from the frangipani trees. My head hurts. In the big stained-glass window there are shadows moving, if you look hard enough. I raise my hand and wave. Why not? Why not, right?

Only, it looks like the shadows wave back. Is that her? Is that Julianna? Am I Julianna? Or am I Rachel, Rachel Lian, waving at my own death?

My head hurts. I let myself fall. I think it hurts my knees. I'm not sure. Sweep, sweep, sweep, sweep, sweep. *I am so tired,* I think, *so tired of everything.* The sweeping comes closer. My head hurts. Mother would say, *Get up, Rachel, right now.*

Mother would say, *You are not a child. Why are you acting like one?* Mother would say, *The ground is dirty. You are getting dirt all over your pinafore. What is wrong with you?* Mother would say . . .

Mother would say . . .

The sweeping stops. I look up. The sweeper is looking at me, and it's the girl, it's Julianna, and it isn't. Her eyes are all black. At first I think her face is covered in wrinkles, and then I realize that the lines aren't wrinkles; they're cracks, creeping in from all sides of her face, thin little lines branching across her pale, pale skin. Within the white of her hair there are ribbons, woven in and out, trailing in the breeze.

"I'm so tired," I whisper.

And in answer the sweeper opens her mouth, and I think she's going to scream, but she doesn't. She just keeps opening it, wider and wider and wider, until she swallows me up.

Until everything is black.

~Khad

Hey are you there?
I think I figured out something import-
ant. Something big
I wanted to tell you
Like NEED to tell you
Are you okay?
Hello?
I hope you're resting or something.
Send me a text when you get this.
Hey, I'm really worried now. Can you call
me or something? Anything?
Rachel?
Rachel?

Khadijah

She's gone.

I looked for her this morning, dying to tell her what I've discovered, what connections I've made. I want to talk to her about Julianna, about Mr. B. I walked in step with Sumi and Flo up the hill toward St. Bernadette's. Rachel never answered a single one of my messages. But I thought surely she'd be here. Surely she'd be here.

But she isn't. She wasn't at the gate waiting for us. She isn't in the assembly hall. She isn't backstage with the other prefects.

"Can I help you?" said Jane in her snottiest voice, but I ignored her.

Sumi and Flo know exactly who I'm looking for. And for once I don't feel them radiating judgment. They just help. They ask around. They use their voices where I cannot use mine.

"I'm sure she's around somewhere," Flo says, looping her arm through mine. "Don't worry, she'll turn up."

"Maybe she's sick," Sumi says. "Or maybe she didn't feel like going to school today. There's been a lot going on."

I nod. My stomach feels heavy with worry.

Then it's time for the announcements. Mrs. Beatrice comes to the mic. And she says the thing I never wanted to hear her say. "It is with deepest regret that I must announce another disappearance among our students," she says. The hall immediately breaks out in frantic whispers. I feel my heart lodge itself in my throat. It's suddenly hard to breathe. "If anybody has any information on the whereabouts of Rachel Lian . . ."

The room suddenly spins. The black shadow pulses on the edge of my vision like it's mocking me.

Rachel Lian. Rachel. They took Rachel.

I was supposed to be her buddy.

I was supposed to protect her. But I didn't. And now she's one of them, one of the missing screamers. I didn't protect her. I failed. And now she's gone.

I don't realize I'm keeling over until Sumi reaches out to catch me. "It's okay, Khad," she whispers. "I've got you. It's okay."

But it's not.

They call my mother. Talk in hushed whispers outside the sickroom about something "triggering" my trauma. I didn't want to be a screamer before this, but now all I want to do is scream. Sumi and Flo sit with me, each holding one of my hands. The teachers tell them to go back to class, but they refuse. At some point Aishah turns up. Since there are no more hands to hold, she just sits with us quietly, waiting for Mak to come and bring us home.

I start to cry in the car. I cannot seem to stop. Not even

when we get home and they have to help me inside because the tears turn everything into a blur. Mak comes and sits beside me on the sofa, rubbing slow circles on my back.

"It's okay, sayang," she says. "Everything is going to be okay." She doesn't ask me any questions. Between sobs I am grateful for this small mercy. I have no answers, no answers for anyone.

"Thank you," I whisper, and for a moment her hand stills. Then she continues, holding me just a little closer than before.

"You're welcome," she whispers back. It feels just right, somehow.

When night comes, I curl up on the sofa like I always do. Aishah comes to sleep on the floor beside me, and holds my hand. She tries to stay awake so that I will fall asleep first. But this has never worked. Eventually her breaths are deep and even, and her eyes are closed.

I am not crying anymore. And once the tears have dried up, all that is left is rage.

Rachel Lian is missing, and I am the angriest I have ever been.

The sickroom is next to the admin office. I heard them talking. Her mother told the school that Rachel asked to go back to St. Bernadette's last night. Rachel's mother waited and waited in the idling car, and Rachel never came out. The mother walked in and searched the school with Pakcik Saiful. Rachel was nowhere to be found. Nowhere at all.

I think of St. Bernadette's, standing silent and watchful on the hill. I think of the dark shadows that flicker behind its swooping arches.

What have you done? Are you sated yet?

My anger makes me restless. As Aishah snores gently, I pick up my phone. Open WhatsApp and scroll through the screamers group. I've ignored it for the past couple of days; it's full of messages I haven't seen. The latest ones are messages about Rachel. About how scared they are, about what could possibly be happening and who could be taking all these girls. Our friends.

~NN
I don't know what to do.

~Amalina Izzati
U all ok?

~Selena.Marie
I'm anxious all the time now, and it feels like nobody is doing anything to help us.

~FazNFurious
What do we do? Stay home? Wait until this is all over?

~NN
How can we know when it's over?

~Ranjeetha P
Are they going to get those girls back?

I scroll upward past all of these, my chest too tight to read anything about Rachel.

And then I pause. And look closer.

And I read and read, long into the night.

Khadijah

Not all the answers are the same.

Some people talk about going to see Mr. B in the counseling room. Or seeing him before they screamed. Some people insist they never crossed paths with him at all. Some remember nothing. But some talk of the shade of a girl who lurked in reflections. A girl with pink lips and white ribbons in her hair. And all of them talk about two things: a dark shadow that breathed, and a sound that wouldn't stop, a sound that grew and grew until it set their teeth on edge. I thought it was going to drive me insane, one girl typed. I felt like it was going to make me claw my face off.

The sound of sweeping.

I think about this all the way to school in the back of Mak's car. She offered to let us stay home.

"I won't force you to," she said gently. "But you can, if you want. If it would make you feel better. It would certainly make *me* feel better."

I wish I could grant her this small relief. But I have to face this. "Save us," the girl told Rachel. If Rachel isn't here, then I have to be the one to save us all.

If not me, who else?

Julianna disappeared sweeping. We all heard sweeping before we screamed. If I find the sweeping, if I figure out where it's coming from, will I be able to find out what happened? Will I find Rachel? Find Fatihah and Lavinia? Find Julianna herself? Or will I find the shadow, the one that Fatihah called jinn, jembalang, hantu? Aishah reaches out to squeeze my hand. I stare at her hand as if I'm trying to memorize its contours. If I don't find out what's happening, will Aishah disappear too?

Sumi and Flo are waiting for us at the school gates. They greet me with open arms and worried expressions.

"You okay?" Sumi asks, uncharacteristically gentle. I nod. "I'm sorry I was being so . . . you know." She runs a hand through her curls, all embarrassed. "Weird, I guess. Overprotective. Jealous." She can barely look at me. I know how hard it is for her to say these words. I reach out a hand, and she takes it.

Flo clears her throat. "Stop it, you two," she says. "If you start crying right here in public, I'm going to pretend I don't know either one of you."

"But what will you do without any friends?" Sumi asks. Flo reaches over to smack the back of her head lightly. "Ow!"

"Not the time, Sumitra."

"Sorry, sorry." Sumi subsides, shamefaced. "I know we shouldn't be joking around right now." She takes a deep breath. "Call it a coping mechanism. I'm scared too, you know? Scared for Rachel, scared for Khad. Scared for all of us."

"And that's okay," Flo says softly. "It's okay to be scared. We can be scared together." She leans her head on my shoulder. "You don't have to talk, Khad. But if you want to, we'll listen."

In answer I lean my head on hers and inhale the apple scent of her shampoo. "I love you guys," I say softly. It only takes a second for them to engulf me in their arms.

During English I raise my hand in the middle of class.

"Yes, Khadijah?" Puan Ramlah asks. Then, "Bathroom?" My teachers have gotten used to filling in my blanks. I nod. "All right. Go, then."

I walk out the door and down the stairs. Trying to act like I'm actually going to the bathroom. Trying to walk like a girl who just needs to go pee. But as soon as I'm outside, my anger propels me forward. Gives me purpose. Sharpens my vision so that I can see exactly what I need to do.

I let it carry me onward, all the way to a closed door.

I take a deep breath. Then I knock.

"Enter," a voice says, and I do.

The last time I was here, I was panicking, voiceless, painted into a corner and desperate for escape. This time I look directly at the occupant of the room. And I open my mouth. And I speak.

"Tell me what happened to Julianna Chin, Mrs. Beatrice."

She looks up then. "Excuse me?" Her voice is calm, and cool, and betrays nothing. It only makes me angrier.

"I know you know something about what happened to her. What's happening to all the missing girls." I thought it would be harder to speak than this. I thought I would be more scared. But anger pushes the words out of me, gives them shape and force and depth.

"That," Mrs. Beatrice says, "is very presumptuous of you, Khadijah."

"What happened to them?"

"What happens to any girl who runs away?" Mrs. Beatrice shrugs. "How can I possibly know that?"

I fight for some measure of calm. For the ability to breathe, to articulate. I know emotion makes me easy to dismiss. I've been down this road before. "You refused to work with Julianna's mother. To help her figure out how her own daughter disappeared. You wouldn't let anyone from the school even talk to her."

"I stopped a woman driven mad by grief and sadness over her daughter's disappearance from harassing our teachers, our staff, and our students," Mrs. Beatrice corrects me. "I prevented her from sullying the school's reputation, and her own."

"It is your job to protect us!" I explode. "Not the school, not its reputation. Us."

She simply looks at me, fingers steepled beneath her chin. When she finally speaks, her words are laced with steel. "It is my job to make sure St. Bernadette's girls succeed out there in the real world. And I am very good at it."

"There is no success for girls who disappear."

"And how sad it is for them and their families," Mrs. Beatrice says smoothly. "But as headmistress it is my duty to ensure the welfare of all the girls who remain. As we have been doing."

I am trembling now. So desperate for her to understand. So desperate to crack this perfect, polished veneer that covers up whoever she is beneath. "But the missing girls aren't just something you can set aside and forget about!" I slam my fist onto her table. "Julianna is a person. Rachel is a person. All the girls are! They're loved and missed and cherished and wanted." I rub my aching forehead, knocking my hijab askew. "We shouldn't have to pay for St. Bernadette's reputation with our bodies," I tell her. "We're worth more than that. So much more."

Mrs. Beatrice rises to her feet. Pushes her chair back. Rests her hands on the opposite corners of her desk. "I will only say this once, and I expect you to listen," she says, so low that I have to lean forward to hear her. "A girl's body is already a commodity. That has nothing to do with me, or with St. Bernadette's; that is simply the truth. You might not see it now, but as soon as you step out of this bubble you live in, this world where you're safe and protected, you will see it, and you will understand. This is the system we are rooted in. But what we can do, and do well here, is to make it so our girls are superlative. Best, brightest, smartest, shiniest. Polish you up so that your bodies have value. So that you have leverage. What you are worth? Is what we determine you are worth, right here at this school." She straightens up. Tugs at the jacket of her lilac suit so that it smooths out the wrinkles. "There is no girl like a St. Bernadette's girl. That is your armor, your calling card, your currency. And that, I will do anything to protect." She looks at me, her eyes hard. Then she sits down and turns her attention back to her work. "It's been a long time since we've heard you speak, Khadijah. I do hope this is not the kind of conversation you mean to waste your precious words on from now on."

I recognize a dismissal when I hear it. And there's nothing else I can do but turn and leave.

I walk outside the building and stand there for a long time. I shut my eyes. Take deep breaths. Try to calm the roiling in my chest. Try not to let my rage carry me into depths beyond my capabilities. This anger is so familiar to me; I know too well how it can burn me if I let it.

And then my whole body stills.

Because I hear it, right there, ever so faintly.

Sweep, sweep, sweep.

I whirl around. Where is it coming from? Where is the sound coming from? I start to run, chasing the sweeping that lingers right on the edge of my hearing. Just beyond reach. Here? Or here? The closer I get, the more desperate I get, the louder it becomes.

It's calling me. It wants me to find it.

There must be a connection, I think feverishly as I scan every corner of the school. Something that ties the sweeping to Mr. B, to the screamers. To Rachel. There must be a way to still save her. Save us all.

"Who is the sweeper?" I say out loud. "Who are you?"

Nobody answers. Girls and teachers look at me askance as I run past them. My eyes wild, my movements frantic, following the sound I know nobody else can hear, because this time it is meant for me. Only for me.

When my feet finally stop moving, I know before I even look up where they have taken me.

Brede's House.

And in the stained-glass window above, a shadow moves, as if it knows I'm here. As if it's been waiting for me all along.

The sweeping is loud now, so loud that it makes my head hurt. I can see the shadow clearly; it's reaching out for me from Brede's House, first in wisps and tendrils, then in thick waves billowing like smoke. Sweep, sweep, sweep, sweep. My head hurts so much. But even though the shadow makes it hard to see; even though the pain makes my eyes water until everything is a blur; even then, even still, I know I must face the beast. I take step after torturous step to the double doors of Brede's House.

When I lay my hands on the handles, they burn like they're branding their shapes into my skin.

Sweep, sweep, sweep, sweep, sweep. The darkness swirls all around me like a tornado; the pain is so intense now that it's hard for me to breathe.

I wrench the doors open with all my strength.

On the other side the sweeper awaits with her broom of twigs, the darkness circling her like a halo. Her face is Julianna's, round and pink-lipped, with ribbons in her hair; then it is mine, the me that I was before the incident, smiling and fresh-faced and tentative; then an old woman with a maze of wrinkles. She looks straight at me, and I gasp for air; her eyes are nothing but black all over, with not a speck of white to be seen.

She bares her teeth at me, all yellowing and cracked, and I don't know, I cannot tell if it's a grimace or a smile, or which I want it to be. Her broom never moves, but the sweeping is louder than ever, and I don't know how to explain it but it makes my brain itch, and it hurts, everything hurts, and I bite my lip so hard that I taste blood, because I know that if I don't, all I'll do is scream. And I don't . . . I don't want to . . .

"I don't want to scream anymore." I shout to be heard over the sweeping and the darkness and the pain slicing through my head like daggers. "And I don't want to not talk anymore. I don't want everyone else to decide what happens to us, to our voices, to our bodies. To tell us how to use them. Please, just give me my friends back. Give me myself back." My throat is sore and my voice is hoarse and everything hurts and, and, and

And the sweeper is just looking at me with those dark, dark eyes.

And then she smiles.

And she lunges.

And the darkness swallows me whole.

Khadijah

I open my eyes to darkness.

The inability to see anything kicks my fight-or-flight reflex into high gear. My heart starts pounding and pounding, as if it's fighting to get out of my chest. I have to take a few deep breaths to steady myself. *Don't panic, Khad. Calm down. You can figure this out.*

I take stock of my body, running through sections one by one, assessing for any damages. The pain in my head has receded to a dull ache, but nothing else seems to be hurt or broken.

"That's a relief," I say into the silence.

Silence.

I sit bolt upright. There is no more sweeping.

Where am I?

My eyes are adjusting now. It's not completely dark in here, I'm realizing. There are a couple of kerosene lamps, giving off a weak, warm light. I'm lying on some kind of raised platform—maybe a table?—in a long, narrow room. And all around me there are shapes, shapes I can't quite make out at first, but that slowly come into focus as my eyes grow accustomed to the dim light.

When I realize what they are, I almost want to throw up.

All around me are the girls.

The missing girls—Fatihah, Lavinia—with glassy eyes and gentle smiles on their faces, all staring straight at me. And right there at my feet, hands clasped, is Rachel.

"Rachel?" I whisper. The tremble in my voice betrays me. I want to grab her hand and run. But I don't even know where I am or what I'd be running away from.

"Hi, Khadijah," she says softly.

"Hi, Khadijah," the other girls echo.

"I'm so glad you're here," Rachel says, and I know she means it, I know she does, but there's something strange and dream-like about the way she's talking. About the way all of them are talking.

"Where's 'here'?" I ask.

She smiles. "The tunnels, of course."

I blink. *The tunnels? The tunnels are real?*

I swing my legs around to get off the table, and grab Rachel's hands. I search her face for any sign of . . . anything, really. Pain, or distress. Something that gives me some kind of clue to what's happening, what she's gone through. But all I see is that smile, serene and calm.

I shiver.

"Rachel, what's going on?" I ask her. "Are you okay? Is everyone here okay?" I scan their faces, but they just look at me, serene, silent. The girls we've been searching for and praying for and afraid for. They're here. They're really here. "What happened?"

Rachel's smile grows even wider. "What happened is that we were saved, Khadijah. What happened is that it kept us safe. Protected us, just like it always has."

I stare at her. "Who? Who is protecting us?"

"Don't you see? Don't you understand?" Rachel squeezes my hand. "Close your eyes, Khadijah. Can you feel it?"

I'm not sure what to expect, but I do as she asks.

All around me they begin to whisper, "Feel it, Khadijah. Feel it."

They sound like the breeze weaving through the frangipani leaves.

"What do you feel?" Rachel asks softly.

I focus, trying my best to understand, trying to feel what she wants me to feel.

And then I do. I am warm and cozy, as if I'm in a cocoon; I am drowsy and as content as a cat in a sunbeam; I am . . . I am . . .

I am safe.

I open my eyes. "What is this?" I whisper. "What is happening?"

"It keeps us safe," Fatihah says, her eyes gleaming in the dim light. "Don't you see?"

I look around at the girls, at their intense expressions, and then beyond to the walls of the room. For the first time I notice that they pulse slightly. As if they're alive.

I look back at Rachel, and understanding begins to dawn for the first time. "Is the thing protecting us . . . Is it . . ."

"St. Bernadette's." Rachel's expression is one of a proud mother when a child takes their first step all by themselves. "You see now, don't you?"

I shake my head, which still has the slightest hint of an ache blossoming in it, and sit back down on the table. "I'm not sure I do."

Rachel sits beside me and holds my hand. The other two girls just watch. Their smiles never leave their faces. "The school senses a danger to its girls," Rachel says. "It tried to help us, at first, by helping us to scream when he first started to come around. To raise the alarm. But when that didn't work, when the wolf still kept slipping in through the gates, the school had to remove some of us from the situation instead. The ones it knew were in more danger than the others. The ones the wolf had his eye on. And here we are."

"The wolf?" I frown. "Who is the wolf?"

The dreamlike atmosphere shifts. Everyone look unsure for the first time. When the silence breaks, it is Fatihah who breaks it. Her voice is hard, belligerent. "He is the villain. The one the school is protecting us from." Then, in a whisper, "He is a bad, bad man."

"Then we have to tell someone!" I whirl around, trying to look directly at each of them. Trying to make them see. But they're agitated now, their eyes restless, refusing to meet mine. "We have to stop him from doing this again. We have to protect them. The other girls."

"Why?" Fatihah flings back. "Nobody protected us. Nobody even listened."

"You can't stay here forever!"

"We can stay as long as St. Bernadette's lets us," she says, and for the first time I see her, really see this version of her. She's different here. She's calmer. More resolute. More edged with steel. "Out there, people don't believe in our stories, or our pain. They tell us we're imagining things. That we cause trouble. That we're . . . hysterical." Her mouth twists as she says the word, as if it tastes bitter on her tongue. "They'd rather believe in jinn, or jembalang, or hantu. Instead of . . . instead of . . ." She bites her lip.

"You can say it, Fatihah," Rachel says gently.

"Instead of real-life monsters," Fatihah spits out finally.

"What do you mean, real-life monsters?" I ask.

The girls turn somber, and I see them all exchanging looks. Fatihah stares down at the ground as if she might cry.

Rachel sighs. "It's him. The danger we're being protected from. The wolf within the walls."

"Mr. B?" I ask. It's hard to keep the tremor out of my voice.

"Mr. B?" Rachel raises an eyebrow at me. "No, not him. It's that man."

"Who?" I ask. "Who?"

Rachel puts out a hand to caress my cheek gently. So gently. "Datuk Shah," she says softly. "Uncle. It's Uncle."

The room spins slightly. The dreamy atmosphere is completely gone. The girls watch me, wide-eyed and serious. Uncle, so involved, so charming, so interested. Uncle, so eager to help coach us to victory. Uncle, so easy with his smile, with his deep voice.

"Yes," Fatihah says quietly. "Him. The PTA guy, the debate coach, the well-connected datuk." She pauses. "Uncle. My uncle."

And for just a moment the shadows seem to lean closer, as if to keep anything from getting to us.

"He's not a good man," Fatihah says quietly, her face now cast in shadow. "He touches me, you know. When nobody's around. He gets too close. He puts his hands where . . . nobody's hands should be." The girls hold out their own hands to her, as if they can erase her body's memory of the touches it never wanted. I close my eyes, trying to steel myself against the pain in her voice, the way it rips through my own memories. As she talks, I feel it all over again, that heavy weight on my body, the wet breath in my ear, the smell of cigarettes. His hands, where nobody's hands should be.

"Julianna?" I whisper.

The girls' faces turn somber. As if in agreement, as if they planned it, they turn.

And I see her.

She is nothing more than a skeleton. Bones picked clean. Flesh gnawed away by nature and time. There are no white ribbons, no lips to paint her beloved bright pink. But around her neck hangs a little silver heart. Just like in her newspaper picture.

Julianna Chin, who was here all along, in the tunnels that nobody ever discovered. Nobody, save for one man.

"He did it," Rachel says, and her voice is wet with tears. "He found her sweeping around Brede's House. His daughter had told him all the stories and rumors about tunnels. He figured out where they were. Brought her in here. And he had his way with her, and then he left her here to die."

"How?" I whisper. "How do you know?"

Lavinia lays a hand on my shoulder. Her expression is grim. "She told us so."

"Julianna?" I whisper.

"St. Bernadette's," Lavinia replies. "I can't explain how. I don't really understand it. But she showed us. I think she wanted us to not be afraid, to understand that she wanted to help us."

"I think," Rachel says, "that she just wanted to make sure Julianna was found. And I think it hurt her that Julianna had to wait for so long. That one of her girls was abused and alone."

The room will not stop spinning. I cannot help myself. I turn away and throw up, and the girls avert their eyes as if to give me space for my sorrow.

"That's why St. Bernadette's did what it did," Rachel continues, her voice nearly a whisper now. "Why she took us. Why the warnings were always the same. Those very first screams . . . We were her canaries."

"Canaries?"

"In the old days, miners brought canaries with them into coal mines. Canaries are sensitive. When the air got even the slightest bit toxic, the birds would drop right off their perches, and the miners would know it was dangerous, that they had to get out and save themselves." Rachel gestures to the girls. "We—and the other screamers—were more sensitive, easier for her to get a hold of, to make us scream."

"The leaves?" I ask. "The sweeping?"

"She wanted us to make that connection to Julianna," Lavinia says softly. "She wanted someone to remember."

"He laid low, after that. After Julianna." Fatihah swallows hard before she continues. "Pak Su. Uncle. Whatever you call him. He was younger, impulsive. I guess he was worried he'd get caught. But they never did figure out it was him. I guess by the time I came along, by the time I presented an opportunity, he thought he was safe, that he could get away with anything. He got brave." The words twist her mouth into a sneer.

"I tried to tell my parents," she says, continuing. "Of course. You should tell your parents, right? That's what they tell you. Tell your parents. So I did. And they . . . they laughed. They said I was overtired. Imagining things. I wanted to talk to the counselor at my old school. They found out. Transferred me here. Said I was . . . I was having a breakdown. 'Your Pak Su has done so much for us,' they said. 'He's rich. Successful. This big shot with his big car. He pulled the strings so you could come here. To this amazing school. Why must you be so ungrateful? You're imagining it. Or you misunderstood. Or you're a liar.'" The more agitated she gets, the faster and shorter her sentences, like a piano in staccato mode. "My mother, that's her baby brother. Nobody can convince her he's bad. But he is. He's a bad, bad man." Fatihah stops. Her chest heaves up and down, up and down. "I want to stay here," she whispers. "Call me a coward. I don't care. I want to stay. Just let me stay."

It takes me a long time to pull myself out of my own remembered hell, but when I do, I get down from the table and put my arm around Fatihah's shoulder. "Listen," I tell her. "Listen to me. I know what you're going through, okay? I'm right there with you. It happened to me too. We're the same, you and me." Fatihah's eyes widen, and I press on. "Only, I got lucky. When I talked, people listened. They believed me. I'm so, so sorry they didn't believe you. I'm so sorry the people who were supposed to protect you failed to do that. But that's their failure, not yours."

I take in a deep, ragged breath. "This terrible thing was done to you. But that's just it. It was done to you. Not because of you. None of this is your fault, do you hear me? None of it. Not yours and not mine." I pause, searching for the right words. "But I am going to tell you this, and I want you to hear it, okay? Are you listening?"

She nods. I bend low so I can see her, really see her.

"You are not a coward," I tell her firmly. "You went through something horrific, something no kid should ever have to go through. And you're here. Still standing. Surviving through it all. Do you know how much strength that takes? Isn't that amazing?" I lean in and whisper this, just for her, "You're not a coward, Fatihah. You're a miracle. Everyone who survives is."

When I pull back, her face is streaked with tears. But she's smiling. "Thank you," she whispers back.

"You're welcome." I straighten up and sigh. "St. Bernadette's tried to warn us, and then it tried to keep us hidden so the danger wouldn't find us. But I don't want to hide. Hiding makes it seem like I'm the one who did something wrong, and I didn't. None of us did."

Lavinia shifts on her feet; Fatihah squares her shoulders; Rachel bites her lip. The gentle smiles, the blank expressions—they're gone now. It's as if they're waking up, all three of them.

"You don't have to come with me," I say quietly. "You can stay if you want, okay? It's your body, your own person, your choice to make. And nobody gets to tell you if it's the wrong or right one, because they don't get to decide that for you. But my choice is to get out there and face him. To use my voice again." I can feel tears prickling behind my eyes, ready to fall. "I haven't done that in a long time," I say. "And I hope there are some of you who can help me, because I know it's going to be hard. But if you can't, that's okay. It really is. I'll do it anyway. I'll do it for us. For all of us."

There is a snort, and it's so loud and so out of place in this emotionally charged moment that I whip around, to see Rachel, arms crossed, a smirk on her face.

"Did you just . . . snort at me?" I ask her.

"Ya." She smiles. "I appreciate the dramatic speech and everything, but did you really think we were going to let you do this on your own? Mangkuk."

I let slip an incredulous laugh. I can't help it. "What?"

"It's okay if not all of us want to get out there," she says. "That part I agree with. But I'm going to stand with you. You don't have to face him alone. Nobody should have to do that."

"Me too." Lavinia folds her arms and nods firmly. "Safety in numbers, what."

Only Fatihah stays silent.

Around us the walls continue to pulse gently, as if St. Bernadette's itself is listening to us.

I let out a breath. "Okay, then," I say. "Okay. If you want to come with me, let's go. Fatihah can stay here, we—"

"I'm coming too."

Fatihah straightens up to look at us. There are still tracks on her cheeks from the tears that streamed down her face just moments ago; she wipes them away with the sleeve of her baju kurung. There's a determination on her face that I haven't seen before. "I'm coming too," she says again, louder this time.

I smile at her. "All right," I say. "Then let's go."

I reach out my hand, and she takes it. And we make our way out of the tunnels, to the world above. St. Bernadette's opens the door, and together we step out to face the wolf.

Khadijah

We cluster in front of Brede's House, the girls and I, blinking at the sudden rush of sunlight. Beyond the cluster of trees and the slope that separates us from the rest of St. Bernadette's, I can hear the sounds of panicked searching.

They're searching for me, I realize. The last of the screamers. The last of the disappearing girls.

I should let them know. Yell out that we're here, all of us, safe and sound.

But I don't speak. None of us do.

We are waiting. We know St. Bernadette's will bring him to us.

And eventually he comes.

I've been banking on this. I knew he'd be here. I've been missing for hours at this point, and he was due to come to the school for debate practice. It would make sense for him to join the search, have himself look like a good guy. Concerned and earnest, good old Uncle, who is always here for the girls.

Beside me Fatihah stiffens, and I grab her hand in mine.

St. Bernadette's tried to give us a voice when we couldn't use our own. It tried to warn us, to warn everybody. But screams alone won't do the job.

I'm going to have to speak.

"Fatihah!" Uncle walks up to her, to us all, his arms open as wide as his smile. "Girls! Alhamdulillah! Your parents will be so happy. We've all been so worried—"

Fatihah takes a step back from him, and we girls circle her protectively.

Uncle's smile falters. "Fatihah? It's Pak Su. Let me take you home. Your parents have been suffering so much—"

I swallow hard. And find my voice. "What about her suffering?" I ask.

He frowns. "Her suffering?"

"You know." I force myself to look him straight in the eye, my heart pounding. "From everything that's happened to her. Everything you did to her. To Julianna. Everything you would have done to us."

"Julianna? Who is that?" His eyes harden. "And what exactly did my niece say that I did to her?"

I glance at Fatihah, but her head is bowed and she's trembling. I can't make her say it. I can't do that to her. "You know," I tell him again. "You know what you did."

Uncle's entire demeanor transforms; he's suddenly somber and sympathetic and warm as he shakes his head sorrowfully. "She's clearly gone through some kind of trauma," he says, and somehow everything about his voice manages to convey sincere concern. "You all have. We should get you home safe to your parents. You're just young girls, after all."

He's so good at this, so good at bending the world to his words, and I want to vomit. I want to retch at the idea that this works. This works. Because of course it does. One charming, worldly, influential man against a bunch of hysterical teens. Who would you believe?

You're just young girls, after all.

Everything we've gone through, and this is it?

This is what we've been reduced to?

"I *have* gone through some kind of trauma."

Everyone stops and stares, including me. Because it's not me talking.

It's Fatihah, hands clenched into fists, face bright red, trembling so hard that it takes a couple of other girls to shore her up. But it's Fatihah, in all her incandescent rage and glory.

"I have gone through some kind of trauma," she says again. "But it's not what you think. It's the trauma of what you did to me. My own uncle! It's the trauma of having you wandering around this school, with me knowing what you did, what you could be doing to other girls. Knowing that me staying quiet was putting them in danger. Hating myself, but not knowing what to do when nobody would believe me." She's talking fast now, almost spitting out the words, so eager to get them out that it's like they've just been waiting. "But I'm done. I'm done staying quiet, and I'm done hiding. I'm not ashamed." She tilts her head back in a gesture of defiance. "I'm not ashamed, do you hear me? I didn't do anything wrong. The only one who should feel any shame or guilt here is you."

There is silence.

Then Uncle laughs, loud and hearty, a laugh designed to break the tension and get people on his side. "Fatihah, sayang, you don't know what you're talking about," he says, ever the fond uncle, eyes twinkling as if he's saying, *Come now, everyone, let's just play along with the child.* "You're overtired and over-stressed," he says. "I'll talk to your parents. We'll find you a good psychiatrist, get you the help you need. Get you better."

"I don't need a psychiatrist," Fatihah bites out, her chest heaving up and down, up and down, up and down. "I need you to stay away from me and my family and this school. I need you locked up so you're never near another young girl again. That's what I need." I'm so proud of her, I think my heart may actually burst.

Uncle smiles at her, solicitous, sympathetic. "Now, Fatihah," he says. "Calm down. You're getting quite hysterical."

Hysterical.

That man used the same word. My stepfather. "Control your daughter. She's hysterical. She's out of her mind. She doesn't know what she's saying. She's a liar."

I am done being silent. "That's what they say to make sure nobody listens to us," I spit out. "Us *young girls.* Men like you use every trick you've got to make sure nobody believes us. But I don't care what you say, or what people believe. It doesn't matter. What matters is what I know to be true. What we"—I gesture to the girls behind me—"know to be true."

"And what is that?" he says. In the golden light of late afternoon, his smile almost looks like a snarl.

"That St. Bernadette's protects us, and that we protect ourselves."

He laughs. "And what ridiculous danger do you believe yourselves to be in? You privileged bunch of brats, spinning your tall tales, trying to damage my reputation. As if you could." His eyes don't twinkle now; they gleam. "Answer me, you little witch. What is it that you're trying to protect yourselves from?"

"The wolf within the walls," I say quietly. And as if we are one, the screamers part, and the old sweeper, her face contorted into something twisted and gnarled and monstrous beyond description, lunges from our midst and wraps her arms around Uncle, and a tornado of darkness whirls around us, so inky black that it almost blocks out the sun, and the sound of sweeping and the howling wind is so loud that it makes us cover our ears, but it's not enough to block out one sound, the one sound that we can all hear, loud and clear and filled with dread and terror.

The sound of the final scream.

Then, in an instant, the darkness disappears. And where Datuk Shah was standing is nothing but an empty space.

From somewhere nearby I hear a sudden shriek. "It's them! They're here, they're here, look, it's them!"

And suddenly people come running to us from all directions, us disappeared girls who have somehow reappeared again, all at once, together, right here on the grounds of St. Bernadette's.

Sumi and Flo reach me first. Flo is sobbing as she embraces me. "You just left the class and never came back," she says into my shoulder. "We've been searching all over the place for hours."

"I swear I must have looked around and inside Brede's House, like, ten times," Sumi says, her hug so tight, I think she may choke me. "Where the hell were you guys?" When they let go, it is only to give way to my sister, and to my mother, who wraps me in her arms and says over and over again: "Alhamdulillah, Alhamdulillah, thank God you're safe."

I want to speak, to tell them everything. There is so much to say to the both of them. To everyone. To make up for the time we lost.

But it will have to wait, after all. The crowd parts, and teachers begin to appear—Puan Ramlah, and Mrs. Dev, all clucking over us like worried hens, asking, "Where were you?" And "What happened?" And "Are you all right?"

The teachers eventually get us all to move, to head back to our own homes, and it's hours later before anyone thinks to ask about Datuk Shah, about where he's gone and why he isn't answering his phone, about who saw him last.

Nobody asks us, of course, us poor traumatized girls, we who reappeared. And for weeks afterward we are all very, very careful not to look at Brede's House, up to the stained-glass window where shadows move restlessly, as if someone is trapped in there.

But nobody ever goes into Brede's House, after all. So I guess we'll never know what that could be.

Oh well.

ACKNOWLEDGMENTS

As always, thank you to Victoria Marini for her steadfast belief in my ideas, even—especially—the ones I text her randomly at odd hours of the day or night. I blame the time difference.

Thank you to the one and only Deeba Zargarpur, both editor and friend, and equally brilliant in both spheres, for guiding me through yet another complicated project, until I figured out what I was actually trying to say.

My greatest gratitude to the team at Salaam Reads/Simon & Schuster: Dainese Santos, Sarah Creech, Kaitlyn San Miguel, Sara Berko, Emily Ritter, Nicole Valdez, Karina Itzel, Kendra Levin, Justin Chanda, and Anne Zafian.

It is rare that you will meet a Malaysian who a) does not have their own ghost story and b) will not willingly share it with the slightest of nudges. I am equal parts grateful and mad about the sleepless nights caused by my friends happily sharing the tales of their own hauntings with me.

Most will read this book as a ghost story. Some may read it for what it is: a love letter to my own mission school days. Thank you, CBN.

And finally: this last line always belongs to you. Thanks for always reaching into the shadows and pulling me back out. I love you, Umar.